# INSIDe THE HOTEL BENTMOORE: TRAINING ELLA

## SHELBY CROSS

ISBN-13: 978-1481116046
ISBN-10: 1481116045

First Print Edition: December 2012
Cover and Formatting: Streetlight Graphics

Like the cover? Please visit LibertineEraPhotographic (http://www.libertineera.com/) to see more images like this one. Want more kink? Check out Provillain.com (http://www.provillain.com/).

# TABLE OF CONTENTS

# DEDICATED TO

*Shadow, UncleAbdul, delightspirit, mr_fish, PurryLady, Vicki, TailStrike, tailstruck, doctorwhat, SteveV, raven_skye, HelKat, Carmen, Miz_t, SeaDove331, JB, Elizabeth, SanguineEffect, ConflictedSwitch, GrizzlyPete, NorthStarr, industrious, kamichan, Mockingbird_Lane, Admiral_Kel-Paten, Luis, and all the other regulars at the Usual Suspects Munch.*

*And, as always, to my Husband.*

*Special thanks to Anonymisslily, The Swallowologist, and Aerin33 for their thoughtful editing help.*

# PART I: MR. LAMONT

# CHAPTER ONE:
# WELCOME TO THE
# HOTEL BENTMOORE

**T**HE ELDERLY MAN KNOCKED THREE times on the thick oak door. Without waiting for a response, he slipped inside the quiet room. He was expected; and even if he had not been, he still would have come inside. He was one of the few people free to come and go as he pleased.

His shoes made no noise as he walked up to the edge of the elegant desk. When he got there, he stood straight ahead, stiff and somber, looking crisp in his flawless three-piece suit.

"She has arrived," he said, his face devoid of any emotion. "The valet has already taken possession of her car. She is being shown to her room as we speak."

"Very good," Mr. Bentmoore replied. "Did you get a look at her? How did she seem to you?"

"Nervous. But they're always nervous when

they first arrive. She's observant—she's taking note of everything."

"Interesting. What is she wearing?"

"A simple black dress, but I believe it's designer. Her shoes look expensive, too." He paused. "She has brought only one suitcase."

"Now that is *very* interesting." Mr. Bentmoore leaned back in his chair. "I wonder why that is."

Mr. Bentmoore knew, just as Mr. Trowlege did, that the way a woman made her first entrance into the Hotel Bentmoore often said a lot about her. Even the smallest detail could reveal much: what she thought of herself, what she thought of those around her, and what kind of demons she was there to fight.

The new woman was taking notice of everything.

They were taking notice of her, too.

It was far from typical for a woman to bring so few things with her, especially when she knew she was going to be staying for a while. For extended visits, women often brought two suitcases, sometimes more.

This particular woman had been told to plan on staying at the hotel for at least a month. They should have needed a cart to bring down all her things.

She was proving to be an enigma...but then, she had been an interesting case from the start. It was why Mr. Bentmoore had agreed to take her on in the first place.

"Shall we confiscate the suitcase?" Mr. Trowlege asked in his bland tone.

Mr. Bentmoore gave it some thought. "No," he replied. "Let her hold onto it."

"And the tour?"

"Skip the tour for now. Give her half an hour to settle herself in, then send her to me. And have Lamont ready for her. If she's as eager as she claims to be, there's no reason for her to wait."

Mr. Bentmoore smiled wickedly. The woman was safely trapped inside his hotel now. She had no idea what she had just gotten herself into, of that Mr. Bentmoore was sure.

Ella looked around the sparse room, frowning at what she saw. The décor was nice enough, done up in the neutral shades of a standard hotel room. The walls were painted a flat beige, but adorned with elegant white crown molding. Thick beige carpet padded the floor in every square inch. Ample recessed lighting illuminated the room in soft, hazy, yellow light.

There was a small chest of drawers sitting against one wall, with an old-style corded telephone sitting on top. Her bed sat against the opposite wall. A simple upholstered chair, padded in the same neutral beige as the walls, took up a small corner. But Ella quickly noticed that there was no television, no paintings hanging on the walls, not even a clock....

And no window.

Which made sense, Ella thought. Her room was well below ground. They had shown her into the hotel through the lobby, located on the ground floor, but the strange little butler who had escorted her onto the elevator had brought them *down* to her room. So the floor she was now on was subterranean.

*Could this be a room on the infamous dungeon floor of the Hotel Bentmoore?* She thought to herself. *If so, it is nothing like what I thought it would be.*

There were no lengths of rope or chain in the drawers, no sex toys, no hidden kinky objects waiting for her pleasure. Ella had checked. (Of course, there had been no bible in the drawers, either. Ella had laughed at the thought of finding one.) The room failed to give off any hint of bawdiness or sex. Even the full-sized bed didn't look particularly welcoming. The sheets and blankets had been folded down for her, but their color matched the walls almost exactly, dull and bland.

In fact, if she had to use one word to describe the room, it would have been *boring*. The whole place looked rather bleak in the artificial light. While she knew it was only three o'clock in the afternoon, down here, it may as well have been three o'clock in the morning. Looking at the bed reminded her how tired she was.

But she couldn't rest, not yet. She had to stay alert. She was there with a purpose in mind: she had a job to do.

Ella put her small suitcase on the bed, unzipped it, and carefully removed the laptop packed safely inside. Then she began to pull out all the cords and plugs she would need to get the computer to work.

First day at the Hotel Bentmoore. Time to get to work.

They had made her wait in a narrow empty corridor on a hard wooden chair for over two hours. There had been no secretary sitting at a desk nearby, no visible sign of any other people; just the muted sounds coming from the lobby, on the other side of the corridor.

Every so often, a woman would walk down the dim corridor and ask Ella if she was okay. The woman was tall, lanky, and gorgeous; just the kind of woman Ella expected to find working at the Hotel Bentmoore. She wondered perversely if the woman was one of the famed mistresses of the hotel, there to have freaky sex with countless men.

In response to the question, Ella would always say yes, she was fine, thank you for asking...but her answers were beginning to sound more and more sarcastic.

Ella dared not inquire how much longer her

wait would be. The woman would surely remind her she was there of her own volition, and free to leave at any time. Ella was the one pressing for this meeting, not the other way around.

After two and a half hours, the woman came her way again, but this time she had a smile on her face.

"Mr. Bentmoore will see you now," she said. "You may knock and go in."

Ella's expression grew nervous as she rose from her chair and stretched a bit on her feet. Then she stepped toward the door. She had to pee, but she would hold it. She was not going to lose this opportunity.

She knocked twice on the door, and heard a male voice say something from the other side. Ella opened the door, took a breath, and walked through.

A middle-aged man, one who looked old enough to be Ella's father, sat behind a large, majestic, and beautifully carved desk. His hair was laced heavily with grey, and laugh lines bordered his eyes and mouth.

"Close the door and have a seat," he said.

Ella obeyed without a word, taking a seat directly across the desk. At least this chair was plush and wide, with padded armrests; much more comfortable than the seat she had been occupying for the last two and a half hours.

Ella was surprised to see there was another man in the room, standing to the right of the man behind the desk. He looked very old—not just by his face, although that was pronounced enough—but by his bearing. What little hair he had left on his head was shiny silver, but trimmed impeccably. His arms hung down at his sides, and he stood stock-still inside his classic three-piece suit of dark grey. The man was old, but not withered. He was aged like fine wine.

He was not smiling, but not frowning, either; Ella realized she could not detect any emotion on the man's face at all, except, perhaps, a touch of curiosity. But his eyes...his eyes revealed his insight, years of knowledge and experience, wisdom gleaned from things he had learned in his many travels. Ella wondered what paths he had walked in life to look upon her with eyes like that.

The man sitting behind the desk cleared his throat. "Now, Miss...."

"Peterson. Ella Peterson."

"Yes, Miss Peterson. I understand from your letter, you would like to work at the Hotel Bentmoore."

"Yes Sir," Ella said. She has no idea why she was calling him "Sir," but as soon as she said it, she knew it was the right thing to do. The man looked surprised, but pleased by her answer. "I would very much like to work at your hotel."

Mr. Bentmoore scanned her face, taking in her appearance. Ella knew he would approve of what he saw: with her light blonde hair, startling blue eyes, her pert nose, fat pink lips, and rounded breasts, Ella had been told many times she was a strikingly attractive woman. She worked out to keep her body sleek and toned, and had learned over the years how to hold herself with dignified grace no matter the company she was in.

But Mr. Bentmoore served her with cool, detached appraisal. "Can you tell me why you want to work here, Miss Peterson? And what makes you think you'd be a good fit for us? You've never even been to our hotel before—I believe this is the first time you've ever set foot inside."

"Yes, Sir, that's true," Ella admitted. "But your hotel's reputation precedes you. I believe I'm the kind of girl you're looking for, the kind this place needs."

His eyebrows went up. "Oh, really? And what kind of girl is that, Miss Peterson? Who, exactly, do you think we're looking for?"

Ella had prepared for this question. "Someone fun, someone creative, someone who can show a man a good time in bed, and someone who can keep her mouth shut."

"I see," Mr. Bentmoore murmured. "And you think you are this kind of woman? The kind who can show a man a good time in bed?"

"Yes. Absolutely." Ella was proud of the way she managed to say it with a straight face. She had been practicing in front of a mirror.

But Ella saw that the man standing by the window was frowning now, and divulging a new emotion: doubt. Ella decided to take the offensive.

She looked directly at the strange little man and said, "I'm sorry, I didn't catch your name."

He gave her a look of surprise. "My name is Mr. Trowlege, miss."

"Mr. Trowlege," Ella said, "it is nice to meet you."

"It is nice to meet you too, miss."

Ella smiled, feeling like she had managed to throw off the seasoned steward and regain the upper hand.

Mr. Bentmoore turned around to pass a look to his associate, Mr. Trowlege. Then he peered at Ella from across his desk.

"Tell me, Miss Peterson, do you always introduce yourself in such an aggressive way to every person you see?"

"Uh, no Sir," Ella said, caught off guard. "I wasn't trying to be aggressive. I just thought introducing myself would be the right thing to do."

"Why? To be polite? Or to try to give us the impression you have some power here, despite the fact that you are the one sitting on that side of the desk, and we are the ones on this side?"

"Sir, I didn't think of it like that...I don't know what you're talking about...I'm sorry...." Ella could feel her face getting red as she stammered.

The situation had changed so drastically...had she just blown the entire interview?

"There is no need to apologize," Mr. Bentmoore said, surprising her once again. "Asserting yourself is often a good thing, and sometimes, even necessary. It is good to have confidence in yourself, so long as that confidence doesn't spill into arrogance. Don't you agree?"

"No Sir. I mean yes Sir. I mean...thank you, Sir." Ella snapped her mouth shut.

"Tell me, Miss Peterson, have you ever been spanked?"

Ella gaped at him in surprise by the sudden question. Then she closed her mouth, recovering quickly.

"I have," she said.

"With what?"

"With my boyfriend's hand."

"What else?"

"What else?" Ella repeated, caught off guard. "What else would he have used?"

"Mmm." Mr. Bentmoore leaned back into his chair, and Ella realized she had blundered again somehow.

"It felt really good," she added quickly, "I enjoyed it a lot." That part was true enough. The spankings had been amazing, just like the sex. But when he had started getting into tying her up with rope, Ella had made excuses to put an end to that relationship, not because she didn't like the rope, but because she liked it too much. It scared her, the way she felt being that vulnerable to another human being.

Of course, that had been a long time ago. When she had finally felt ready to open herself up to another man, it had ended with disaster. Ella's experiences in romance had taught her a harsh lesson: never reveal yourself completely to anyone.

Mr. Bentmoore sighed. "Let me show you something, Miss Peterson," he said.

He pulled open his desk drawer. Very carefully, with both hands, he brought out something to the top of his desk, and lay it down slowly.

"Do you know what this is, Miss Peterson?"

"It's a flogger," Ella whispered, looking down at it. She had seen pictures of floggers on the Internet, but had never seen one close up. Now, looking down at the beautifully braided and polished leather flogger in front of her, she couldn't tear her eyes away. It looked like a piece of fine art, not like a weapon of sexual hedonism.

Without her realizing it, Mr. Bentmoore was studying her expression. "Would you like to know what it feels like?"

"What?" Ella's eyes snapped up. Both Mr. Bentmoore and Mr. Trowlege were looking at her intently. "What do you mean?"

"I could show you what it feels like to be flogged. All you have to do is come around here and bend over my desk. You don't even have to raise your skirt, I can flog you over it. Just to give you a taste of it, you understand."

Ella gazed at the flogger. Mr. Bentmoore's offer hung in the air. She wondered if this was some kind of test, a sort of entrance exam: if she agreed to be flogged, her score would go up. If she refused, she might very well fail.

Ella rose from her chair. "I would like that, thank you," she said.

"Very good," Mr. Bentmoore replied, rising as well. "Just come around the other side here... and lean down."

Ella walked around the desk and put both her palms flat down, keeping her head up and her eyes straight ahead. She did not want to look at either of these men in the face. She had known, when she had thought up this crazy plan of hers, that she would have to endure some amount of sadomasochism. The Hotel Bentmoore had a reputation for being the sort of place where people could go to indulge in that kind of thing. But she had not thought for one moment she would have to face it at the interview!

She could take it; she could handle some pain. How much, exactly, she wasn't sure. But if things got out of control, if it became too difficult, she could always quit. Until then, she would pretend to enjoy it.

She would pretend to enjoy everything they did to her, everything they put her through, and meanwhile, she would document it all. It couldn't be that hard to fake sexual pleasure, could it? Women faked it all the time.

And really, when it came right down to it, did it matter if she enjoyed it or not? Would they care? Ella thought not. All these men cared about was getting their rocks off.

She leaned over and thrust her ass back, adopting what she hoped looked like a wanton pose, and spread her legs as wide as her dress would allow.

Mr. Bentmoore took his place by her side, holding the heavy flogger in his hand. "I'll start out slow, and increase the strength as I go," he said, his voice light. "We can stop at any time, whenever you wish. Do you understand?"

"Yes, Sir," Ella said, understanding full well. By agreeing to this humiliating spectacle, she had passed the first test. Now it would be a test of endurance.

"Let's begin then. Relax your back, Miss Peterson."

Ella took a deep breath and relaxed. A second later, she felt the strands of the flogger brush across her lower back.

"How was that?"

"Fine," Ella said, confused by the question. She had barely felt it; the hit she had been bracing for had felt more like a caress.

"Good. Then I'll keep going. Remember, you can stop me at any time."

Mr. Bentmoore did not wait for her to answer,

but began to flog her once more, with gentle, easy strokes.

Ella was surprised by the sensations the flogger wrought. It prickled some, but not much; and after every hit, a warmth would spread across her skin where the flogger had hit, radiating from her back all the way down to her toes. Mr. Bentmoore was focusing primarily on her lower back, but now and then, he would swat her bottom, too.

Ella began to relax her whole body, feeling languid and pampered. This didn't feel like a beating; this felt like a massage. She was supposed to be afraid of this? She could handle this no problem.

"It's going to get harder now, Miss Peterson," Mr. Bentmoore warned her.

Ella answered by dipping her head further down, locking her elbows in, and closing her eyes.

True to his word, the hits began to come harder and faster, with more force, and more bite. The strands of leather began to feel like tiny needles stinging her skin, but only briefly, only long enough to make her cringe and gasp. Once impact had been made, lines of tingling warmth would flow.

Slowly, the swats built up in intensity, and migrated down until Mr. Bentmoore was putting all his focus on Ella's bottom. Her muscles trembled, and her shoulders shuddered with each hit. The pain had built up so gradually, now that it was blooming inside her head and clouding all her thoughts, Ella could not think clearly...and she had not noticed the effect it was having on her.

Mr. Bentmoore hit her with a particularly vicious swat, right under her left buttock, and Ella's whole body stiffened. She lifted her head up and let out a short, mournful cry.

She began to twist her head to the side, undulating her hips, waving her waist like a belly dancer. But as she began to let herself go, out of the corner of her eye, she caught sight of Mr. Trowlege.

He was staring at her in rapt attention. He was finding this entertaining, she realized. No: he was finding *her* entertaining. Ella quickly saw herself through his eyes, what she must look like, and her whole body froze up.

"Stop!" she yelled. She looked over her shoulder at Mr. Bentmoore before he could swing the flogger again. "Please stop."

Immediately, Mr. Bentmoore lowered the flogger to his side. "Did it start to hurt too much?" He whispered.

"No," she shook her head. "No, it didn't hurt too much."

"Then what was it? Why did you ask me to stop?"

"I just...I just wanted you to." She looked directly into his eyes, daring him to argue with her.

He did not. "Interesting," came his bland reply. "How do you feel?"

"Fine." Ella straightened up to her full height and smoothed down her dress, trying to sound blasé. "I feel fine."

She felt far from fine, but she would bite her teeth through her lip before admitting it to this man. Dear God, she had been enjoying the flogging! She had barely caught herself in time before getting lost completely in the pleasure of it. What kind of allure did this man have?

She could think about that later. Right now, she had to get her head back in the game.

"Are you sure you're fine?" Mr. Bentmoore asked her, clearly concerned. "Can we get you a cup of water?"

"No, thank you. I'll just have a seat," she replied, grabbing onto the chair.

The deed was easier said than done. Even through her skirt, her bottom ached and burned.

"Well, Miss Peterson, let's get back down to business then," Mr. Bentmoore said, reclaiming his own seat and acting as if they had not just been in the throes of a lewd scene, completely improper for any job interview, and filled with a power Ella could not understand. "You say you are the kind of girl we are looking for, but I think you are mistaken. We usually hire women who are experienced, who are known in our general community, or at least, come with references."

"I have references. If you had looked at my résumé, you would have noticed I have lots of references. My college professors, work colleagues—"

"Those are not the kinds of references I'm referring to," Mr. Bentmoore cut in, stifling a smile. "I'm talking about references in the kink community. Someone who has an established reputation."

"Oh," Ella said, deflated and thinking to herself: there really was something called a kink community? It wasn't all made up? "What I lack in experience, I make up for in determination. You'll see, Mr. Bentmoore. I can be whoever you need me to be. I'm very good at adapting to new situations, I think I've proven that."

"Yes, you have," he had to agree. "You might be able to handle the things we throw at you." He smiled at his own pun. "But I'm not sure—"

"It's because I introduced myself to Mr. Trowlege before, isn't it?" Ella pursed her lips. "I tried to assert myself. You didn't like that. You don't like it when women speak when they're not supposed to, do you, Mr. Bentmoore?"

"Now hold on there, young lady," Mr. Bentmoore said, raising his brows and frowning. "As I told you before, what you did was completely acceptable. There is nothing wrong with having some self-confidence."

"But not showing it off, not without permission. Right?"

"That would definitely be true in certain circumstances," he said, holding back another lecherous grin. "But not this one. This is just an interview."

"Ha! You bent me over your desk and beat me with that, that...."

"Flogger?"

"Flogger, and you call this just an interview?"

Now Mr. Bentmoore looked angry. "I did not bend you over my desk, as you so elegantly put it, Miss Peterson. You did that all on your own. You were free to refuse."

"Ah. I see. As if it wouldn't have mattered if I had refused. As if you wouldn't have ended the interview right then. You men never take responsibility for your own actions, do you? No matter what happens, it's always the woman's fault for getting herself into these things."

"Miss Peterson, I suggest you watch your tone." Mr. Bentmoore's eyes took on a hard gleam, and his lips pressed together. Ella knew she had crossed the line.

She had ruined everything.

"You're right, Mr. Bentmoore, I'm not the right girl for this place," she said rising from her chair, trying to stop the moisture pooling in her eyes. "I'm clearly too confident for my own good. You need a girl who knows when to shut up and do as she's told, someone who has a reputation for that sort of thing. I'm sorry I came here with the wrong impression."

"Miss Peterson—"

"Thank you for the lesson with the flogger, Sir. It's not one I'll soon forget. I'll show myself out."

"Miss Peterson, stop right there!" Mr. Bentmoore's booming voice halted Ella in her tracks. Slowly, she turned around. Mr. Bentmoore looked at her sharply. "Do you have any understanding of what you came here asking for, young lady? Do you realize what kind of place this is? The services we provide?"

"You provide sex, pleasure...indulgence in its most basic, physical form."

"Not only, Miss Peterson. Not only." He shook his head. "You should have done a better job doing your homework about us before you got here. Or maybe...maybe you did just enough."

At that point, Ella felt like crying. She was done trying to figure out the man's riddles. "Thank you for your time, Mr. Bentmoore. Have a good afternoon."

This time, when she made her way to the door, Mr. Bentmoore didn't try to stop her, and Ella closed the door softly behind her.

Mr. Bentmoore and Mr. Trowlege both stared at the door.

"Did you notice?" Mr. Bentmoore asked his long-time friend.

"Yes," Mr. Trowlege replied. There was a long pause. "Will you help her?"

"I believe I will," came Mr. Bentmoore's answer. "But I'll let her keep up the ruse as long she chooses." He smiled wickedly. "It will make things more interesting."

By the time Ella got home, she felt spent, dejected, and crestfallen. She had put all her hopes on this one prospect, this one opportunity. Now what was she going to do?

As she put her purse down, her phone began to vibrate inside. Ella pulled out the phone and glanced at the screen: she saw she had missed three calls.

"Hello?"

"Miss Peterson, you are not an easy person to reach," Mr. Bentmoore's voice came through. He was more than a little annoyed.

"I'm sorry, Sir," Ella said, scowling as the words came out of her mouth. Why was she still calling the man Sir? "I didn't hear my phone ring. It was on vibrate."

"Do you understand, if we agree to hire you, what this job will include?" He asked without preamble. "You will have to be trained. You will be paid for your time, of course, but the training period will be rigorous, strict, and very demanding, both mentally and physically. Frankly, not many women are able to get through it."

"I will," Ella stated. "I know I can."

"We shall see, Miss Peterson. If you are serious about taking on this job, you will have to pack up your things and have someone else watch your house for a while. We have facilities here for our trainees; until we're done with you, you will not be allowed to leave the hotel at any time, not without permission."

"I understand," Ella breathed.

"Do you," Mr. Bentmoore said, giving Ella the impression he was shaking his head. "One more thing. You will have to go through a detailed medical checkup. We don't allow any STDs here, Miss Peterson. You don't have any, do you?"

"No, Sir."

"When was the last time you got tested?"

She swallowed. "About six months ago, Sir. But I haven't had any sex since then."

His voice grew softer. "I understand." Ire built in Ella's chest at his patronizing tone, but she said nothing. "You'll be tested again; many doctors don't bother doing a full panel. What about birth control?"

"I'm on the pill."

"Good. I'm going to give you the number of one of our doctors. Make an appointment. As soon as he clears you, we'll let you know when you should come back to start your training... assuming you still want the job."

"Oh yes, Sir," Ella said. "Yes, I do."

"Very well then. Oh, and one more thing, Miss Peterson: from this moment on, you're not allowed to have sex with anyone, and I do mean anyone. Understand?"

"Yes, Sir."

"Then I'm sure we'll see you again soon. And welcome to the Hotel Bentmoore, Miss Peterson."

He hung up, and the line went dead. Ella stared at her phone for a moment, a little bit shocked by what had just happened. Then she whooped with joy.

⌒⌒⌒⌒

That had been two weeks ago. Ella had survived through the invasive medical checkup, answering all the doctor's questions, enduring the gynecological exam, and giving enough blood to feed a hungry vampire. Then she received the call.

"Pack your things, Miss Peterson," the female voice on the other end said. "It's time to start your training at the Hotel Bentmoore. You do have someone ready to watch your house, feed the pets?"

Ella smiled. "I have someone to watch my place," she said, "and I don't have any pets."

"Good then. We'll be expecting you soon."

The car ride to the hotel had been long and hot. The air conditioning in Ella's car had given out weeks before, but she had no money to fix it. By the time she got to the hotel, Ella was sweaty, tired, and needed a nice hot shower... but she was excited, too.

Ella was an investigative reporter, a newly self-employed freelance journalist, one who had yet to make a name for herself in the industry. She had been trying to find jobs here and there, struggling to make ends meet, but all that was about to come to an end.

She was going to blow the top off this despicable place. She was going to tell the world everything that went on inside the secretive, perverse, and sordid Hotel Bentmoore.

After that, her troubles would be over.

But first, she had to plug in her computer.

Ella looked around the walls of the room, and realized for the first time that there were no outlets.

Panicking, she ran around the room, checking all the walls. There were no outlets to be found, not even in the bathroom. Once her computer ran out of power, it would be nothing but a paperweight.

Thank God, she had prepared for this scenario. Ella had brought a few brand new notebooks with her, fresh and ready to go, along with an array of pens and pencils.

They might be able to stop her from documenting anything digitally, but they couldn't stop the handwritten word!

Ella packed all her computer things back into her bag, feeling smug and self-confident. They hadn't managed to outwit her, but the game was definitely on, and she would have to stay on her toes. With no computer at her disposal, she had limited ways of contacting the outside world. In fact....

Ella picked up her cell phone and stared at the screen, eyeing the empty space in the corner that was usually filled with a tiny row of bars. Dread skipped merrily up her spine. She pressed in some buttons, trying to check her email, waited for the screen to refresh, and got—

Nothing. She had no reception.

A thought popped into her head: *Of course I have no reception. I'm underground.* And then another thought emerged: *I am officially cut off from the outside world.*

Fear reared its ugly head, but she tamped it down. She would not be cowered! They could force her into isolation, try to wear out her resolve, but she would not give up. She had more strength than that. And really, when it came right down to it, there was a limit to what they could do to her. If she insisted they let her leave, well then, they would have to let her go. They couldn't exactly tie her up and keep her there against her will, could they?

Could they?

Ella ran to the door and studied the knob. It had no lock at all—not on the inside, but not on the outside, either. She could not lock them out...and they could not lock her in. She breathed a sigh of relief.

Then she thought: there was probably not

much time before someone would be knocking on her door, asking for her presence. After that long drive, she felt like a sweaty, dirty, thirsty wreck. She had to clean herself up...but she took a few minutes to open up one of the new notebooks, grab a pencil, and quickly jot down some of her initial first impressions of the furtive Hotel Bentmoore. Only then did she brush her teeth, fix her hair, apply a fresh coat of lipstick, and dab on some perfume.

She heard the knock at the door just as she was fixing her pantyhose. Ella opened it, and was somehow not surprised to see Mr. Trowlege standing before her, the same bland expression plastered over his face.

"Mr. Bentmoore would like to see you," he announced.

"Hold on, let me just grab my purse."

"What for?"

Realizing the man had a point—there was nothing in there she would need, not her wallet, and certainly not her cellphone—Ella shrugged, and stepped into the hallway. Then she gazed at the door, and gave Mr. Trowlege a questioning look.

"No one will enter your room," he said, reading her expression. "Your things are completely safe."

Ella frowned. She hated the idea anyone could come into her room at any time. But she didn't think it would be wise to complain.

"Please, Mr. Trowlege," she said. "Lead the way."

He looked at her for another brief moment, then began to stride down the hallway. Ella followed behind, breathing hard, trying to prepare herself for what was to come.

Mr. Trowlege led her to a difference set of elevator doors this time. These doors were well hidden: built into an enclave and painted exactly the same shade as the walls, they disappeared almost completely.

Mr. Trowlege held the elevator door open as Ella walked through. Then he pressed a button as the doors closed, and the elevator ascended.

The two people inside stood in silence, facing the mirrored doors. Ella didn't bother asking any questions; she had a feeling Mr. Trowlege would only tell her to wait, and ask her questions to Mr. Bentmoore.

As the doors opened, she stepped out, and saw with shock that were back inside Mr. Bentmoore's private office. Mr. Bentmoore was sitting at his desk, just as he had been the last time she had seen him, looking fresh and composed.

"You have your own private elevator?" She asked him before she could stop herself.

"Of course," Mr. Bentmoore replied.

"Of course," Ella repeated softly. It made sense. If her room was on the same floor as the famed "activity rooms," then Mr. Bentmoore would want his own private way down. He probably used that elevator often, she thought, to sneak away and play with his female staff. Maybe he didn't fool around with the mistresses; maybe he fooled around with the men, the ones the hotel called the "hosts."

During her research of the Hotel Bentmoore, Ella had learned that Mr. Bentmoore was a married man, and had been since the re-opening of the hotel, when it had turned into the place it was now. But that didn't necessarily mean only women appealed to him, and it certainly didn't mean he was monogamous.

In fact, based on the elevator alone, it was now obvious to Ella he was not. Her opinion of him slipped down a few notches.

From across the room, another man stepped forward, and Ella's eyes widened at the sight of him. Tall, thin, and graceful, wearing a clean-cut black suit and crisp yellow shirt, he looked like he had just walked out of a model's photo shoot. Ella was truck by his limber physique, narrow shoulders, and tight hips. His hair was a rich brown, and matched his eyes almost exactly. He looked very young, like a boy fresh out of the schoolroom. There was also an innocent air about him; a playful smile curved up his delicate lips.

"Miss Peterson, this is Mr. Lamont," Mr. Bentmoore said, motioning the other man forward with his hand. "Should you decide you still want to continue this endeavor of yours after our talk, Mr. Lamont will be your introductory trainer. He will prepare you for the weeks ahead."

Mr. Bentmoore's statement raised a dozen alarm bells in Ella's head. "Prepare me?" She asked. "And my *introductory* trainer? How many trainers will I have?"

"Many," Mr. Bentmoore replied. "Let me explain. The Hotel Bentmoore upholds the highest standards in the services we provide our guests. We must therefore have equally high expectations of our own staff. Groomed appearance, physical prowess, mental self-discipline, dexterity of the body and mind—all these things are important if we are to maintain the reputation we have earned. To that end, you will also be expected to rise to our standards. We will work on your appearance, your skills...and your sexual prowess. Endurance, creativity, restraint—all these things need to be heightened and augmented—not to mention, basic knowledge and aptitude. Those need to be worked on, too. By the time we're done with you, you will be a proficient and well-versed sexual connoisseur, worthy of calling yourself a mistress of the Hotel Bentmoore."

Mr. Bentmoore's words filled Ella with rancor. *They are going to try to teach me how to be a well-groomed and well-trained whore,* she thought. But she wisely kept her mouth shut.

"Mr. Lamont is one of our Masters," Mr. Bentmoore continued.

"Masters?" Ella interrupted. "Masters of what?"

"Oh, you'll find out," Mr. Bentmoore replied, giving her a wicked smile. Ella looked at Mr. Lamont, and saw that he was smiling, too. "All our Masters have earned the title for one reason or another," Mr. Bentmoore said. "They have a very diverse set of skills. You'll get to know all of them in due time—should you decide to stay on and work with us. But before you agree, I need to make sure you understand the rules."

"Rules?"

"Yes, rules. These rules are the basic tenets of our agreement, should you stay here. Rule number one: you are not allowed to go anywhere around the hotel without express permission. You will have access to the lobby floor, most of the hotel grounds, and certainly the dungeon floor, where your room is located. But you will never go anywhere you have not been granted permission, and you will never, ever, visit the private guest rooms upstairs. Those floors are off limits. You will go where you have been ordered to go, and that is all. Do you understand?"

*She was under house arrest.* "Yes, Sir," Ella replied.

"Two: you will follow our orders completely, to the letter, and without exception. Since you are in the training process, it is natural for you to have many questions. My Masters will be able to answer them, or help you onto the path to find the right answers for yourself. But that does not mean you will be allowed to refuse their requests. Any act of disobedience may well be enough to get you dismissed from the hotel. Understand?"

Ella clenched her teeth together. "Yes, Sir."

"Good. And one final thing: I don't know if you've noticed it by now, but you have no reception in your room—"

"I've noticed."

Mr. Bentmoore stopped and looked at her through slitted eyelids. "Do not interrupt me again, Miss Peterson."

Ella looked down and gnashed her teeth. "I'm sorry, Sir."

Mr. Bentmoore paused before continuing. "The reason you have no reception in your room is because we don't want you to. Your room is your sanctuary, your safe place, where no one can bother you or distract you from what you are here to do. It is not the place for you to watch television or chat with your friends. You will go there to sleep, wash, dress, and reflect. That is all."

When he stopped, Ella felt safe to talk. "So where do I go to use my cell phone?"

"You don't. Cell phones are restricted inside the hotel. Anything with camera capability is not allowed. If you need to make a phone call, you can call from my office. Do you need to call anyone right now?"

"No," Ella said before she had time to think.

"Nobody? A friend? Relative? Someone who might need to know you arrived okay?"

"No, no one."

"Well, in that case." Mr. Bentmoore motioned Mr. Lamont over. "I'll let you two get acquainted. Mr. Lamont, you know what to do."

"Yes, Mr. Bentmoore." He gave Ella another wide smile, and this time, it was ravenous. "Come with me, Ella. We have a lot to do."

# CHAPTER TWO: ELLA GETS ACQUAINTED

**M**R. LAMONT LED HER BACK onto Mr. Bentmoore's private elevator and pressed the button to send them down. Ella noted the panel on this elevator didn't need any key access to get to the dungeon floor; Mr. Bentmoore didn't have any restrictions like that. And why would he, Ella thought wryly. It was his hotel.

Ella stood with her feet together, trying hard not to fidget. "Mr. Lamont, could you please tell me where we're going?"

"Sir."

"What?"

"From now on, you should call me Sir. Once your training period is over, you can call me Mr. Lamont, or just Lamont, since everyone here calls each other by their last name."

"But for now, I should call you Sir."

"Yes."

"Why?"

Mr. Lamont gazed at her. "Because it is

proper," he said, "to show respect." He waited to see if she would argue. Ella, thinking better of it, kept her mouth shut.

When they got to the dungeon floor, Mr. Lamont led her down the dimly lit corridor to another side room, and this time, he did have to take a card-key out of his pocket and slide it through the lock on the side of the door to open it.

As Ella crossed the threshold into the wide room, shock rose in her throat, and her heartbeat began to drum in her chest painfully.

*This* was a real dungeon room: not a fake one, not a movie set, and certainly not some picture she had glimpsed on the internet. This was a place where people were beaten, mauled, and tortured. What really dumbfounded Ella was that they came here *willingly*.

Then she remembered: she had come here willingly, too.

Ella had thought she had known what she was getting herself into by taking on this challenge. Now, she was not so sure, but there was no going back. She began to wonder for the first time if she really had any idea what she had gotten herself into. But she had made her deal with the devil, and it was time to pay up. She swallowed down her fear, trying to get her nerves under control.

She could do this. She could.

But when she spoke, her voice squeaked like

a scared mouse.

"Are you going to beat me now?"

Mr. Lamont smiled. "Do you want me to?"

The question caught Ella off guard. "No," she said, shaking her head vigorously. "I don't."

Mr. Lamont frowned, then shrugged. "Then I won't," he said. "That wasn't what I had been planning to start you with, anyway. I just thought I would indulge you if that's what you wanted."

*Why would I want that?* Ella almost asked. But she stopped, remembering the role she supposed to be playing. She was supposed to be a "sub," a submissive woman, and a masochist to boot. She was supposed to like that sort of thing.

And then Ella had a flashback of the beating Mr. Bentmoore had given her inside his office, the flogging that had felt so good, especially at the end: naughty, thrilling, and so, so erotic. Thank God she had put a stop to it before it got too far.

But what did "too far" mean? What would have happened to her? And what if they did that to her again, and she wasn't able to stop it in time?

She vowed, then and there, she would not let any of these people flog her or beat her or whatever they wanted to call it—she would not let them wear her down so hard, she could not pull herself back up. She would maintain control. She would not let them violate her.

With that vow firmly in place in her mind, Ella stood up a fraction taller, and faced her trainer head on.

"What were you planning then, Sir?"

Mr. Lamont raised his eyebrows, detecting the subtle change in her. "First things first," he said. "Would you like me to show you any of the equipment?"

"Yes." She wanted to know every piece, every detail, so she could write them down later in her notebook when she got back to her room.

Mr. Lamont drew her attention to the large cross. "This is a St. Andrew's Cross," he said. "You've probably seen one before, yes?"

"Yes," Ella said, the lie slipping easily from her lips.

"Over here," he continued, striding over, "is one of our spanking benches. This is my favorite one."

"Why?"

"The pads are a little thicker, and the straps a little thinner, than some of our other spanking benches. Little details like that can make a huge difference in the results. The legs on this one aren't adjustable, but that's okay with me. Some of the other hosts like adjustable legs."

"Why?"

"Better access."

Ella thought wisely not to ask what he meant; she had a feeling she didn't want to know. She would probably find out eventually anyway.

"Over here is a suspension bar," Mr. Lamont continued, "and there is a restraining chair. That's an exam table, as I'm sure you could guess just looking at it."

*Perverts playing doctor*, Ella thought, and turned away. "What's in there?" She asked, pointing to the enormous wardrobe sitting against the wall right in the center of the room. It was made of a rich mahogany, delicately carved, stunning and completely out of place.

"Ah, that's where we store all our equipment for the room," Mr. Lamont said. "Every activity room has one. We trade things now and then, move some toys from room to room, but every wardrobe is well stocked with all the basics."

"Basics? Like what?"

"Chains, whips, crops, canes, cuffs, leashes, straps, gags, blindfolds, blackout masks, paddles—"

"I get it," Ella snapped. "Thank you Sir."

Mr. Lamont gave her slanted look, looking amused, then pointed to the other side of the room. "That's the bed," he said. "Some of the other beds we have in the other rooms are far more intimidating, but I like to keep things simple."

The bed was, indeed, simple. It was a perfect square, low to the ground, and covered tightly with a fitted black sheet.

Ella had never seen a square bed before. It looked more like...a stage.

"What's that?" She asked, pointing to a

strange contraption next to the bed. It looked like a small bench, but the top of it was humped, not flat. Looking at it more carefully, Ella realized it was made of two different pieces: the bottom, which was the bench itself, and the top, which was the mounted hump. It looked to be some kind of piece of machinery. There was a smooth, wide, tubular shape coming out of the mound, made of shiny pink silicone.

Ella's eyes went wide.

There was no question the phallus coming out of the machine was a dildo.

"That's my favorite toy," Mr. Lamont said. "It's very fun, and you're going to get well acquainted with it today. It's called a Sybian. I take it you've never seen one before?"

"No, never." Ella had never heard of one, either. The look of it scared her.

"Soon enough you're going to get to know it up close and personal. But first: let's get you undressed."

Ella swallowed and glanced away, feeling her face go red. Mr. Lamont gave her an encouraging smile. "Don't be bashful, Ella," he said. "It will be okay, I promise."

Ella nodded, but couldn't stop her nerves from shaking.

The moment had arrived. She was really going to have to do this.

She began to strip off her clothes, one piece at a time, and let them fall to the floor.

"Look at me, Ella," Mr. Lamont said. Ella raised her eyes; they were full of fear. But Mr. Lamont's grin was wide and warm. "I know it can be hard to undress in front of a man you've just met," he said, coming to stand before her. "But it's okay. You look beautiful, you know."

"I know," Ella snapped, her indignation returning.

Mr. Lamont's lips curved down into a frown. "Finish," he ordered. "Take off your bra and panties."

Without tearing her eyes away from his, Ella peeled off her underwear and flung them to the ground. "What now?"

"Now let me look at you." Mr. Lamont began to circle her body, taking slow, measured steps, studying her body with a keen and appreciative eye.

Her breasts, soft and round, sloped gently above her ribcage. Her nipples had hardened in the cool room air. With her hourglass waist, flaring hips, and creamy alabaster skin, she stood before him like a renaissance painting come to life.

As he took in the sight of her, Ella bristled. She felt like she was being examined like a slab of meat, and Mr. Lamont's hungry gaze did nothing to dispel the notion.

"Very nice," he murmured. "Not a blemish on you, not even a scratch. We'll have to fix that."

"What?"

"Nothing." Mr. Lamont shook his head. "Nothing you have to worry about right now. But I do think we need to have a serious talk. Put your clothes on the bench over there and have a seat on the bed, Ella."

Ella put her clothes on the padded bench and sat on the edge of the strange square bed, feeling vulnerable and exposed. Even as Mr. Lamont began to take off his suit jacket and place it neatly next to Ella's pile of clothes, she had to fight the urge to cover her body with her hands.

"Let's start with the basics," he said, fighting the top button on his shirt to get it open, and rolling his head a little once his neck was free. "How many sexual partners have you had in your life?"

"Um...six? Maybe?"

"Good enough. How many long-term relationships?"

"None, I guess. I mean, if they had been long-term, I wouldn't be here now, would I?"

Mr. Lamont had to smile. "I mean, how many of your sexual relationships did you consider significant?"

"Oh...I guess two." Her voice went soft.

So did Mr. Lamont's. "Were they monogamous relationships?"

"Of course."

Mr. Lamont paused to give her that penetrating stare of is, and Ella realized she had somehow just blundered again. "I mean, I think they were monogamous. If they was sleeping with other women, I certainly didn't know about it."

Mr. Lamont sighed. "What's your favorite sexual position?"

"On top."

This time, he grinned. "That's very common, but by the time we're done with you, you'll be able to say 'all of them.' What words do you use to label yourself?"

"Label myself?"

"Words you give to describe yourself."

"Um...I guess I'm smart, and stubborn—"

"No, no, no." Mr. Lamont laughed. "I mean, words you use to describe what you are in the *scene*."

"I don't understand."

Mr. Lamont narrowed his eyes. "Ella, are you sub? A Domme? A Top, bottom, masochist, sadist, switch?" He paused. "Or do you just not like to put labels on yourself? Some people don't, and that's okay."

"Yup, that's me, I don't like to put labels on myself," Ella answered quickly. She had no idea what some of those labels even meant.

But Mr. Lamont looked at her in surprise. "You must think of yourself as a sub, or at least a bottom, or Mr. Bentmoore wouldn't have asked me to train you. If you were a Domme, he would have given you to Marissa. Are you any kind of masochist at all?" When Ella failed to answer right away, his eyebrows rose even more. "Do you like pain?"

"I...." Ella swallowed hard. "I guess I do." The realization startled her.

Mr. Lamont scrutinized her expression. "You're embarrassed to admit it," he whispered. "Interesting. But we'll fix that, too. What have you had used on you?"

"Used on me?" She was sinking fast now, flailing in her own ignorance. *Oh God, please don't let him see through my disguise,* she thought.

"Whips? Paddles? Floggers?"

"Flogger," Ella said loudly. "I've had a flogger used on me." No need to tell him her first time with it had been in his boss's office, she thought. "And my boyfriend used his hand."

"Hands are effective," Mr. Lamont said. "With the right Top, they are all that's needed. I'm a paddle guy myself...especially impression paddles." His eyes clouded with lust, then cleared. "But it sounds like you've had very little worked on you. This is excellent."

"It is?"

"Yes, it is. It means I can break you in exactly how I want to." His smile was wicked. "One last thing. Any hard or soft limits you want to tell me about?"

"Um...."

"Come now, there must be something your boyfriend did to you that you didn't like."

"No, not really. I mean, if I didn't like it, I

just told him to stop." Mr. Lamont stared at her in disbelief, and Ella realized she would have to say something, and fast. "One time he wanted to come on my breasts. I told him no. I thought the idea was gross."

"So he didn't do it?"

"No. Like I said, I told him not to."

"Huh. Sounds like you two had a very easygoing relationship."

"What the hell is that supposed to mean?"

"Nothing," Mr. Lamont sighed. "I'm asking you about hard limits now. Do you know if you have any?"

Ella shook her head, and Mr. Lamont gave her a good-natured grin. "That's okay," he said. "We can start finding them out together." Devilish light danced in his eyes. Ella suspected he knew very well she had no clue what "hard limits" meant, and was fiendishly letting her flounder.

"That would be good," Ella said, her voice clipped.

"Excellent!" Mr. Lamont rubbed his hand together, and Ella noted his hands were wide and veined, with well-trimmed nails. "Well then, let's get started." He motioned her to the Sybian. "Say hello to my little friend."

"Um, hello?" Ella didn't know if he had been serious or not.

Mr. Lamont laughed. "Oh, Ella, this is going to be fun. Now then: the Sybian is meant to be straddled, like a saddle. I would like you to get on."

Ella came around the strange contraption, staring down at it like it might pounce on her. As she looked it over, she realized the bench had been cut to the exact dimensions of the machinery sitting on top, with the legs of the bench measured to be just the right height, Ella realized, for squatting.

Wary now, Ella lifted her leg over the Sybian, centered herself, and plopped down. She knew Mr. Lamont was watching her, and had gotten a nice glimpse of her shaved slit as she spread her legs. Now that she was straddled across the strange machine, her pussy lips were pressed into the smooth curved surface.

"Very good, Ella," Mr. Lamont said, "But you're not on yet quite right. You're supposed to be sitting on top of the attachment." He pointed to the long phallus in front of her.

"What?" Ella squeaked.

"The attachment goes inside your cunt."

"My *what?*"

Mr. Lamont shook his head. "So bashful. We will have to work on this modesty of yours." He pointed. "Just stand up, position yourself on it, and sit back down. It's not hard. Well, it is hard, but it's not difficult." He laughed at his own little joke. "If you need lube, I can provide some. Are you wet enough?"

"I...I don't know."

"Soon enough, you'll be creaming every time

you look at it. But for now...." He went to the bedside table, retrieved a small bottle of lube, and squirted some on his fingers. Then he came over to the rigid springy dildo sitting atop the machine, and ran his fingers up and down the smooth shaft. "There," he said. "Get on."

Ella touched the "attachment" with weak fingers. Trembling, feeling like her knees were about to give way, she lifted up her body, angled herself just so...and slowly, very slowly, slid her body back down on the hard blunt plastic that filled up her pussy. As she felt her butt touch bottom, she bit her lip, trying to get used to the strange sensation of the large dildo inside her.

"*Very* good, Ella," Mr. Lamont said, pleased. "Now that you're sitting, let me tell you what this little machine can do: it can help you get the best orgasms you've ever had." He laughed when Ella gave him a startled look. "Oh yes, this machine can show you what your body is truly capable of, and in no time at all. But there's no reason I should try to convince you. I'm going to show you."

"How?"

Mr. Lamont picked up a control panel that had been sitting on the floor, snaking away from the machine. "This knob here controls rotation," he said, showing her the black panel. "And this one controls the vibration. For your first time, I'm going to work the controls. But later, I'll hand the reigns over to you, and you'll be able to experiment and see what you like." He held his fingers to the knobs. "Are you ready?"

"I don't know."

"Just try it, Ella. It's not going to hurt you."

Ella nodded. "Okay."

Mr. Lamont turned on the machine, and a loud noise started up. Ella wasn't expecting the noise. Then again, she wasn't expecting the incredible vibrations spreading inside her pussy, either. The machine hummed between her legs, coursing delicious prickles of pleasure up her spine and down her legs. Ella gasped.

Mr. Lamont gave her a minute to get used to the new sensations. Then he held up the panel again, his finger on the other knob. "I'm going to start the rotation now," he warned her. "I'll start it out slow, and work my way up."

Ella felt the dildo begin to make tiny little circles inside her. Her eyes went wide. It tickled and pulled, grazing and teasing her insides in the most fascinating way. Ella closed her eyes and leaned forward.

Immediately, she jacked her head up and cried out. When she had leaned forward, the machine had touched her in a new, unfamiliar way—a way that felt amazing.

Ella leaned forward again, testing the strange sensation.

Then she leaned forward again. And again.

Ella began to rock her hips and sway on top of the astounding machine that had managed to seduce her in no time at all with its magic. She bit her lip to stop herself from crying out as she moved her hips in a slow, languid circle that quickly built up speed.

"Stop!" She yelled. "Stop!"

Mr. Lamont immediately turned off the machine. "What?" He said, alarmed. "What happened?"

"It was...I was about...."

"Yes?"

"I was going to come," Ella said, her whole body blushing.

Mr. Lamont cocked his brow. "That was the *point*, Ella."

"I know, but...." She bit her lip and looked away.

"I understand." Mr. Lamont's voice was soft. "Many women are embarrassed to come while a strange man watches them from afar. Not everyone is a born exhibitionist. But you can be trained, Ella. It's another thing I'm here to teach you."

Ella's face filled with fear. "Please, Sir, I...I don't know if I can."

"You can, and you will. Let me show you." And he turned on the machine again.

For an instant, Ella thought of jumping off the machine, and dealing with whatever consequences might come. But that thought soon fled as the heavenly vibrations taking over her body trapped her in place once more. The dildo rotated, jolting her with a steady rhythm of pure bliss, and this time, Ella did cry out.

"That's it, Ella," Mr. Lamont encouraged her. "Feel it. Let it take you. Ride it out."

"Oh, God!"

Mr. Lamont's voice was low and direct. "Come for me now."

The short order set her off, and Ella's pleasure exploded. Atop the machine, she shuddered and yelled. The Sybian kept up its ministrations as Ella came, joining in the magnificent performance between woman and machine. She had never felt anything like it.

She swayed on the Sybian like a snake dancer, undulating her body as tiny aftershocks wracked her body. When she was done, she sat very still, breathing hard. Her clit throbbed; she felt very sensitive.

"You did beautifully, Ella." Mr. Lamont said, turning off the machine. "I'll give you a short break."

Ella heaved for breath, looking startled. "A short break?"

Mr. Lamont smiled. "Oh, we are far from done. But just close your eyes and rest now."

Ella did close her eyes, too weak to protest. She was still trying to process what had just happened. She was used to needing time, and a lot of foreplay, to reach an orgasm.

All the orgasms she had ever felt in her relatively young life had been *nothing* compared to what she had just felt with the Sybian. Mr. Lamont had made her come in under three minutes.

No, not Mr. Lamont, she thought. The machine. The Sybian. Mr. Lamont hadn't even touched her.

Dear God, what would happen if he *did* touch her while she was riding this thing?

She opened her eyes when she heard him go to the large wardrobe and open it, and looked up to see what he was holding in his hands.

"They're nipple clamps," he told her before she could even ask. "I can tell by your face you've never seen them before. It's going to be fun being your trainer, Ella."

"Are they going to hurt?" Her voice was ragged and low. Perhaps it was her weak state, or perhaps it was the surreal effect of the situation, but Ella wasn't fearful of the idea of pain. In fact, she was curious.

"Yes," Mr. Lamont said. "They will hurt some. But how much they hurt is up to you right now. They're adjustable. I'm going to let you decide how tight I make them, and then give you reign over the Sybian. You'll have complete control. Sounds good?"

"Yes, Sir."

Mr. Lamont smiled at her ready answer. Then his focus shifted to her breasts, and his expression changed. With one hand, he picked up the end of the nipple clamps. With his other large hand, he carefully plucked up her left nipple.

Ella gasped. She looked down to see what he was doing, and watch every little movement of his blunt fingers. Mr. Lamont pinched her nipple a few times, getting it nice and hard. Then he pulled at it, distending it outward. Ella moaned, and momentarily closed her eyes; but she opened them quickly to watch Mr. Lamont fit the nipple clamp.

It pinched some, but not too much. The weight of it felt more odd than the clamp itself.

Once the first nipple was clamped, Mr. Lamont went through the same process with the second. When Ella's nipples were both clamped, he stepped back to admire the view. The thin silver chain dangling between the clamps hung between her breasts like a piece of fine jewelry.

"How's that? Too tight?"

"No, Sir. It's fine."

"Too loose?" He looked at her shrewdly.

"It's fine."

"I think we can make them tighter."

Reaching over, he turned the tiny screw inside one of the clamps, tightening it up considerably. Ella made a sound like a moue.

"That's much better. Let's do the other."

When he stepped back again, both clamps felt twice as tight as they did before, and Ella's nipples were noticeably stiffer.

"Now I'll give you the controls over the

Sybian," he said, handing her the small black box. "Remember, this one is for rotation. This one is for vibration." He stepped away from her. "Have fun."

For a moment, Ella just stared at the box. Then, she slowly turned up the vibration, just to see what would happen. She felt the Sybian begin to hum and shake beneath her once more. The dildo, still lodged up her cunt, vibrated with life.

Ella adjusted the rotation setting, and felt the dildo begin to gyrate inside her pussy, still sensitive and engorged from her recent orgasm. She groaned and leaned forward on her free hand, trying to adjust to the invasive, but not unpleasant, sensations. She turned the rotation up further, making the dildo twist harder and faster inside her.

"That's good, Ella. But remember, you're in no hurry. Take your time."

Ella didn't answer. She was completely absorbed in what she was doing—and what she was feeling. Her passion rose rapidly with each tight circle of the dildo, and she began to bob up and down on the machine, slapping her thighs against the smooth surface with each jerk of her body.

A painful jolt from her nipple refocused her attention, and Ella looked down. Mr. Lamont had grabbed the clamp, and was now tightening it even further, bit by delicious bit. Sweet agony shot through her nipple, down her spine, and straight to her clit.

As Mr. Lamont tightened up the other clamp, watching the way Ella bobbed and shook and swayed in complete abandon, he encouraged her further.

"Tell me what you're feeling right now, Ella. Do you like it?"

"Yes, Sir. Oh God, I like it...."

"What do you like?"

"The clamps, the machine...the way it feels...." She couldn't continue, as all words escaped her. She bounded on the machine, making it go faster and faster; and as she did, Mr. Lamont grabbed the chain between her nipples and pulled on the clamps.

Ella screamed this time as she came. If she thought her last orgasm was powerful, it was nothing compared to this one; white light exploded inside her head. She curled into the machine and continued to cry out with each jolting shock of pleasure.

As she calmed down, Mr. Lamont was already removing the nipple clamps. Ella turned off the machine as soon as she could get her hands to move, bending herself forward and back. She felt like she had no bones left in her body. She felt flushed, limp, thirsty...and wonderful.

"Would you like some water?"

"Yes, Sir. Thank you." Ella smiled languidly, watching Mr. Lamont disappear behind a door around the wardrobe to get her a glass of water.

She had nothing but good feelings for her trainer now. Mr. Lamont could do whatever he wanted with her, as long as he let her ride his glorious machine.

He returned with the water, and Ella gulped it down, breathing hard as she handed him back the empty glass. He put it absently on the bedside table.

When he turned back to her, Ella saw his expression had changed. His brows were furrowed, and his smile was voracious.

"We're going to try something different now," he said. "I'm going to control the Sybian again. You are going to try hard *not* to come. Understand?"

"I *shouldn't* come?" Ella asked, alarmed. "How do I do that?"

"Fight it. Relax your body, think of something else, do whatever you need to do, but don't come, not for as long as you can. Think of this as a test, Ella."

"But I'll fail. Eventually, I'll come." It scared her a little to admit it, how much her outlook on things had changed, and just since getting on the Sybian.

"I know," Mr. Lamont said. "But this is where you start to train your brain to control your own responses. When you came before, your body was going through its natural processes and reactions. Now you'll start to learn how to recognize those reactions, control them, and get your body to react the way you want it to. You'll get better at it as time goes on, but for now, I want you to just try it, and get an idea what I'm talking about."

Ella nodded. "Okay."

She saw his fingers move against the control box ever so slightly, and underneath her sweaty, tingling body, Ella felt the machine spring back to life. Her eyes widened, and she bit her lip.

But as Mr. Lamont stared at her with half-hooded eyes, watching with great interest as she fought the thrilling ecstasy resonating throughout her body, Ella's mettle rose, and her tenacity returned. She braced herself against the machine, preparing herself for battle.

She would not come. Not until she could do it on her own terms. Not until she saw that smug look disappear from Mr. Lamont's face.

Ella kept her body very still, and strained to put as much of her weight as she could on her hands. The Sybian quivered and twirled beneath her, and Ella fought to ignore it. She stared hard at Mr. Lamont.

Their eyes met. His expression helped anchor her and hone her in while the machine wreaked havoc with her senses.

When she caught him turning up the machine, she closed her eyes and bit her lip, but then held his gaze once more, letting him know with her steady glare that she would not be giving up anytime soon.

Ella's breathing came hard and fast as Mr. Lamont continued to turn up the machine. Ella held her body rigid, careful not to move the slightest bit. She feared if she did, she would succumb to her growing need to rock against the diabolical dildo tormenting her needy clit.

The minutes ticked by. Sweat poured from Ella's face and dripped down her sides. Her breathing came in tight, high-pitched wheezes. The noise of the Sybian was vibrant inside the open room. Mr. Lamont stared at her with growing enthrallment.

Ella held on.

He held up the control box to her eyes, making sure she was looking at what he was about to do. As she watched in dread, Mr. Lamont turned the vibration knob up all the way, giving her a lecherous grin. Beneath her, the Sybian began to dance.

"No...." A loud plea escaped her lips. Ella fought hard against the rising onslaught, closing her eyes and focusing all her energy on fighting the pleasure, the urgency, the need to come.

And for a while, she succeeded. Mr. Lamont's expression went from intrigue to fascination as Ella's body shook and rattled over the machine, looking seized. But the harder she fought, the greater her need grew. She knew eventually, the dam would burst, and the rush building inside her would be unleashed. It was only a matter of time.

It was about to happen. She couldn't hold back any longer.

But she would still do it her way.

"I'm going to come," she said, leaning forward.

"Hold on."

"No."

"I said hold on, Ella."

"No! I *want* to come." She met her trainer's look, and their eyes did a battle of wills. Mr. Lamont was staring at her in astonishment—but also, Ella thought, with new respect.

It was the respect she saw there that finally released the gates. Smiling broadly, she came with a roar, leaning all the way over the machine. Her orgasm was so intense, it felt like tiny synapses in her brain were exploding. As her cry carried on, a look of anguish mixed with bliss covered her delicate features, and she arched her body in a perfect bow. Then she slumped against the machine.

Mr. Lamont quickly turned off the Sybian and rushed forward to help her down. Ella leaned on him as he led her to the soft bed.

"I think we're done here for today," Mr. Lamont said, looking down at her quivering, sweat-soaked, and lanky body. "When you're ready, I'll take you back to your room."

"Thank you Sir. Did I pass the test?"

"Oh, yes, Ella. You passed."

Mr. Lamont stood in front of Mr. Bentmoore's desk, his arms crossed, his eyes looking somewhere in the distance. "She has no idea what she is, or what she's capable of. She's either ignorant, or oblivious."

"I think it's a bit of both," Mr. Bentmoore replied from his seat, looking up at the tall thin man. "The basic knowledge will be easy to teach her—she's a smart woman. But how she reacts to it all will be hard to predict."

Mr. Lamont frowned. "Her control is amazing," he whispered. "I've never seen anything like it. In time, she will find it an incredible asset. But for now, I think she will try to turn it against us."

"Then we will have to break her of it."

"It will take time, and a lot of work." Mr. Lamont's grin was wide and fiendish.

"I'm sure you and the others are up to the task. It is, after all, why she is here." Mr. Bentmoore gave Mr. Lamont a pointed stare. "Tomorrow morning, start on the toys. Floggers, paddles, belt...you know the drill. But no whips, not yet. She's too new. We shouldn't get ahead of ourselves."

Mr. Lamont's smile returned. "It will be my pleasure, Sir."

# CHAPTER THREE: THE HITACHI

**T**HE NEXT DAY, **ELLA WAS** brought back to Mr. Lamont's activity room bright and early. Of course, she only knew it was bright and early because she had managed to catch a few rays of the rising sun shining through the extravagant windows of the dining room as she had been finishing her breakfast.

Nobody else had been there at that early an hour. Ella had eaten in the posh quiet dining room alone.

She'd managed to write up a few pages of notes when she'd gotten back to her room the day before, after Mr. Lamont's little "test" of her will. But she found describing her feelings of what she'd been put through, what she'd felt as the scene had unfolded, was difficult. All her thoughts were a chaotic mess. So she contented herself with jotting down what had happened in the most clinical terms, using nothing but bullet point statements. Then she had taken a much-needed nap.

She had been awakened a few hours later by the sound of someone knocking on her door. Ella made sure to hide her notebook under her mattress before answering it.

When she opened the door, she was surprised to find a tall, svelte, and beautifully vibrant young woman looking back at her, smiling and holding a dome-covered tray.

The woman introduced herself as Stacey. But she didn't wait for Ella to reply before walking through the door with a happy bounce in her step. Ella couldn't be angry; the tray obviously hid a huge plate of food. Whatever it was, it smelled delicious, and made Ella's stomach rumble. (Since becoming a freelance journalist, money had been very tight for Ella, and she'd often had to make some painful food choices.)

As Stacey put down the tray and removed the dome, Ella sat down on the bed. Her eyes widened at the meal set before her: steak, vegetables, and noodles, all of it still steaming hot, all of it looking delicious. Stacey gave her a few minutes to dig into her dinner; then she began to give Ella the real reason for her visit.

"After you eat, you're supposed to come with me to the seamstress."

"Seamstress?" Ella asked between bites. "What seamstress?"

"Our seamstress. She needs to take your measurements."

"Why?"

"For clothes, silly. You need to be fitted for bras, panties, corsets, dresses...all the basics every mistress of the Hotel Bentmoore needs. It's easier to have her make all that stuff for us here, instead of having to order it out."

"I see," Ella said thoughtfully. "I guess it's like having a personal uniform."

"No," Stacey said, shaking her head. "It's not the hotel telling us what to wear. Some of the outfits are just really popular with the guests, like the crotchless panties, and the corsets." She tilted her head. "Say, have you met Mr. Harden yet? He loves doing corset training."

Ella's throat constricted, and she had to swallow hard to get her bite of food down. "Corset *training*?"

"Never mind," Stacey said, taking in Ella's alarm. "When you're done eating, I'll take you to the seamstress, and then I can give you a short tour of the hotel."

Ella finished her food quickly, and Stacey ordered her to leave the tray outside the door. Then they stepped out into the corridor, and Stacey shut the door behind them.

As they walked down the corridor to the elevators, Ella could hear horrible screams and moans ricocheting off the doors lining the hall, and she cringed. Stacey seemed unaffected.

The visit with the seamstress was short, but educational. Ella learned that while certain articles of clothing were considered staples for the mistresses' wardrobes, the women could also request any kind of costume or lingerie outfit they wanted. Of course, requests made by guests were put at the head of the list.

Clothes the women bought outside the hotel still had to go through a fitting process with the seamstress, to make sure they fit perfectly, showing off every feminine curve and supple limb. Mistresses of the Hotel Bentmoore always had to look their best.

Ella grew skeptical when she was handed a shapeless red dress and told to put it on. She felt like she was wearing a muumuu—until the seamstress gave her the belt. At least with the belt on, her waist was cinched in, and Ella felt a little prettier.

Then she remembered: she wasn't supposed to care if she looked pretty or not.

The seamstress watched as Ella posed in the dress, checking herself out in the full-length mirror. "From now on, you should wear this inside the hotel," she said. "Your breasts are high enough you won't need a bra, but I can give you a thin one if you want, if your trainer says it's okay. But from now on, no panties under the dress."

"What?"

"No panties from now on," the seamstress repeated. "No underpants allowed."

Ella spluttered. "But I brought my own. You don't need to give me any."

"That's not the point," Stacey cut in. "From now on, you don't wear your own clothes. You only wear what we give you, and we're not giving you any underpants. You go bear under the skirt."

"But—"

"Trust me, Ella. You don't want to wear anything without approval."

"Oh...okay," Ella said.

As she walked out of the seamstress's office wearing nothing but the loose dress and a pair of matching slip-on shoes, Ella felt very naked underneath.

She had a feeling that was the point.

Stacey's tour of the hotel was brisk, but even so, it took a lot longer than Ella thought it would. She learned that the hotel was much bigger than just the front main building: there were quite a few other structures across the lavish grounds.

Inside the main building, Ella already knew about the decadent dining room and lobby, but Stacey showed her the well-equipped fitness room, a retro-style game room, a few conference rooms, an indoor pool, and a dim, tastefully furnished bar.

Then they made their way outside, and Stacey showed her around the tennis courts, running tracks, stables, and two more pools, not to mention all the secluded and manicured lawns spread out around the hotel. She had not even bothered to show Ella all there was to see, but there was no way Ella could remember it all.

"You don't have to worry about learning your way around yet," Stacey said as they made their way back inside the hotel. "There'll always be someone to escort you around."

"Until when?" Ella asked. "I mean, at some point I'll be trusted to be on my own, won't I?"

"That's up to Mr. Bentmoore to decide." Stacey opened the door to Ella's room and motioning her in. "I suggest you get some sleep. You'll be woken up early to resume your training."

Ella stopped her outside the door. "Stacey, can I ask you a personal question?"

"Sure."

"How long have you been working at the Bentmoore?"

Stacey creased her brows. "Not that long...a few months now."

"But you must've gone through the training process, too. So...how long does it last?"

Stacey was quiet for a moment. "That really depends on the person."

Ella's voice fell to a whisper. "Does it get really hard?"

Stacey studied her face. "Yes, it gets hard. Not many women can finish it. The hotel doesn't hire just anyone."

Ella sighed. "I see."

Stacey made a face, like she was debating what she was about to say. "My best advice to you is to take it one day at a time, and don't worry about what's to come. There's no point. I really can't explain to you what it's like; but you'll learn for yourself soon enough. Every woman goes through a different process, anyway. Just remember that this was only your first day, Ella. It gets harder, but in some ways, it gets easier, too." With that, she waved Ella goodbye, and shut the door behind her.

Ella had a hard time falling asleep after that. She managed to write down a few more pages of notes, but her thoughts were muddled with emotion, not cold hard facts. Ella soon gave up, vowing to write more the next day.

When Mr. Trowlege had woken her up the next morning, telling her to be ready to go in fifteen minutes, it felt like she had hardly slept at all. But she managed to brush her teeth and put on her shapeless dress before Mr. Trowlege requested her presence again in the hallway.

He escorted her to the dining room, told her she had exactly twenty minutes to eat breakfast, and walked away. Ella had not been allowed to pick her own breakfast; a tray had been brought to her. Although the food was delicious, Ella began to wonder if this was to be a regular thing, not being allowed to choose her own food.

After that, Mr. Trowlege had brought her back to the elevator and asked her if there was any reason why she might need more time in her room before presenting herself to Mr. Lamont.

"No," Ella answered, thinking she could catch up on her notes later. "I can see Mr. Lamont right now."

Ella had a teasing suspicion her anticipation over resuming her "training" on the Sybian was clouding her thoughts, but she ignored it. Excitement was unfurling in her belly, but she tried to ignore that, too.

Mr. Lamont was waiting for her in the same activity room, and wearing the same style suit. He even had the same expression on his face, playful and naughty. But there was a deeper look of sensuality behind his eyes, a hint of things to come.

A collection of evil-looking weapons, tools of the Bentmoore's trade, lay spread across the bed. Ella barely glanced at them; after her eyes caught sight of a flogger closely resembling the one used on her weeks ago in Mr. Bentmoore's office, her fear got the better of her, and she looked away.

She didn't want to dwell on whether it was the promise of what lay in store for her that scared her so...or the thick rush of fresh excitement that pulsed through her veins.

"Good morning, Ella," Mr. Lamont began. "I trust you slept well, and had a good breakfast?"

"Yes, Sir."

"And I see you're wearing a Bentmoore dress, which means you must have been to the seamstress yesterday. Tell me, did she explain the rules about clothes?"

"I—I believe so, Sir."

"What did she tell you?"

"That I shouldn't wear anything without permission."

"Correct—which means you shouldn't be wearing anything underneath that dress. Show me: take it off."

Casting her eyes down at the floor, Ella unzipped the dress and stepped out of it. Then, trying to act casual, she draped the dress over her elbow and held her arm in front of her, using the dress as a shield to cover her naked body. Even after everything that had transpired between them yesterday, after everything Mr. Lamont had put her through, she still felt shy in front of him.

"Oh, Ella," Mr. Lamont said. "You don't have to cover up your body from me. Put the dress away. Lower your arms to your sides." When Ella didn't obey right away, a cold gleam entered his eyes. "I said, put the dress down and your arms to your sides, Ella."

This time, Ella complied, albeit slowly. She flung the dress to the bed, and relaxed her arms at her sides.

Mr. Lamont's smile returned. "That's it. Soon, we will train you how to use every inch of your flesh to tantalize and titillate. But first, you have to get over your modesty. There is no reason to be ashamed of your body. It is quite pleasing, you know."

"I know." Ella's voice was hard. She picked her head up to fix her eyes on Mr. Lamont, giving him an insolent look.

Mr. Lamont crossed his arms and sighed. "Do you want to tell me where your body issues come from?"

"I don't know what you're talking about, Sir."

"Is that so? Well, I'm sure I'll learn of them eventually. Both I, and all the other hosts here, are quite good at getting to the bottom of things." He smiled at the double entendre. "But if you want to keep your secrets for now, that's fine. We'll move on."

He walked over to the bed and waved his hand over all the toys splayed out. "Today, we will begin reviewing some of the equipment we use at the Hotel Bentmoore. Since you're so green, we have a lot to cover. I expect you to pay attention. You may well be tested later on what you've learned, and the consequences of failure would be...painful." His grin was ominous. "Have a seat," he said, motioning her over to the Sybian.

Ella looked over the Sybian, and noticed the dildo that had been sitting atop it yesterday was gone. Where the phallus used to be, there was now a piece of square rubber, covered with short, flat, blunt bristles.

Ella only briefly looked over the strange square before swinging a leg over the hump of the machine and sitting down on it hard. Her eyes widened as she accustomed herself to the strange feeling of the small bristles digging into her skin, tickling her nerve-rich flesh. Mr. Lamont gave her a moment to settle in; then he put his hands on his hips.

"As you see, I took off the dildo. The Sybian has a wide array of attachments; I'm hoping you are with me long enough to try them all."

"Long enough with you? You mean, you don't know how long you'll be my trainer?"

"That's up to you and Mr. Bentmoore. When he thinks you're ready for another trainer, you'll move on."

"To whom?"

"I think we should focus on your lessons right now, Ella."

"Sorry, Sir."

Mr. Lamont cleared his throat. "Now then. I think yesterday you learned very well the full potential of this machine. But more importantly, you got a taste of the untapped potential of your own body. You probably had the best orgasm of your life, and in the shortest amount of time, am I correct?"

Ella nodded. "Yes, Sir."

"Today we're going to focus on learning some of the basic tools we use here at the hotel, and the Sybian is going to help us."

"How?"

"Let me show you." Mr. Lamont picked up

the small black control box and turned it on. Instantly, the Sybian shot to life. A low hum echoed from the machine as it vibrated between Ella's legs, causing the pliant satiny bristles to shake and pulse against her delicate flesh.

Ella gasped, squirmed, and then gasped again. Her squirming had not made her more comfortable; it had only sent a short current of arousal up her body.

Mr. Lamont looked pleased with her reaction. "With no dildo, the Sybian will not stimulate your g-spot, but with the flat bristles, it *will* stimulate your clit," he said above the muted hum. "It's on the lowest setting now, and I think we'll keep it there for a while. Cook you on a low simmer." He gave her a twisted grin, and Ella's jaw opened as understanding dawned.

Mr. Lamont was going to start teaching her about all the tools he had laid out on the bed, all the strange sex toys...and meanwhile, the Sybian would keep her in a low, constant state of arousal.

"Sir, why do you have to teach me this way? Why can't I just sit on a chair, or on the bed...?"

"I have my reasons."

He went to the bed and picked up what looked like a table-tennis paddle. "Let's start with this," he said. "It's one of my favorites: your average, standard paddle. As you can see, it has a thin layer of padding, but underneath that is just a simple piece of wood...."

Ella did her best to focus all her attention on Mr. Lamont, and not on the rascally bristles rippling beneath her.

He held up another one. "This is a leather paddle. This one is more flexible than a wooden one; it's pliable, and can bend around flesh. But don't let that fool you, the leather paddle can still be a formidable tool in the right hands...."

Ella nodded as he continued, even as lines of strain began to appear across her forehead.

"Now, this one right here is a type of impression paddle. As you can see, it has the word SLUT engraved across it. The word is backwards, of course, so that when the paddle hits the skin, the word is impressed onto the flesh the correct way across. There are many types of impression paddles...."

Mr. Lamont's lesson droned on, and all Ella could do was sit still across the machine, put all her energy into listening to his flat and steady monotone voice, and try her best to ignore the tortuous tingling going on in her nether regions.

"So as you can see, there are many types, shapes, and styles of paddles. Ella, are you listening?"

"Yes, Sir," Ella croaked. Her upper lip was beaded with sweat, and her lower lip was pressed between her two even, white front teeth.

"You don't look like it. Tell me, do you need to come?"

Dignity fled her. "Oh, yes, please Sir!"

Mr. Lamont shook his head and tsked. "Well, you lasted quite a while, I'll give you that." He dropped the paddle he had been holding, grabbed the control box, and turned the vibration up full blast. Immediately, the Sybian began to shake and thrum violently beneath her. Ella squealed.

"Go ahead," Mr. Lamont said above the noise. "Come."

Ella didn't have to be told twice, or ask what to do. She grinded her cunt into the plucky bristles, mashing her soft inner folds into the supple spikes. It only took her a moment to find her rhythm, and when she did, she rode the Sybian to quick and complete release.

As she came down from her climax, rolling her head in circles atop her shoulders, Mr. Lamont turned the Sybian back down to the setting it had been at before.

"Better?"

"Oh God." Ella cleared her throat. "I mean, yes, Sir."

"Good. I expect you to last longer this time, Ella. We're going to talk about floggers now."

Mr. Lamont's lesson continued, and Ella sat up straight in her spot, with renewed vigor and sense of purpose. Between her thighs, the Sybian shook, but she didn't care.

She had already come. She could ignore it.

Her resolve remained firm and uncompromising for about twenty minutes. Then it began to crack, just as Mr. Lamont was moving on from leather floggers to rubber ones.

"...While leather floggers come in varying strengths and malleability, rubber floggers are a different breed: no matter how long or thick they are, the strands will sting. They have a lot of bite to them. Of course, one can change the potency of the sting, depending on the strike. Take this pussy flogger, for instance...."

As Mr. Lamont held up flogger after flogger, going on and on in his matter-of-fact voice, Ella's whole demeanor began to change. Her face went from flushed to pale, her toes began to curl and uncurl, and her knees began to shake. Her firm control, so confident and assured only a short time ago, was now slipping away once more.

"Mr. Lamont...Mr. Lamont, I can't...I can't... oh, no!" An orgasm burst out of her core without warning, and Ella wasn't ready for it. She leaned all her weight forward and cried out from the surprising force.

"You weren't expecting that one, were you?" Mr. Lamont asked softly. "Good. That means your body is getting the hang of it."

"The hang of what? My God, what are you doing to me?" Ella's voice cracked under the strain. The orgasm receded just as quickly as it had engulfed her, and now she felt drained, and somehow empty.

"We're engraining your brain with new sensory paths, and training your body with new muscle memory," Mr. Lamont said. "The process takes time, but you're off to a great start."

"Oh, God."

"Let's move on to restraints, shall we? I think collars and leashes are the things to start with...."

Ella heard Mr. Lamont's voice, but it came from somewhere far away, somewhere far beyond her focus. Her legs were slippery against the machine now, her pussy and inner thighs coated with her juices. It was embarrassing, but at the same time, it filled her with wonder.

She was not used to getting so wet; lubrication had often been a problem for her. But here she was, fairly swimming in her own oils, trying to maintain her balance on top of the slippery and sleek machine that was now also quite warm, thanks to the heat radiating from her cunt.

She had come without warning, without expecting it at all. She thought only men suffered from that sort of thing. The question lurking in the back of her head surfaced once more: what the hell were they doing to her?

"Ella, you are not paying attention," Mr. Lamont said. Ella's eyes sharpened.

"I'm sorry, Sir. I guess I'm feeling a little overwhelmed right now." That was true enough.

Mr. Lamont's eyes furrowed. "Very well. We'll give you a break from the Sybian. You may dismount." He turned off the machine.

Ella's movements were slow and ungainly, as her legs were feeling wobbly after so much time on the machine...not to mention her two mind-wracking orgasms.

Once she was off, she headed straight to the bed, and collapsed on her back. Her whole body felt warm, and her inner thighs and pussy lips felt tingly hot. Her clit throbbed. Her legs were wet and shiny from her own body fluids.

She didn't care.

"We're going to try one more thing before I let you take a rest," Mr. Lamont decided. "As soon as you're ready, I want you to get on the spanking bench."

"Sir?"

"I just need to get something." He went to the wardrobe, and when he came back, he was holding what Ella recognized (or thought she recognized) as a back massager.

As she watched with half-hooded eyes, Mr. Lamont plugged the massager into a nearby outlet, and patted the bench. "You ready to get on?"

Ella pushed herself off the bed, a small smile playing across her mouth, thinking she was about to be treated to a back massage. The spanking bench was covered in smooth, cool leather that felt marvelous against her hot skin. Ella relaxed her body over it, ready for some pampering.

She squeaked when she felt Mr. Lamont press the massager into the apex of her thighs.

"This is a Hitachi," he said. "It's another type

of vibrating sex toy. Spread your legs wider, Ella."

Ella whimpered. "Please, Sir, I can't." She didn't mean she couldn't spread her legs; she meant she couldn't come again.

"Yes, you can," Mr. Lamont said, understand her completely. When she didn't obey, his voice became sharp. "Ella, Mr. Bentmoore let you start your training with me because I have a reputation for being the most lenient of all the hosts. But if you can't follow my orders, you're going to have an impossible time later with the others. Now spread your legs."

With a tight grimace, Ella spread her legs. Mr. Lamont couldn't see her expression, of course. He was too busy snuggling the large head of the Hitachi into Ella's plump and wet pussy lips from behind.

Ella whined when he turned it on.

"Are you in pain?"

"No," Ella said in a high-pitched voice. "But I'm afraid."

"Why?"

"I've never come this way before...and so many times...it's so...." She couldn't finish.

Mr. Lamont's voice softened. "I understand," he said. "It can be overwhelming at first. But you're doing great. Now, I want you to hold the handle of the Hitachi between your legs."

"What? Why?"

"You're going to play with it. Move it up and down, in and out, whatever you want. I'm going to flog you—very lightly, you understand. Nothing hard, nothing too painful."

Ella wanted to cry. She was too tired and too spent to do anything other than plead. "Please, Sir, I can't," she repeated.

"You liked it when you were flogged before, didn't you?"

"Yes." Her voice was barely a whisper.

"I'm not even going to flog you that hard, Ella. Just a steady, soft rhythm. As soon as you come, we'll be done. Understand?"

"But I have to come, right?"

"That's right. Come one more time. But how you do it, how long it takes, is completely up to you."

A moment later, she felt the long soft stands of the flogger brush into the space of her lower back.

Ella squeezed the handle of the Hitachi in her hand and leaned her shoulder into the padded bench. True to his word, Mr. Lamont did not hit her hard; but still, Ella cried out every time the satiny ribbons glided across her skin.

Her face flitted with expressions as her emotions did a short battle within her. She wanted to come, she wanted this torment to be over, but at the same time, she feared if she did come again, she would be reduced to a ball of raw nerves.

And a small part of her, a part she was trying very hard to bury deep despite it getting increasingly harder to do so, was telling her she wanted this torture to go on, she wanted it to last for as long as possible, because it felt so good. In fact, that voice was now telling her the only thing that could make this scene even better would be if Mr. Lamont flogged her harder.

"Please, Sir, hit me harder."

Ella braced her legs apart and pressed the Hitachi hard against her clit, gasping at the penetrating thrills.

"Are you sure, Ella? You want me to go harder?"

"Please, Sir!" Her voice was more of a command than a request. Mr. Lamont was the one flogging her, but Ella still felt like she was the one controlling the scene. After all, she was the one controlling the Hitachi, and deciding when and how she came.

Mr. Lamont was more than willing to oblige the terse request. "As you wish," he said.

Ella could hear the satisfaction in his voice, but let it go. He was happy to be flogging her harder, but that didn't matter. Nothing else mattered now but the mingling delights of the Hitachi lodged against her cunt and the flogger biting into her skin.

Mr. Lamont began to flog her with great sweeps of his arm. The strands collided with her skin, making her gulp for air with hissing breaths. But Ella held the Hitachi against her pussy with steady pressure. The pleasure built at an alarming rate.

"My ass," she said. "Flog my ass!"

Mr. Lamont moved the flogger down to the curves of her ass, and Ella began to move the Hitachi wand up and down against her trembling, sopping wet pussy.

Ella got caught up in the sounds of the flogger whistling through the air, the smack of the heavy strands hitting her skin, and the feel of the Hitachi vibrating against her clit. The pain and pleasure mingled inside her head as the pressure rose, and finally crested.

As she came, she pushed herself against the bench, jerking the Hitachi against her pussy and clit in a blur of speed. Mr. Lamont kept flogging her as her orgasm burst, and Ella came with a coarse cry. But as soon as it was over, Mr. Lamont stopped.

"You okay, Ella?"

Ella couldn't answer right away. She was still trying to catch her breath. She finally managed a soft, "I'm okay, Sir."

"Just breathe for now. When you're ready, I'll help you dress. You did wonderfully, by the way."

"Thank you," she said, her voice high and shaky. "I don't think I'll need help getting dressed, if you'll just give me a minute."

"Let me decide that."

In the end, he did help her zip up her dress, not because she couldn't do it, but because she was too tired to protest.

But he did take note of the look of renewed resistance in her eyes.

"I'll escort you to your room," he said, crossing his arms in front of himself. "You can have the rest of the afternoon to yourself."

"Thank you, Sir. I think I need to have a long rest."

"Sleep if you need to, and have a good lunch. We'll resume your training this evening."

Ella swallowed down a choke. "Yes, Sir."

*"She's doing remarkably well, especially for one so woefully ignorant. She's quick—in body, and in mind."*

*"I thought she would be."*

*"I gave her a taste of the Hitachi today, and the flogger."*

*"How did she react to them?"*

*"Surprisingly eager. I worked her over hard—she didn't even notice how hard. And she still had some fight left in her afterwards." He paused. "She'll prove a handful later, Sir."*

*"One scene at a time, Lamont, one scene at a time. Let's not get ahead of ourselves."*

# CHAPTER FOUR: FEAR AND REALIZATION

**E**LLA FELL ASLEEP AS SOON as she got to her room. When she woke up, she had no idea what time it was, and had to call the front desk to ask.

"It's two o'clock in the afternoon, miss," the seductive female voice on the other end said. "I see here you haven't eaten lunch yet. Would you like me to have your meal sent down, or would you like to have someone escort you to the dining room?"

"Neither, at least not yet," Ella replied. "I'm going to shower first. I'll call back when I'm ready."

"Very good, miss."

Ella took a long time catching up on her notes and writing down everything she'd gone through since the day before. As she wrote, she was surprised by how much she remembered from Mr. Lamont's long-winded and provocative "lessons." She thought for sure she would have forgotten most of it, especially by the way the lessons had been administered, but she was wrong.

When she got to the point in her notes where she had to describe how she'd been flogged while holding the Hitachi to her pussy, she had to put the pen down for a while. Her breathing quickened, and her skin grew hot. But she got her body under control, and picked up the pen again. As the words flowed onto the page, she could feel her muscles contract inside her pelvis and around her pussy.

She was turned on. Just the memory of what she had done that morning aroused her more than she could ever remember. The flogging, the multiple orgasms, all of it was stirring her up and making her feel sensual and needy.

Ella closed her notebook with a snap.

She retreated to the shower, where she let the hard water relax her body. But when she tried to slip her hand between her thighs to wash herself there, she gasped. Her clit, even after her long rest, was still very sensitive to the touch.

She stayed clear of it, washing around it instead, delving deep inside her pussy lips.

Even her pussy lips were sensitized, she realized. They were swollen, too. Slippery from the soap, they felt extra soft, and she ran her hand up and down inside her silky velvet folds, marveling at the feeling.

Then she stopped.

Never in her life had she behaved like this before. What was happening to her? Was she merely being trained, as they claimed, or was something more sinister going on? It felt like she was being reprogrammed, like a machine, like a robot...

Like a human sex toy.

Ella turned off the shower and got out quickly, standing naked and shivering in the cold air.

She would not let them do this to her. She would play the role, and pretend to be what they wanted her to be; but when she walked out of this hotel, she would be the same woman, the same Ella.

It was a promise to herself she refused to break.

When Ella got to the activity room later that evening, the first thing she noticed was that the Sybian was gone. Mr. Lamont stood in the spot where it previously resided, wearing his sensuous smile.

"Where's the Sybian?" Ella asked before she could stop herself.

"We're done with that part of your training," Mr. Lamont said. "Time to move on to other things. Here, let me show you." He pointed her attention toward the bed, where a large, mechanical-looking apparatus was already set up next to it.

Ella's eyes immediately focused on the end, where a long purple dildo, thin but curved like a finger, pointed out.

"It's another type of fucking machine," Mr. Lamont explained. "In case you haven't heard by now, I'm an expert on fucking machines. Give me some metal, a motor, and enough time, and I can create for you a device that can spread open the gates of heaven. This one here I modified for my own uses. I call it The Juicer." He let out a chuckle. "You'll figure out why very soon. Now please, get on the bed."

"Um, how?"

"On all fours, with your backside facing the dildo. I'll adjust the height once you're on the bed."

Ella eyed the strange contraption nervously.

"Now now, Ella, no more shyness," Mr. Lamont admonished her as he went to the large wardrobe to retrieve some things. "I think we've moved beyond that, don't you?"

Ella gave herself a mental shrug, and began to take off her dress. The machine looked menacing, but couldn't be any worse than the Sybian; and Mr. Lamont was right, they were beyond any notions of modesty or propriety.

Once she was naked, she climbed up on the bed. But her positioning wasn't quite right for Mr. Lamont, and he fixed it quickly.

"Move back a little bit...that's it...keep your hips steady, head up...Perfect. I'm going to insert the dildo now from behind you. Don't move."

Ella felt Mr. Lamont's warm fingers touch her between her spread thighs, and she inhaled sharply. She realized with a start that it was the first time Mr. Lamont had ever touched her cunt.

As he spread open her pussy lips to gently fit the tip of the dildo inside, Ella held her breath.

"The machine is ready," he said. "I'm going to turn it on now, and get the dildo all the way in. Ready?" He didn't wait for her to answer, but flipped a switch, and Ella felt the dildo slide forward into her pussy. It was thinner than the attachment he had used on the Sybian, but curved, and hit her vaginal wall in an odd way that left her breathless.

Mr. Lamont turned another switch, and the dildo began to vibrate inside her with a low steady hum, tickling her innards.

"There we go," he said. "We'll just leave it on that setting for now. Try to ignore it. I'm going to start teaching you about canes and crops today."

*Try to ignore it?* Ella thought. She was trying her best not to *move*. She felt silly being on all fours across the bed, her breasts dangling beneath her, the brazen toy working away inside her from behind. "Sir, I really think I'd have an easier time sitting on a chair."

"True, but that would not give us the same results. Now then, I want you to look at what I brought out to show you." He lined up all the toys in front of her and, despite the absurdity of the situation, began his lesson.

"Canes come in a few basic materials: wood, metal, and plastic. Of the wood variety, there are many different types, like cedar, bamboo, cherry...but rattan has the reputation as being the meanest cane. Of course, that depends on the feelings of the bottom getting caned, as well as the technique of the top wielding it...."

The lesson continued just as it had the day before, and Ella concentrated as hard as she could.

Despite the humiliating position she was in, and despite the surreal (and in her opinion, ludicrous) quality of the scene, Ella thought she was doing a good job comporting herself. She kept her body still, and her eyes focused on her trainer.

But gradually, in sure degrees, the teasing finger of the machine fluttering inside her began to be felt. It was pressing against the top wall of her cunt in the most vexing way, unpleasant only because the pressure that had been easily overlooked before was now becoming too light and fleeting. She wanted it to press harder.

Ella could no longer ignore the toy oscillating inside her, but she couldn't do what she really wanted to do, either, which was to press herself against it.

As Mr. Lamont droned on about the flexibility of bamboo canes, Ella tried to adjust her stance just the tiniest bit by spreading her knees a little wider and shifting her hips to push back her ass. Her eyes widened. The humming dildo had touched her in a most amazing way, and a shock of pleasure jolted her.

"Ella, what are you doing?" Mr. Lamont eyed her suspiciously.

"Nothing, Sir," Ella replied, trying to refocus.

"Mmm." His face grew shrewd. "I think I should give you a little quiz, just to make sure you've been paying attention. But first—" Putting down the cane he had been holding, Mr. Lamont picked up the control box and turned a knob. The probing dildo began to vibrate faster, hitting Ella's cunt walls with thrumming speed.

"Tell me, Ella, what kind of cane is this?" He held up the cane in front of her cloudy eyes that were quickly filling with distress.

"It's nylon, Sir," Ella gasped.

"And this?" He held up another.

"Stainless steel."

"And this?"

"Rattan—oh!"

"Which one is more flexible?"

"The—oh god—the nylon one, Sir."

"And which one is more durable?"

"The stainless steel...."

"Very good, Ella," Mr. Lamont smiled. "You passed the quiz. You get your reward—and another lesson." He moved around the bed to stand next to Ella's side.

Ella felt, rather than saw, him turn up the

tortuous machine. The finger began to vibrate even faster, but worse, it began to pump in and out of her pussy. Ella's cunt was now so wet, she could hear the juicy sucking noises the dildo made as it flowed in and out of her cunt.

Mr. Lamont began to taunt her. "You want to move, don't you Ella?"

"Yes, Sir, I do." She bowed her head in shame, even as she thrust her hips and ass back against the fucking machine.

"I bet you do," Mr. Lamont whispered. Then Ella felt a hiss through the air, as something hard stung her ass.

"Ow!"

"Your first taste of a cane," he said. "I'm just going to tap you with it, just to give you an idea what kind of power it wields." He tapped her again, and Ella flinched and moaned. "You want to move, go ahead. But you'll move with the cane tapping your ass."

He began to drum the cane against Ella's creamy soft skin. He didn't strike her hard; in fact, he was barely flicking his wrist. But the taps stung like bee stings, and Ella jerked to try to get away from the prickling bite.

At the same time, the dildo inside her kept up its determined assault. It raked across her vaginal walls, grazing her most sensitive nerve endings, and Ella could feel her muscles tightening all around it, trying to hold it still inside. But the finger would not be caught, no matter how Ella chased after it with her cunt and thighs.

At least the steadfast rhythm of the cane was becoming more bearable. No, not just bearable, Ella realized: the shocking nips of pain were making her reflexively squeeze her cunt muscles, making her tighten around the mechanical dildo. They were also complementing her steadily growing pleasure in the most astonishing way.

The pain of the cane was increasing her pleasure, and making her come faster.

Ella swayed against the machine, jerking now and then from the taps of the cane, and groaned.

"That's it, Ella," Mr. Lamont said, his voice breaking through her haze. "Use the pleasure and the pain to guide you. Work for your release."

Ella moved her hips now in wide circles, undulating her torso and jerking her head around as if she were in a trance. The cane danced across her ass and thighs, beating to the rhythm of the machine, and the brazen dildo fucked her cunt with unwavering tenacity.

Ella pushed back her whole body, lodging the purple finger deep inside her womb, and came with shuddering jerks and flicks of her head. Her hair whipped around as her shoulders weaved.

For Mr. Lamont, it was an incredibly erotic scene to watch.

He stopped his light tapping of the cane and turned off the machine as Ella came down from her orgasm. She pulled herself forward and fell on her stomach, breathing hard. Behind her, the purple dildo dripped, coated with her slick juices.

"Look behind you, Ella," Mr. Lamont ordered. "Look at the dildo. I want you to see what your body does when it's aroused."

Ella turned around and looked at the dildo with surprise clear all over her face. "I got that wet? That's...."

"That's beautiful," Mr. Lamont finished for her. "That's the sign of an aroused woman. Touch it, see what it feels like."

Ella cocked her eyebrow, giving her trainer a wary look. But her curiosity won out, and she pointed a single finger to run it along the slippery dildo. She pressed her fingers together.

"It's so...wet," she said, amazed.

"Yes. Now taste it."

Her eyes went wide. *What?*

"Go ahead, put your finger in your mouth. Taste your own juices."

"No." Ella voice was calm, but firm.

It was the first time she had flat-out refused Mr. Lamont, and it was clear he didn't like it. He gave her a piercing stare. "I said taste it."

"No!" Ella said again, louder this time. "It's disgusting. I won't do it!"

For a moment, their eyes did a battle of wills. But then, to Ella's surprise, Mr. Lamont smiled. "Now we're making some real progress," he said. "Now you're starting to think about limits."

Ella gaped at him. "Limits?"

"Soft limits, hard limits; every woman has them. You can't negotiate with a Top if you don't know what your limits are as a bottom."

Ella was now thoroughly confused. "Sir?"

But Mr. Lamont shook his head. "That's it for today. Get dressed. I'll take you back to your room."

*"She got a taste of the cane today, and one of my personalized fucking machines."*

*"And?"*

*"And, she did beautifully. I didn't go very hard with the cane, of course. I didn't restrain her, either. I'll do that tomorrow. But she did refuse me something."*

*"Oh?"*

*"She refused to taste her own cunt juices. She said it's disgusting."*

*Both men laughed.*

*"Well, she needs some work, obviously," Mr. Bentmoore said. "But it's good she's thinking about boundaries. It means she's getting over her initial fear and denial. You're doing good work, Mr. Lamont. Carry on."*

Ella was a jumble of emotions when she got back to her room. She felt tired, frustrated, overwhelmed, and a little bit panicked. Her conviction had been cracked wide open today, and it made her feel shaky and unsure of herself.

She had been caned.

She had liked it.

The pain hadn't been too bad at all. Mr. Lamont had promised to just "give her taste," and he had been true to his word. But the pain had been undeniable...as was the fact that she *had* enjoyed it.

Ella was in a quandary now. Her notes were supposed to be an impartial report of what the hotel was like, what kind of people she was meeting, what they were making her do...but she had always planned her investigative report to be an exposition of how vulgar and obscene the secret affairs of the Hotel Bentmoore really were. This place was supposed to be the den of iniquity itself, brimming with scandal and disgrace.

How could she hold the hotel in contempt if she was enjoying herself? She wasn't acting anymore, and she could no longer pretend she was. She liked being here. She liked what they were doing to her.

But that didn't have to change the goal of her mission, she decided. She was there to report on the inner workings of the Hotel Bentmoore, and she could still do that...even if she understood now how people could like this sort of thing.

But her newfound feelings scared her. Her body's unexpected reactions to Mr. Lamont's strange machines and "lessons" scared her even more.

This place was not changing her, it was *exposing* her, stripping away all her inhibitions and reserve, and showing her all her hidden desires, shrouded fantasies, and deep, potent, thrilling passion.

That was what scared her most of all.

# CHAPTER FIVE: THE BARN

**T**HE NEXT FEW DAYS PASSED by in a blur, as Mr. Lamont continued to teach her all about sex toys, bdsm equipment, and what kinds of things Ella might experience as a masochist and as a sub.

His lessons were straightforward and thorough, punctuated now and then by Ella's need to come. She didn't need the machine anymore to become aroused; just looking at all the sex toys made her wet.

Mr. Lamont was proud of her progress. "Most people need months in the scene to learn everything you've learned in the last few days," he told her.

"Thank you Sir," Ella replied.

"You're welcome," he said, grinning. "You know, with your beauty and your brains, you'll make a fine mistress of the hotel."

Ella had no response to that. The compliment had touched her heart in a way she hadn't expected, and she locked it away in a safe place where she kept all her cherished memories.

She was beginning to feel a little guilty for the way she was misleading everyone, especially Mr. Lamont. Not enough to stop what she was doing, of course. She needed this story, or she might be living on the street next month. But the people here were definitely not the kind of lowlifes she had been expecting. And they acted as if she was one of them, or at least would be, eventually.

A few days later, the seamstress finished most of Ella's wardrobe. Stacey brought the clothes down to Ella's room for her, acting more excited about the apparel than Ella.

"Aren't the corsets beautiful?" She asked as she held one up, her eyes liquid and dreamy in awe. "Try one on!"

Ella held up one of the other corsets to her torso and looked down at it. "I don't know how to put it on."

"That's what I'm here for, Ella. I'm going to teach you how to put on a corset by yourself. You'll be wearing them a lot, and you won't always have someone to help you. Here, take your dress off."

"Uh...."

"Don't be shy, Ella. It's just us girls."

Ella shrugged her shoulders and unzipped her dress. As it fell to the floor, unveiling her nakedness, a moment of discomposure made Ella blush. But Stacey's bubbly and matter-of-fact demeanor quickly dispelled it, and soon, the two women were giggling in excited camaraderie.

"Ooh, look at the lacing on this one," Stacey remarked, holding up the gleaming silk and lace. "I'm going to have to ask the seamstress to make me one like this! Here, turn around, let me help you into it."

"What do I do?"

"Just stand still. I'll let you know when to hold your breath."

Putting on a corset, Ella learned, was an involved process. Hooks had to be snapped closed, material had to be adjusted, and strings had to be pulled. As Stacey tightened up the corset, Ella went through a couple moments of panic when she feared her ribs would implode, but Stacey quickly loosened up the lacings so Ella could breathe again, chuckling at Ella's expression.

When the process was done, the strings tied and tucked in, Stacey told Ella to go look at herself in the full-length bathroom mirror.

"Just look at your waist! And your chest! I wish I had breasts like yours. You look so beautiful."

"Thank you," Ella said, taken aback. It was the first time another woman had ever complimented her on her breasts. Men had complimented them, of course; but those compliments meant nothing. Hearing a woman compliment her chest felt different, and strangely heartwarming.

As Ella gazed at herself in the mirror, she

had to agree: the corset did wonderful things to her figure. Her breasts, already perky before, now snuggled side by side inside the tight corset, like soft pillows pressing against each other. Her hips, too high and square for her liking, now flared below her waist in a perfect hourglass shape.

Ella circled her waist with her hands, and found she could almost enclose it. When she turned around, she noticed the curve of her back, sleek and smooth, now sloped gracefully to show off the contours of her butt. Her soft white buttocks rounded out under the hem of the corset.

She turned to face front, and her eyes travelled down to her pussy. She had been ordered to keep it shaved and smooth, and she had to admit, she liked it that way.

With her blonde hair cascading down her back, her blue eyes bright, her skin gleaming, Ella looked like a sleek, sexy debutant. For a moment, she admired her reflection, feeling beautiful.

Then she realized what she was doing: preening at herself in front of the mirror, acting like a wanton slut! What the hell was wrong with her?

"Can I take it off now?" She called out, turning away from the mirror in disgust.

"I guess," Stacey said, frowning at the change in Ella's tone. "Let me show you how to take it off, and then I'll show you how to put it on by yourself. We'll practice a few times together."

"Okay." Ella's voice was less than enthusiastic, but Stacey pursed her lips and set herself to the task she had been sent to do.

She showed Ella how to hook and unhook the corset in the front, and then instructed her the best way to tighten it up the back. It took Ella half a dozen tries, and by the time she was done, she was sweaty and irritable, all her composure gone; but she finally felt like she could do it on her own.

"For now, you don't have to wear a corset unless one of the trainers tells you to. That probably won't be until Shern or Harden," Stacey said, as Ella put back on her dress.

"Thank God. I can't imagine walking around in this thing all day."

"If you wear it long enough, your body conforms, and it doesn't bother you so much."

"Oh." Ella tried to smile, but the smile never reached her eyes.

"I'm to take you to breakfast now," Stacey said, "and then you're supposed to get some exercise. Mr. Lamont has ordered you to go for a swim."

"Sounds lovely."

"Good. Let's head upstairs for some breakfast. I hear the chef is experimenting with a new recipe for Belgium waffles."

"And will I be allowed to try it?"

Stacey paused. "I forgot you're on food restriction," she said. "But don't worry, once the training period is over, all that stops."

*That is truer than you know*, Ella thought, thinking that once her training period was over, she would be gone from this place anyway.

In the end, Ella was allowed a plate of the waffles, but Stacey warned her Mr. Lamont was much more lax in what he allowed the "new recruits" to eat than some of the other trainers.

"Mr. Shern likes to control *everything* you eat, down to the salt and pepper. But at least it's just food. When you compare him to someone like Cox? God, Cox can be *such* an asshole. I almost didn't...." She pressed her lips shut. "Never mind. I shouldn't be putting ideas in your head about the other trainers before you've met them. Let me take you back to your room, and you can relax for a while. I'll pick you up to take you to the pool in half an hour."

"I didn't bring a bathing suit," Ella said, feeling foolish for overlooking it.

"Don't worry, I was going to give you one from the hotel, anyway."

A half hour later, Ella was looking at the tiny scraps Stacey was claiming made up a bathing suit. In another life, the two-piece outfit might have been some kind of bikini, but so much of the fabric had been snipped away, it now looked like a bunch of string held together with wisps of blue cloth.

"I can't wear this," Ella protested. "It won't cover me at all!"

"Mr. Lamont warned me you're still dealing with some modesty issues. He said this would help you."

"Oh, did he!"

"It's not a big deal, Ella," Stacey said, trying to appease her. "It's the style here. Why don't you try it on, and see how you look for yourself?"

Realizing she had no choice in the matter, Ella took the scraps of slinky fabric into the bathroom, and shut the door behind her. When she was done putting on the bathing suit, she turned in the mirror, and took in her reflection.

The suit (what there was of it) was a cobalt blue, and fit over her butt and breasts like second skin. The color managed to complement her eyes. But the top barely covered her nipples, and the material in the back was so thin and narrow, it wedged up her butt. Ella kept trying to pull it out of the crack of her ass.

Stacey stepped into the bathroom and caught sight of Ella's futile attempt to shield more of her bottom. "It's supposed to do that," she laughed. "You have a nice ass, you should show it off. C'mon, I'll take you to the pool."

"I can't walk around the hotel in this thing!"

"You'll get used to it." Stacey didn't wait for her to reply, but abandoned her in the bathroom to wait for her in the hallway. Ella, giving a last look over her shoulder to the pale contours of her ass curving around the tight bikini bottom, sighed, slipped on the matching flip-flops Stacey had oh-so generously provided, and followed behind.

But as she walked out of the bathroom, she grabbed a towel from the rack and draped it around her body. Stacey didn't say anything.

She led Ella upstairs and through a narrow corridor Ella had never been through before. A simple glass door at the end of the hallway released them outside, and Stacey led the way to the pool.

When they got there, Ella was grateful to see it was completely empty of guests.

"I'll come back in about an hour," Stacey said. "Make sure to do some laps—don't just sit in the sun and do nothing. Okay?"

"Sure," Ella replied, surprised she was being trusted alone. "I'll get in my dose of exercise."

"Good." Stacey waved and left.

Keeping true to her word, Ella did ten laps across the pool. When she felt like she had fulfilled her obligation, she got out, grabbed one of the wide padded lounge chairs, lay down, and relaxed.

Time went by. Ella began to feel hot in the glaring sun. She wanted to get back to the hotel and take a shower. She wondered how much time was left of that hour Stacey had promised her—

And then she heard a loud, hair-curling scream.

Ella sat straight up and looked around. The

scream had sounded close.

Another piercing scream rent the air. Ella scanned the horizon, every nerve ending on her body tingling. She got up and began to walk away from the pool, straight ahead, through a field of grass.

A small knobby hill rose in front of her. Climbing it quickly, she gazed down upon two buildings below. One was the stables, where the hotel kept all their purebred horses. The other was one Stacey had not bothered to show Ella on her tour: it looked like an old, dilapidated barn.

Another scream carried over the breeze, and Ella headed toward the barn.

As she passed the stables, she could hear the horses neighing and clapping their hoofs inside. She wondered why no one had run out from the stables to check the source of the screaming. Perhaps there was no one in there?

As she got closer to the derelict barn, Ella slowed down. Here and there, pieces of the wood siding were drooping to the ground, looking like they were about to break off. Large holes were broken through the high-topped roof, letting the sun stream down inside. The whole structure looked unkempt and abandoned. Even the ground around the barn was gravelly and scattered with weeds.

For a moment, it was quiet.

Then Ella heard a low moan, followed by a choked-off sob. Fearful now, she crept up to the wall, and found a small, filthy window. Crouching down to find a tiny clean spot on the glass through which she could look through, Ella peered inside.

The interior of the barn was even more run down. Dust and rubble were everywhere and coated everything, from the open paneled floor to the wood rafters. Two thick concrete columns rose up to the ceiling, probably to support the decrepit structure.

Ella caught sight of some movement from the far column, and looked that way.

There, tied to the column with thick rope, was a woman.

Her face was blindfolded with a simple black sash, tied to the back of her head. She was standing upright, but naked, looking ethereal in the dusty ray of light coming through the hole in the roof above.

Her arms were hugging the pillar, her wrists tied firmly together on the other side with another matching sash. The knot in the sash was very tight, Ella saw, probably a result of the woman scissoring her hands and pulling on her restraints. Her hair, bleached white and cropped short at the jaw, hung in disarray, and stuck here and there to her sweaty face. Her breasts were flattened against the pillar, her cheek pressed to the side. She was anchored securely, and could not take a single step away.

Ella noticed the way the woman's back

rose and fell, the way her ribs expanded and compressed for breath, the way her soft mouth opened, her lips curling in as she gasped for air. She was breathing hard, heaving and moaning at the same time.

A hiss went through the air, and Ella heard a muted snap. The woman convulsed and cried out, stiffening her arms and hugging the pillar tight. Something had hit the woman's back, something thin and quick.

Ella looked past the woman, and her mouth opened in shock. A man was standing behind her, holding up something Ella had only seen in movies.

It was a whip.

The man was average height, perhaps half a head taller than Ella. His hair was a creamy brown, his eyes a shade darker. Ella noticed a subtle slant to them, just enough to make him look foreign and, in Ella's opinion, deeply compelling. Or perhaps it was the way his eyes were filled with lustrous brilliance, shining in the reflected sunlight. His brows were furrowed with concentration, but his lips were curved in a wicked grin.

He was naked.

His arms, toned and smooth with muscle, gleamed in the streaming sunlight. His wide chest, bare and smooth, stretched between broad shoulders. His waist was narrow and chiseled, and his strong thighs bulged with muscle.

He was sporting a massive erection. His cock aimed up to the ceiling, and in his movements, rubbed against his stomach.

The man swung his arm, flicked his wrist, and let the whip fly. A split second later, the woman let out another piercing scream.

Fascinated by what she was seeing, Ella moved to the other stained window, trying to get a better view of the sordid scene unfolding inside the dusky barn.

Now she could clearly make out the woman's back, ass, legs and thighs; they were covered with long red angry lines of the whip. No part of the tied woman was left unscathed, although her ass had been gifted with the brunt of the man's workmanship. It was crisscrossed with crimson strokes.

As Ella watched, the man flung the whip again with a wave of his arm, and another scarlet line flushed along the woman's quivering skin.

Now the blindfolded woman let out a desperate sob as the man began to whip her quickly, mercilessly, with effortless flicks of elbow and wrist. Her reedy back trembled from the onslaught; her knees shook, and her thighs rippled, as if all strength had left her. Her arms slumped as she leaned her body into the pillar, her only source of support.

The whip flew faster, a whirlwind of strikes, and the tone of the woman's cries began to change. They grew more frenzied, and more fervent; they were cries of unending torture and insatiable need.

Ella knew the woman was not just crying out in pain, she was crying out in crazed passion. She was aroused by the tortuous whipping.

So was Ella.

Sensing the change in the woman's cries, the man stopped his whipping and came to stand behind the panting, trembling female. Pressing his chest into her clammy, raw, and welted back, he whispered some words into her ear. The woman nodded her head vigorously and let out a breathy "yes, Sir," scrunching up her face beneath the blindfold. Immediately, the man came around to the other side of the pillar and began to untie her wrists.

A moment later, she was free from her bonds. Ella was amazed the man could untie her so quickly when her restraints had been pulled so tight.

As soon as she was free, the woman crumpled to her knees.

The man rushed around to support her, but did not help her to stand. Instead, he pulled her up under her arms just enough to straighten her back, so that her mouth would be level with his straining cock. Then, putting both hands on either side of her face, he tugged at her cheeks until her lips spread apart.

He pushed his cock inside.

The woman pushed against the man's thighs

with both hands, fighting and gagging against the thick prick being rammed down her throat. But the man grabbed a fistful of hair at the back of her head and held her still, pressing even further in with his hips until she had his full length, all the way to his balls, down her long, slender throat.

The woman beat her fists against his legs, making muffled cries around his cock. The man pulled out of her mouth, slowly, inch by inch, just enough until the helmeted tip remained inside and the woman could take a few desperate breaths. But as soon as that was done, he rammed back in, getting nothing but silence out of the straining woman.

The man did this a few times, retreating slowly to let her breathe, then shoving back in, holding himself still inside her hot dripping mouth until she fought for release.

After a few moments, the woman's struggles grew weak, and she stopped reacting in panic every time he plunged his cock down the back of her throat. Subdued now, beaten down by his steady force and calm authority, she lowered her hands to her sides and accepted his cock into her mouth and throat without protest.

But this wasn't enough for the man. As soon as she had settled down and yielded to his forceful intrusion, he pulled away from her soft lips completely, popping free his thick erection, and pulled her up by the hair.

The woman howled, trying to grab onto the fingers gripping her hair with such brute force. But she was dragged up to a standing position until she was tipping her head back, grimacing in pain.

As soon as she was on her feet, she was pushed toward the pillar, and only given a split second of warning to put her hands out before she was shoved face first into the column. Ella noticed the force of the shove was not that strong, only enough to shock the woman into obedience; she quickly caught herself against the pillar.

And the ploy worked. As soon as the man tapped the inside of the woman's feet with his own, she spread hers wide, without protest, heaving against the pillar.

The man pulled her back by the hips, until the diamond of her dusky pink cunt lips peaked out between her thighs. The man stepped up right behind her, nestled his cock between her pussy lips, and thrust inside.

The woman pulled up, shocked by the brutal thrust. Holding her bent by the hips, the man kept her from making any kind of escape, and grinded his groin against her ass.

He began to fuck her hard, with loud smacks of skin hitting skin. Soon, the woman began to push back, moaning and crying as she tried to swallow him up inside her hungry pussy with violent rocks of her body.

The couple's rhythmic, violent fucking went on and on as Ella watched from the sanctity of the window.

The woman was clearly overcome now by her need for release; she pushed her body back and forth with all her might, trying to impale herself on the man's rigid cock and bring herself off. If the man had wanted to, he could have let the woman fuck herself on his hard tool, and have her do all the work for both of them.

But that was clearly not what he wanted: he lowered his hands to grip her hips and ass hard, holding them still with his wide spread hands, not letting her gain an inch of control. At the same time, he kept up his own steady pumping, furrowing his brows and making sounds of delight each time his prick disappeared up her swollen, wet cunt.

Only when it was clear the man was about to come did he let go of the woman's hips and let her thrust her butt back against him, skewering herself on his steely prick. A second later, she was crying out in shattering release, the woman reaching her climax a split second before the man.

She screamed as she came, stiffening her whole body, her smeared mouth forming a perfect O in her face. The man grunted and pounded into her, shuddering in blinding pleasure.

He recovered before she did. As her knees buckled beneath her, he pulled her into his arms.

As Ella watched, enthralled, he picked her up in his arms like a baby, hefted her a little to ensure he had her securely in his arms, and carried her to the corner of the barn. Ella saw now that there was a mattress sitting on the floor, nudged into the corner. It looked clean and soft, covered with a silky yellow sheet, matching pillows, and a thin cotton blanket.

The man lay the woman gently down on the mattress, carefully pulled the blindfold off her head, and looked for any sign of distress on the woman's face. She gave him a soft smile, but did not open her eyes as she turned her body to her side, looking spent.

Leaning over the women's face (and giving Ella a very nice view of his flawless ass), the man whispered another few words into the woman's ear. She nodded slightly, and the man pulled the blanket up over her naked body. All Ella could see of her now was the back of her bleach blonde head, and the gentle rise and fall of her side. The man got up off the mattress and stepped away.

To Ella's confusion, he disappeared somewhere else inside the barn. Ella could no longer see him—the tiny hole in the window did not allow her to see that far. Ella waited for the man to come back, wondering why he had left the sleeping woman lying there, and where he could have gone.

Her answer came a second later, when she

heard a deep male voice right behind her.

"Well now, aren't you a pretty little thing—for a spy."

Ella managed a tiny squeak of surprise before her breath locked in her chest. For a split second, she thought the man was referring to her disguise and deception—but no, he was referring to the way she was spying on his scene with the woman sleeping inside the barn.

Ella's eyes widened as they travelled up the man's body. For a second, she was left speechless.

He was taller than she had expected him to be. He had also managed to slip on a pair of pants before coming outside. They were unzipped in the front, showing off a nice expanse of flat lower stomach, and a thin line of soft brown hair that disappeared under the pants, right over his crotch.

"You're wearing a hotel bathing suit," the man said, looking her over with scrutiny Ella found disarming. "But you're not hotel staff. I'd know you if you were. So who are you?"

"I'm new, Sir," Ella stammered. Just like with Mr. Bentmoore, Ella's natural reaction was to address this man as Sir. "I'm new. I'm still being trained."

"A trainee? Ah, then you must be Lamont's new toy. What's your name?"

"Ella, Sir."

"Well, Ella, I'm sure you were not instructed to go wandering around the hotel grounds, especially when I booked the barn this morning for my guest. Why aren't you at the pool?"

"How did you know I was supposed to be at the pool?"

"The bathing suit?" He cocked his brow.

"Oh, right, the bathing suit," Ella said, flustered. She felt like she should defend herself somehow, but the man was making her feel too nervous to say much of anything. He had caught her spying on him having a hot raunchy scene with a hotel guest. Why wasn't he chastising her?

"Tell me, did you enjoy your little peep show?" He asked, crossing his thick arms in front of him and looking at her underneath furrowed brows. Ella could feel her whole face go red, but she couldn't look away from his fascinating eyes.

"I'm sorry, Sir, I know I shouldn't be here, it's just—I heard screaming, horrible screaming, and...." Her voice trailed away as the man continued to stare down at her.

"And you just had to check it out and make sure everything was okay." He shifted his feet to widen his stance against her. "Let me explain something to you, Ella. At the Hotel Bentmoore, you are going to hear a lot of screaming, all the time. It's not something you have to worry about—unless you're the one causing the screaming. Are you a masochist?"

"I...."

"You don't know?"

Ella's voice lowered. "I believe I am, Sir."

"Do you like being flogged, paddled, caned?"

"Yes, I do."

"Then you're a masochist. It's not something you have to *believe* in. Does Lamont do those things to you?"

"Yes, Sir," Ella admitted, her face flushing.

His voice lowered to a whisper as his eyes began to dance with sparkling light. "Tell me, has he made you scream?"

The question made Ella's eyes flare up, and she took a tiny gasp.

"I see he has not," the man said, clearly disappointed. "Well, he likes to go easy on his women. Now answer the question: did you like what you saw in there?"

"I...." Again, Ella stammered.

"God you're a timid one," the man said, sighing. "Lamont must love you."

"I am not timid," Ella hissed, gaining some of her courage back. "I'm just...." She shut her mouth as it became clear she had been rendered unable to finish a complete sentence.

"Go back to the pool, Ella," the man said, shaking his head. "I'm sure someone will be looking for you soon, if they are not already." He turned around to walk away.

Ella stopped him. "Are you going to tell anyone you saw me here?"

He looked at her over his shoulder. "No," he

said. "There's no reason to. No harm, no foul. It's not like Lamont would punish you that hard, anyway."

"Thank you, Sir," Ella said, relief thick in her voice.

"Don't bother." He took another step away from her.

Ella's vexation rose. "Who are you?" She called out.

The man stopped. This time, he turned all the way around to face her.

"My name is Mr. Cox," he said. "I am a host of the Hotel Bentmoore. I am a Dom, a Master, and one of the worst sadists you will likely ever meet. So when I say I won't tell anyone I found you here, Ella, rest assured, it's not because I'm doing you a favor. It's because I'm reserving the right to punish you myself. When the time comes and I get my hands on you, Ella, you will be the one screaming. Now get back to the pool."

This time, it was Ella who turned around. She ran all the way back to the pool.

Stacey found her sitting on one of the lounge chairs, breathing hard.

"Are you okay?" She asked, putting her hand on Ella's shoulder.

"Yeah," Ella said. "Just doing some jumping jacks. Getting in my exercise, as ordered."

Stacey's look was skeptical. "It's time to go

back to your room. You have a long afternoon ahead of you."

Ella rose without responding. As she followed Stacey back to the hotel, she gave one last look over her shoulder toward the quiet barn.

# CHAPTER SIX: THE ST. ANDREW'S CROSS

**A**s **Mr. Trowlege escorted her** down the hall to her activity room, Ella noticed something had changed: she was not being brought to the same room she had shared with Mr. Lamont these past many days.

"Where are you taking me?" She asked to Mr. Trowlege's stiff back.

"One of the other rooms," came the reply.

Ella rolled her eyes. "Why?"

"You will see."

A second later, he stopped in front of one of the other doors, went through the motions of unlocking it, and motioned her inside. As soon as Ella had crossed the threshold, the door was shut behind her.

She looked around. The room was filled with strange apparatuses: benches, cages, bars screwed down to narrow tables and laden with cuffs; stocks, pillories, a rack, and more perverse and frightening devices spread across the room. It looked like a torture chamber, updated for

INSIDE THE HOTEL BENTMOORE: TRAINING ELLA

modern day. The only familiar pieces of furniture in the room were the large ornate wardrobe, and the bed, already lined up with floggers and other nefarious tools.

Mr. Lamont stood in the center of the room, looking pleased. "Hello, Ella," he said. "Ready to get started?"

"I don't know," she said, eyeing all the equipment. "Does it matter?"

Mr. Lamont frowned. "Of course it matters," he said. "You should be filled with excitement, not fear."

His answer only filled her with a strange, hollow sadness. "I'm sorry, Sir," Ella said. "I will try harder."

Mr. Lamont's frown deepened. "Get undressed," he said. "Quickly now."

"Yes, Sir." Her words were devoid of inflection.

Ella undressed quickly, but without any enthusiasm or drive. Mr. Lamont pressed his lips together in a fine scowl.

"Ella, is something bothering you? Did something happen this morning?"

"No Sir," Ella said. "Nothing happened."

"Is that so." He gave her a probing stare, trying to see something behind her eyes, but Ella looked back at him blandly, controlling her crisp features with her easy composure.

"Come here," he said. "I want to introduce you to your first piece of bondage equipment."

He pointed her to a large wooden cross

towering in the corner, shaped like a giant X. "The St. Andrew's Cross. Do you remember what I taught you about it?"

"Yes, Sir."

"Good. I want you to stand up against it and face me, arms and legs against the cross."

Ella did as ordered, feeling the first twitter of excitement. She was finally going to experience the St. Andrew's Cross, something she had been both anticipating and dreading for a long time.

"Grab onto the handle bars," Mr. Lamont said softly. "No, don't look down. Keep your eyes on me. That's it." His voice grew thick and husky. "God, you look beautiful." He went to the bed and picked up a flogger. "Let's start you off with a short quiz. What kind of flogger is this?"

"Bullhide braided leather flogger, long tail."

"Very good. And this?" He picked up another one.

"Rubber flogger. I think, ah, teak handle?"

"Very good. And this?"

"Rattan cane."

"Ella, feel your pussy."

"What?"

"Let go of one of the handle bars, reach down, and feel your pussy. I want you to feel how wet you are."

Her brows creased with confusion as Ella lowered one hand between her legs, and slowly pressed it against her pussy lips. She gasped.

Her pussy was not just moist. It was slick,

wet from her own juices that were leaking out of her cunt.

"Do you understand now, Ella? You see the toys of sadomasochism, and your body becomes aroused without conscious thought. It betrays you now. You have no control over your reactions." The satisfaction in his voice was clear, and his rich smile was wide. "Now put your hand back up and grab on."

Ella gripped the cross handles with tight fists. Mr. Lamont retrieved a short rubber flogger from the bed, one Ella had never seen before.

"We've done a fair amount of work on your ass and thighs, but I think we've woefully neglected your breasts," he said. "Time to test how sensitive those nipples really are."

He stepped up to her prone body, took careful aim, and flicked the whippy flogger straight at her left breast.

Ella gasped. The stretchy rubber had bit into her flesh with sharp precision, making the skin mottle and redden. Mr. Lamont whipped the flogger again, this time on the underside of her breast, and got the same gasp of shock.

By the time he moved on to the other breast, Ella knew the kind of pain she was in for, and she cringed away, letting go of the handle.

"Stand straight, Ella. Grab the bar."

Ella fixed her stance, but still cowered in anticipation.

Mr. Lamont beat the top, curve, and

underside of her breast. The flogger whipped through the air with quiet hisses. Ella dodged the last strike and stepped away from the cross, breathing hard, holding her breast, and looking at Mr. Lamont in accusation.

"I'm not hitting you that hard, Ella," he said. "Does it really hurt so much?"

"Yes...no...I don't know," she replied, unable to think clearly. "It's hard to stand still while you're flogging me."

"Just grip the handles tighter. You can make all the noise you want. I had no idea you would react this way to a simple breast flogging—I'm very pleased. But you need to come back to the cross now."

With slow shuffles of her bare feet, Ella stepped back up to the cross, and grabbed the handles once more. Mr. Lamont gave her a delighted grin.

He braced his legs apart, and began to swing the flogger in wide figure eights, striking both her sensitive breasts with easy cadence, never losing his poise.

The same could not be true for Ella. She was scrunching up her face now, lifting her feet, and holding onto the handles with white-knuckled fingers.

When a particularly harsh swing brought the tips of the flogger right onto her left nipple, she cried out, and let go of the handle to shield her breast with her hand. But Mr. Lamont didn't catch her instinctive reaction in time, and he swung the flogger right into the fleshy meat of her fingers. Ella's intake of breath was sharp and loud.

"Why did you let go of the bar?" Mr. Lamont said, very angry now. He dropped the flogger to the floor and grabbed Ella's hand, checking it for damage.

"Because it *hurt*," Ella replied. She looked down at her throbbing and aching hand as Mr. Lamont turned it over and checked both sides of her fingers.

"I cannot risk you thrashing around when I'm flogging you against he cross. You might get seriously hurt."

Ella continued to study her hand as he walked away. "I thought getting hurt was the point," she called out.

"Not the parts I don't want to hurt," he replied as he opened the wardrobe and disappeared behind the door. When he returned, all of Ella's concerns about her hand fled.

He was holding up a pair of leather cuffs, thick and wide. Carabiners were already attached to the rings of the cuffs to lock her wrists to the bars of the cross.

"No," Ella murmured.

"If you're cuffed in, you won't be able to get your hands in the way."

"I don't want you to cuff me." Ella stepped off the cross and away from her trainer.

Mr. Lamont eyed her shrewdly. "What are you afraid of, Ella?"

"I'm not afraid."

"Then why won't you let me cuff you?"

"Because I don't want you to!" Ella's voice rose. Mr. Lamont had taken a step towards her, and she shrank away. "Stop it!"

He paused. "You say you're not afraid, but you sure act like it. Tell me what's going on."

Tears sprung in her eyes. She hated the way she was cowering, the way she was blubbering, but most of all, she hated the turmoil going on inside her head, the maelstrom of conflicting thoughts.

She did want to be cuffed: in fact, she wanted it very badly.

But not like this. This felt *wrong*. She could not submit in this way, not so readily...not to *him.* Her body was willing, but a greater force inside her head would not give in.

"I don't want to be cuffed," she repeated, her voice coarse. "You can't make me!"

Mr. Lamont's brows creased, and his lips pursed in a thin line. "It's true, I'm not going to force you," he said softly. "But I'm not going to continue the scene like this, either. So are we done?"

Ella was quiet, unable to look at him.

"I *said,* Ella, are we *done?*"

Ella peered at him with eyes filled with sadness. "Yes. We're done."

"Very well." His jaw clenched. "I'll take you back to your room."

⎯⎯⎯⎯⎯

*"She hit a wall today. I think I might have discovered a hard limit."*

*"This is excellent news."*

*"Not really: the limit was a pair of cuffs. She wouldn't let me restrain her to the St. Andrew's Cross."*

*Mr. Bentmoore took a moment to digest this. "What happened when you pushed?"*

*"She snapped. She couldn't even look at me." Mr. Lamont's eyes narrowed. "The thing is, I'm not sure it was just about the cuffs. I got the feeling something must have happened this morning."*

*"Such as?"*

*"I have no idea. When she wasn't with me, she was with Stacey. I asked her, but she doesn't know anything. Told me all Ella did all morning was try on corsets and do laps around the pool." He paused. "Do you want me to try to dig deeper?"*

*Mr. Bentmoore gave it a moment of thought, but they both already knew the answer coming. "No. I think you're done, Mr. Lamont. You've made great progress with her, but it's time to move her on to the next trainer."*

*"I understand, Sir." The disappointment in his voice was obvious. "Who do you have in mind?"*

*"Harden. He's strict, but focused. I think he*

*can gain her trust and help her forward."*

*"I hope so, Sir."* Mr. Lamont sighed. *"She will make a beautiful submissive...once she learns to let herself submit."*

Ella turned on the faucet in the bathroom sink and splashed cold water on her face. As she dried herself with the towel, rubbing her cheeks in deep circles, she caught her reflection in the mirror.

She didn't know if she recognized herself anymore.

She had witnessed something that day in the barn, something profound, and she didn't understand it. All she knew was it had something to do with that man, Mr. Cox.

What had Stacey called him? An asshole?

He didn't seem like an asshole to Ella. He seemed...dangerous. Threatening to her senses in a very deep and primal way. He was someone she should stay away from, she decided. Otherwise, she might end up in over her head.

Wasn't she already in over her head?

Ella took a couple of deep, calming breaths. So she was getting a little bit more immersed in this assignment than she had originally planned. That was okay; that was good. Some of the best pieces of journalism in history came out when reporters were able to get immersed in their work.

She could handle it.

But as she grabbed her notebook and began to write down the events of the day, she left out her momentous meeting with the formidable sadist Mr. Cox.

# PART II: MR. HARDEN

# CHAPTER SEVEN:
# AN EPIPHANY

**T**HE NEXT DAY, **E**LLA WAS brought to a new activity room, one with new equipment, new furniture—

And apparently, a new trainer.

"Where is Mr. Lamont?" She asked the man standing in the middle of the room, who was offering her a welcoming smile.

"You're done with him," he said, his smile wavering. "I thought he told you."

Ella stammered. "He told me we were done, but I thought he meant done for the day. I didn't think he meant...." She looked over the new man with greater scrutiny, understanding now he was to be her new trainer.

He was older than Mr. Lamont: his thick hair was a glimmering silver, and laugh lines framed his sparkling green eyes. But his trim and toned figure was obvious under the dark grey suit. He was older, yes, but still a very attractive man, and strong enough to take her down if he had to.

Dear God, where had *that* thought come from?

"Who are you?"

The man raised his eyebrows. "My name is Mr. Harden," he said. "I'm to be your trainer now. It's nice to meet you, Ella."

"It's nice to meet you, too."

"Sir."

"What?"

"'It's nice to meet you, too, Sir.' As your trainer, you will address me properly."

"I'm sorry—Sir. Jeez, why do you people have to stand on ceremony so much?" The question broke from her mouth before she could stop it.

Mr. Harden's smile faded. "We do this, Ella, so everything is clearly defined between us from the start. Rules help us remember our roles. Now why don't you try saying hello to me again, and this time, address me properly."

Ella flushed. "Hello, Sir."

Mr. Harden's smile returned, and a gleam entered his eyes. "There now. That wasn't so hard, was it? Let's take a look at you."

His eyes grazed up and down her lithe form, and he nodded approvingly. "The dress becomes you, but I understand you have been fitted with corsets, correct?"

"Yes, Sir."

"From now on, I want you to wear them. Let's start with, oh, three hours a day? You can wear them in the confines of your room if you want, but I would prefer it if you wore them around the hotel, as well. You should treat them as part of your regular wardrobe now. I'll have Stacey make sure you have matching skirts to complete the outfits when you go out."

Ella gnashed her teeth together. The man was treating her like his own personal dress up doll. "Thank you, Sir."

"You're very welcome. Now get undressed."

Ella's jaw dropped. She supposed she should have been expecting the order—after all, it seemed to be standard for the trainers around here to order her to strip within five minutes of greeting her—but it still shocked her. He had said it so easily, so coolly, like he was asking her for the time.

Ella supposed it was natural for the hosts of the Hotel Bentmoore to expect the women under their "care" to have no shame or reservations about stripping at the merest suggestion, but Ella did not feel so amiable.

Mr. Harden seemed to sense her quandary. "Mr. Lamont told me you have lingering problems with your modesty, and undressing in front of a man."

"I don't. I just...."

"You have nothing to be ashamed of. Your body is beautiful."

"I know, *Sir*." Her voice turned cold.

Mr. Harden paused. "Do you want to be here, Ella?"

"What do you mean?"

"Do you want to be here, at the Hotel

Bentmoore? Do you want this job?"

Ella squirmed. "Yes, Sir."

"Then follow orders. Get undressed, and have a seat on the bed. We'll go over some rules, and hopefully this will clear things up between us."

Ella whipped her hair back and puffed some air through the corner of her mouth. Then she began to unbelt her dress with quick yanks.

"No," Mr. Harden shook his head. "Slowly. Prolong the moment. I'm seeing your body for the first time; let me enjoy it. Tease me with it."

Ella paused. Then, moving at a snail's pace, she finished the job of unbuckling her belt, keeping her eyes locked onto her new trainer.

If he noticed her impudence, the petulance in her eyes, he made no remark upon it. "That's it, Ella," he said. "Slowly."

As Ella pulled down the zipper of the dress, she spread the front open wide, revealing her pale, pink-tipped breasts. The zipper descended further, unveiling her narrow waist, bony hips, and flat, feminine belly. As the dress fell down to the floor, Ella bent one leg in front of the other, put her hands on her hips, and jutted out her chin, giving Mr. Harden a brazen, flashy pose.

His grin was wide as he crossed his arms in front of his chest. "Very nice, Ella," he said. "I don't think modesty is your problem—just motivation. Have a seat on the bed. Let's talk."

Ella sat down and crossed her legs, feeling like her effort to annoy him had been thwarted.

She debated whether she should open her legs and give him a nice teasing view of her cunt, but decided that might be overdoing it.

Or maybe not....

"Don't cross your legs in front of me," he said. "Bend them straight out."

Ella obeyed, biting back a sharp retort.

"Now then: Mr. Lamont, I understand, did a nice job taking you through the first stage of your training. He introduced you to our equipment, taught you the basics of BDSM, and helped you to tap into your inner masochism. You should no longer have any fear of walking into any one of our activity rooms and seeing all our equipment. Am I correct?"

Ella's voice was almost mute as she looked down at the floor. "Yes, Sir."

"Good. The next stage is going to be putting some of that fear back." Ella's eyes snapped up, and he chuckled. "Pain can be an instrument of pleasure, Ella, but it can go to a dangerous place in the wrong hands. You need to learn your thresholds now, how far you can go, how much pain you can take. Everyone has limits. With my help, we will figure out yours. You will also begin to learn sexual techniques, how to entice, how to seduce, how to beguile. You will become an expert of the flesh, and learn how to bring men to the heights of pleasure."

Ella bared her teeth in a scowl. "You make it sound like I'm learning how to be a whore."

"No," Mr. Harden said, shaking his head. "You are no cheap dime whore. You will be like the proud and noble courtesans of royalty: a well-bred and well-educated artist of the trade. You will be sought after by many, but you will choose whom you favor with your talents."

Her surprise was obvious. "I get to choose?"

"Of course you get to choose, Ella. The relationships we foster at the Hotel Bentmoore are intimate affairs. It will be up to you to decide which guests you play with. We offer suggestions, of course, and hope you are willing to experiment and keep an open mind. But in the end, it must be you who agrees, and gives consent."

"And if I don't?"

"You won't have much of a job here. But then, you always have the choice to leave."

Ella's eyes grew stormy blue. She understood now what he was trying to say: play the high-class slut, or be shown the door. "I see."

"No," he shook his head again, "it is clear you don't, but you will. Consent should never be given lightly, Ella. It requires a lot of deliberation, and, especially in the beginning, a lot of negotiation. But the first thing it requires is knowing yourself." He looked at her through slanted eyes as he said softly, "I don't think you know yourself at all."

Ella was quiet.

"There is going to be one major change with my training techniques from what you were used to with Mr. Lamont," he went on. "I'm going to push you harder than he did, which means you're going to need a safeword. Tell me, Ella, do you know what a safeword is?"

Ella had a feeling he knew she had learned about safewords from Mr. Lamont, but was trying to test her knowledge. "It's a word the bottom can use to stop the scene."

"That's right. A safeword is used to grind the scene to a halt. Now, whether play continues after that is up to those playing. Some people take a few minutes to work things out, and continue on with the scene. Others use the safeword to stop all play for the night, and move on to aftercare. But here at the hotel, the basic tenant is that once the bottom uses her safeword, the Top must stop whatever he is doing, and figure out what happened that prompted her to use the safeword."

"I would think it's obvious," Ella said, her voice full of derision. "He went too far."

"That is often true, yes. But there are many ways a Top can go too far, and he has to figure out where he crossed the line. The safeword can be used as a tool, too. It can be used to test the limits of a bottom." Ella blanched as understanding began to set in. "You're going to need a safeword from now on, Ella," Mr. Harden said, "because I'm going start testing your limits."

Ella shifted uncomfortably in her seat. "Sir,

what is my safeword?"

"Eventually, you will think up your own unique safeword, but for now, we will stick with the old standby, 'Red.' Can you remember that, Ella?"

"Yes, Sir. Red."

"Very good. Let's get started, shall we?" With a wave of his hand, he motioned Ella to the other side of the large wardrobe.

Ella walked around the large piece of furniture, looked to what Mr. Harden was motioning her to, and caught her breath.

There, attached to the wall, was a large, pink, silicone dildo. It jutted out from the wall like a vulgar obscenity, and curved upward exactly the way a real cock would.

"What...?"

"One of the fundamental crafts a mistress of the Hotel Bentmoore must master is how to give a good blowjob. Sadly, many women walk in here completely lacking in their skills. So we're going to start with this: I want you to think of that dildo as the best tasting cock in the world, and try to suck it off."

Ella stared at the dildo in horror. "I can't do that!"

"Why not?"

"It's not even real!"

"You think I want to put my cock in your mouth and risk getting bit? No." He shook his head. "Believe me, once I know you have the basic techniques down, I will look forward to moving you onto the real thing. But for now, show me what you've got with that." He pointed her back to the dildo.

Ella stepped up to it, grimacing. Making a face of complete disgust, she pressed her lips to the tip of the smooth plastic cock.

Then she pulled away. "This is ridiculous," she said. "I feel silly."

"You won't once you get used to it. Go on, take it in your mouth." When Ella didn't move, his voice grew hard. "Do it, Ella."

For a second, she scowled, and the scene threatened to take a precarious turn. The silence between them became heavy as they stared at each other.

But finally, Ella turned her face back to the dildo, and this time, when she pressed her lips against the slick silicone, she opened her lips to let the smooth plastic cock slide inside.

"There you go," Mr. Harden murmured, pleased. "Get a feel for it."

Ella stopped when she had the thick helmeted tip well inside her mouth; it felt big and bulbous inside her cheeks. Instinctively, she squeezed her lips around the shaft, trying to accommodate the foreign prick against her tongue.

"That's good, Ella," Mr. Harden encouraged her. "Fold your lips around your teeth so you don't scrape it. Now slide your mouth down."

Ella closed her eyes and pushed her face

forward, getting a heavy mouthful of cock. She squeezed her eyes shut when the sleek dildo hit the back of her throat. Then she released her lips, pulled back, and swallowed the surge of spit in her mouth.

Out of the corner of her eye, she saw Mr. Harden give her a look of displeasure. "You've never deep-throated, have you?"

Ella freed her mouth to answer the question, sucking some spittle off her lip. "No Sir," she said. "I don't even know what that means."

"It means letting a cock go all the way down your throat. You'll need to learn how to do that, but first you need to learn how to control your gag reflex." He furrowed his brows. "We won't start on that now. I just want to get an idea what skills you already have, and what you can do. Keep going, do whatever you would normally do with a cock in your mouth." He pointed back to the dildo.

This time, Ella grabbed the base of the shaft, shoved the dildo into her face, and attacked it with angry gusto, jerking it in and out of her mouth with quick pumps. As she assailed the dildo with her glistening mouth, she shifted her face to the side, just enough to stare furiously at her trainer.

Mr. Harden pursed his lips. "Slow down, Ella," he warned her.

Ella let go of the dildo and stepped away. "You want me to treat it like a cock, right? This is how I would make it come, right?" Her anger continued to bubble to the surface. She had no idea where it was coming from, but it felt good, and she gave into it without restraint.

Mr. Harden shook his head and tsked; then he opened up the wardrobe and retrieved something from inside. At first, Ella couldn't see what it was—the door blocked her view. But as he closed the door, she saw Mr. Harden was now holding a paddle in his hand.

"What's that for?"

"Motivation," he answered. He came around to her side, bent over, and smacked her ass with the paddle.

"Hey!"

"Hey is for horses. Speak like a proper Hotel Bentmoore woman." He smacked her butt again.

"Don't do that!"

"Why not?"

Ella tried hard to think up a valid reason for him, since she knew "it hurts" would not work. "It's hard to concentrate on my—um, work— when you're paddling me."

"Consider it another thing you'll have to get used to." He whacked her with the paddle again, much harder this time, and Ella shrieked. "Get your mouth back on that dildo. Work it!"

Furious now, Ella gobbled up the smooth dildo into her mouth and pumped it with straining jaws. Mr. Harden didn't spank her again.

After a few minutes, she began to get the

hang of the task, and relaxed considerably. She sucked the dildo down her tongue with slow pulls of her cheeks and jaws.

"That's good, Ella," Mr. Harden said, pleased. "Suck it down, like that. Now lick it."

Ella began to lick the thick plastic cock with wide strokes of her tongue, coating it with her saliva.

"Gently now...slowly...that's it, twist your head to get it in there...that's nice, Ella."

She put her hands against the wall on either side of the slippery pink prick and leaned forward, bracing herself so she could get a better handle on the fake cock in her mouth.

As she closed her eyes and continued her measured pumping, Ella's demeanor began to change. Her face flushed, and small beads of sweat appeared over her brow. She pumped her mouth faster, harder, and with hard pulls of her jaws that hallowed out her cheeks every time she pulled back. She worked to take more of the hard rubbery phallus in her mouth, as if she could make it come.

She was beginning to enjoy herself.

"I think you like sucking cock."

Ella stopped and turned her head—as much as she could with the dildo in her mouth—to look at Mr. Harden, who was gazing at her with a measured grin. "Put your fingers between your legs. Feel how wet your pussy is."

Ella slid her hand between her legs, dug

her fingers between her pussy lips, and found that she was drenched. Her fingers came away coated and slippery with her own juices.

"Ahh, watching you touch yourself with that cock in your mouth looks lovely. Keep touching yourself, Ella," Mr. Harden instructed. "Rub your pussy. And keep working that cock, too. Make yourself come as you suck it."

Ella squeezed her eyes shut and whined, shaking her head against the dildo. She could not stand there and pleasure herself as she sucked on a fake cock...she could *not*....

A second later, she felt the *thwack* of the paddle hitting her ass again, biting into her smarting mounds.

"*Move,*" Mr. Harden said.

With another whine, Ella snaked her fingers deeper into her sopping cunt, fitted them right against her clit, and resumed her rabid sucking of the dildo.

After a few moments, she fell into a natural rhythm, and began to pump her face onto the dildo in cadence with her hand rubbing against her clit. Her face bobbed, and her hand rubbed; and every so often, Mr. Harden would smack the paddle against her ass by way of encouragement.

But Ella could tell that he was not deriving any pleasure from her distress; he was only trying to teach her a lesson. There was no passion in his eyes, no satisfaction in his face whenever she cried out in pain.

The fact upset Ella.

She jolted from the shock of her own feelings. What, did she *want* him to enjoy hurting her?

Yes, realized, she did. She wanted him to enjoy hurting her the way Mr. Cox had obviously enjoyed hurting that woman in the barn. Without that merging of stormy passion, that synergy between man and woman, Top and bottom, all she was left with was a feeling of sour dissidence, and deep detachment from her trainer.

But the disconnect she felt from Mr. Harden helped her maintain control. He wanted her to come, and she would, yes—but when *she* was ready, when *she* decided the timing was right, and not before.

Mr. Harden was the one holding the paddle, but Ella was still the one controlling the scene.

A few moments later, when she decided she'd had enough, she let her orgasm go and came with a wail, shuddering and moaning, her mouth fluttering around the hard silicone. Saliva dripped from the dildo as her mouth pressed around the shaft.

As soon as she was done, she pulled her face away from the dildo and leaned her cheek against the cool drywall, breathing hard.

"That was good, Ella," Mr. Harden announced.

"Thank you, Sir." Her voice was polite.

Ella had to agree: it *had* been good. Not because her orgasm had been all that momentous, but because she'd had an amazing epiphany in the process.

She might be a masochist, she might like the pain...but that didn't mean she had to give up control. Giving into the pain did not have to mean giving up herself.

The realization made her smile.

Unfortunately, Mr. Harden didn't see it.

*"We're off to a rather rocky start, I'm afraid. I gave her a small test today of her skills with the wall dildo. As we expected, her technique needs a lot of work."*

*"But that's true for most of the women who come through here. That doesn't explain your worry."*

*Mr. Harden paused. "She did the work, complied with my orders well enough...but I never felt like there was any real submission on her part. She followed orders because she chose to, and in the end, she came because she wanted to, when she was ready. She didn't give up any part of herself—not to me, and not to the scene. Mr. Bentmoore, are you sure she's a submissive?"*

*"Yes, Harden, I'm sure. It's odd she's fighting her true nature so strongly, though. Keep working with her, see if you can make any progress."*

# CHAPTER EIGHT: TOPPING FROM THE BOTTOM

**T**HAT AFTERNOON, ELLA ENTERED HER activity room in high confidence. She was learning a lot about this place, and in the process, she was learning a lot about herself... but she no longer had to fear losing herself to these men, who seemed intent on making her their puppet. She could act the bottom, but still maintain control. The knowledge brought her comfort, and made her feel like she had the upper hand.

As soon as she entered the activity room, her eyes fell upon the long balance beam going across the floor, sitting on short legs about six inches off the ground.

Mr. Harden greeted her from the other side of the room. He held in his hand a long and thin riding crop, reaching from his palm to the floor.

"I hope you had a nice rest and a good lunch," he said, "because we have a long afternoon ahead of us."

Ella said nothing to her trainer's greeting,

but stared at the crop.

Mr. Harden whipped up the crop, pointed the tip under Ella's chin, and forced her face up to look at him.

"Proper Bentmoore etiquette, Ella. Greet me politely."

"Hello, Sir," she responded, her face impassive. When Mr. Harden didn't pull the crop away from her chin, she gave him a fake smile.

"That will do, for now," he said, lowering the crop. "Turn around, let me look at you."

Ella turned in a tight circle, wobbling on her feet with clumsy sways of her hips. She had put on her brand new lavender corset, along with the matching black and lavender skirt she had found waiting for her, crisp and folded, outside her bedroom door.

Her nipples were barely covered up by the top layer of flimsy lace; they threatened to peek out with each movement of her hips. The skirt was tight, and clung to her waist and thighs like second skin. It was also extremely short, and showed off a nice expanse of slender leg. Her calves and ass were stretched and lifted by a pair of new stiletto heels.

"You look lovely," Mr. Harden said.

"Thank you, Sir," Ella replied. She had learned by now she should acknowledge his praise, but appreciation was another matter. There was none in Ella's tone.

Mr. Harden sighed. Then he creased his

brows, studying her form. "You did a good job putting on the corset, but I think we can get it a little tighter. Turn around."

Ella turned, careful in her new wickedly high heels. Mr. Harden untied the bow in the back of Ella's corset, grabbed hold of the strings...and pulled.

Ella sucked in her breath as her ribs compressed. Her back straightened, her neck stretched, and her breasts lifted.

"There we go," Mr. Harden said. "Much better."

Ella would have loved to refute that statement if she had not been putting all her focus on breathing. White rage bubbled up in her chest, and her hands clenched into fists.

She had no idea where this anger was coming from, and why it was causing her to resist her new trainer at every turn. She told herself she had better do a better job of acting the obedient, docile female, and not let anything faze her....

Until Mr. Harden grabbed her skirt by the hips, and yanked it all the way down to her ankles.

"*Much* better," he said. He pulled the skirt away from her feet as Ella skipped and hopped in place, doing her best to maintain her balance. She was now wearing nothing but the tight lacy corset, the vicious shoes, and the lavender ribbon in her hair. Resentment flitted across her features as she fought the urge to cross her legs.

"Don't hide yourself from me. You are a vision

of beauty." He pointed to the balance beam with the crop. "You have a new assignment today. I want you to stand on the beam."

Ella was taken aback. "Sir?"

Mr. Harden cocked his brow. "I said, get up, and stand on the beam."

Ella studied the narrow beam with unease. "Can I take off my shoes?"

"Of course not. That would defeat the purpose of the exercise."

Nervously, Ella stepped onto the slender beam. She had to put one foot in front of the other to stay on, and wobbled inelegantly as she swayed with both arms out.

Mr. Harden looked up at her, tapping the crop in his hand. "A Hotel Bentmoore woman always carries herself with poise and dignity," he said. "She is refined. She is confident. She holds her head up high. No matter where she is, who she is with, or what she is doing, she knows the effect she is having on everyone else around her." He waved down the length of the beam with a swish of the crop. "Now walk."

"Sir, I—" Her sentence was cut off as Mr. Harden struck her backside with the tail end of the crop. Ella stumbled off the beam, crying out and barely catching herself from falling on her face. She looked over her shoulder at her trainer in fury.

"Every time you fall, you will get a taste of the crop," he said. "If you break your composure, you will get the crop. And if you don't listen to my instructions, you will get the crop. Now get back on."

Ella's eyes darted up and down the beam as she paused, tense, unyielding, weighing her options. For a moment, the room was quiet. Mr. Harden's lips pursed as he waited, the crop ready and waiting in his hand.

Finally, with tiny reluctant shuffles of her shoes, Ella stepped back on the beam.

"Good," Mr. Harden said. "Now then: back straight. Face up. Shoulders down. Good, very good. Now walk."

Ella lifted her back foot off the beam, swayed wildly, and fell off. Immediately, she felt the bite of the crop on the curve of her ass.

"Back on," Mr. Harden snapped. "Try again."

Giving him a look of pure venom, Ella stepped back on the beam. Again her trainer had her fix her stance, and again she corrected her posture without a word.

He told her to walk, and this time, Ella managed a single, lumbering step, but the second step saw her crashing to the ground.

She stood up, brushed her legs off, took a deep calming breath...and felt Mr. Harden swipe the crop against her vulnerable ass once more.

"Back on," he said.

Ella gazed at him with murder clear in her eyes. Mr. Harden struck her again with the crop, making her cry out and cringe away from him.

"Back on," he repeated.

Rubbing her ass like a petulant child, Ella climbed back on the beam. It was a little easier now—she was beginning to get the hang of it—and she balanced herself quickly. She managed six single steps.

Then she fell off.

Ella braced herself for the sting of the crop, and felt it in short order.

"Again," Mr. Harden said, swatting her harder.

Ella climbed back on.

Laboriously, and with frequent smacks of the crop against her derriere, Ella figured out how to walk across the detestable beam: with a narrow tread of her feet, and high lifts of her knees. Even after she had resolved how to stay on, Mr. Harden continued to correct her walk and stance, making sure she looked straight ahead at all times, with her face relaxed, her chest out, and her arms down at her sides.

"How am I supposed to see where I'm going if I'm looking straight ahead?" She asked him after falling off the beam once more.

"Widen the scope of your eyes. See everything around you. The beam, the floor, the wall straight ahead, me—everything. Open up your peripheral vision."

"I can't do that."

Mr. Harden tapped the floor with the crop. "Yes, you can. You will learn."

"My eyes don't work that way."

His voice grew hard with impatience. "Do you think you're the first woman to learn how to do this, Ella? Many women have gone through our training procedures, trying to become a mistress of the Hotel Bentmoore. Countless have tried. Most have failed. Do you want to fail? Or do you want to succeed?"

"I want to succeed, Sir." Her voice was quiet.

"Then try again," he said as Ella wobbled and weaved across the beam. "Poise, Ella. Dignity. Grace. Elegance. These are the attributes of a Hotel Bentmoore mistress. Her surroundings are irrelevant; her quality comes from within."

Ella fell off once more, and Mr. Harden smacked her with the crop.

But this time, when she got back on the beam, her efforts showed a renewed sense of determination. Without having to be reminded, Ella stretched her body up, lowered her shoulders, and lifted her head up high. Her steps were confident now, even as she swiveled around the beam. Her hips swaggered, and her lips curved in a beguiling smile.

"I think you've got it," Mr. Harden announced. "Yes, that's it. Now turn...tilt your head a little... yes!" He gave her a wide smile. "You've got it down perfectly! I can see that in time, no man will be able to resist your charm and appeal. You're a vision of sensual beauty, Ella. A true Hotel Bentmoore woman."

Mr. Harden had meant to please Ella with

his praise. In all his years, he had never met a woman who reacted adversely to words of gushing approval.

Until now.

The change in Ella was swift and obvious. Her face hardened, her shoulders squared, and her lips tightened. For a second, she stood on the beam and stared down at her trainer, looking like a cat about to pounce. Then, with a gleam in her eyes, she hopped off the polished wood.

"I'm done," she said.

Mr. Harden's brows rose. "Excuse me, I don't remember saying so. Get back on the beam."

"No." Ella faced him. "I'm not getting back on that thing."

"Ella, I'm warning you, if you don't get back on, there will be consequences."

"Like what? Whatever you're going to do to me, just do it, cause I'm not taking orders like some bitch in obedience training."

Mr. Harden's eyes filled with surprise; then they flooded with anger. Satisfaction welled up deep inside Ella's chest.

He was angry; good. Now she would see what he would do—now she would see what he was capable of. If he wanted her to submit, then by God, he would have to dominate.

His eyes narrowed into hard slits, and his voice lowered to a whisper. "Very well. I suppose, just like I must test your boundaries, you must test mine," he said. "Go to the bed. Lean against it—and brace yourself."

Breathing fast now, Ella moved over to the bed and leaned her body over the edge of the mattress. Her fingers clutched at the sheet, and her legs shifted nervously, but she held herself still as she heard Mr. Harden come to stand beside her.

"Remember, you brought this on yourself," he said. "Widen your legs more. Straighten your toes. And take a breath, because this is going to hurt."

Even as her fear made her shiver, Ella widened her stance and straightened her feet. She would not grovel and cower before this man; she would keep herself composed. He wanted poise? She would show him how poised she could be.

She heard the hiss of the crop as it sliced through the air a second before it sliced into her ass. To Ella, that's exactly how it felt: like a sharp knife slicing into her soft flesh. She gripped the sheet and lifted her head as if looking toward the heavens for help, but she did not cry out.

Another blow of the crop came down, striking her across the thighs, and Ella squealed, but held the pose.

Again, and again, the crop bit into her flesh. Mr. Harden left grill marks across her buttocks, thighs, and hips. A few times, he even aimed lower, hitting her slender legs right above her knees.

Ella began to cry out after each blow, releasing

her pain in a series of high-pitched whines. But otherwise, she said nothing. She did not alter her stance, either, but kept her legs apart and her head down. After a particularly vicious strike, she even jutted her ass out further, as if trying to dare the man on.

Mr. Harden accepted her challenge with another burning swat of the crop that made her stiffen and screech.

But after a few minutes, it was obvious the scene was beginning to take an interesting turn. Ella's grip on the mattress began to ease, and she grazed her slender hands up and down the length of it, caressing the silky sheet. Her eyes, squeezed shut before in grimacing pain, now smoothed out in calm repose. Her sleek ass cheeks spread wider as she relaxed her muscles, no longer fearing the crop.

The agonizing blows of the crop, once so terrible, didn't feel so bad anymore. In fact, they felt kind of...good. Hazy warmth was spreading across her ass and thighs, along with a luscious tingling that heightened every time the thin deadly crop lashed across her reddening, welting skin.

A dreamy smile played across her mouth now. Her head came up and she let out a low moan of delight from the jolting, prickling mix of pain and pleasure.

Mr. Harden paused his strikes to study her. He took in her spread haunches, tranquil features, dreamy eyes, and rich moans.

"You like this, don't you Ella?" He asked.

Ella nodded yes.

"I thought so. Reach down and feel how wet you are."

Ella reached down between her legs, and gasped. Her cunt juices were running down her thighs. Her pussy lips were swollen, and her clit throbbed with arousal.

"That's right, girl, you're dripping with need. I bet it wouldn't take you long at all to make yourself come. Go on, do it: rub yourself off!"

In her hazy state, Ella thought this was a marvelous idea. Pushing her legs back even further and spreading her hips, she widened her stance, giving her fingers easier access inside her pussy. As she fingered her own clit, Mr. Harden began to crop her once more, urging her on with quick, scouring smacks of the crop.

Very soon, Ella was moaning into the mattress, jerking her head from side to side, and pumping her thighs back and forth in abandon.

"You're gorgeous," Mr. Harden said behind her.

Ella had to smile. She *felt* gorgeous.

"Do you want me to go harder?" He asked.

The question surprised her...and filled her with a rush of anger. Why was he even asking her? Why was he giving her the option to say no?

Who was the one in control here?

And then she remembered—she was. That

was how she had wanted it: for her to stay in control, even as she allowed herself to be cropped.

Her mood deflated, and her pleasure in the scene disappeared.

"Yes," she answered him. "Go harder."

"You'll have bruises in the morning."

"I don't care." In that moment, she didn't. All she wanted now was to come, and get this scene over with.

Immediately, Mr. Harden began to crop her harder. As Ella's orgasm built, she gave him quick, direct orders.

"Yes, there, now my other leg...move up a little...a little slower, please...harder...yes...yes...*fuck*!"

Mr. Harden played a symphony on her ass with the mastery of a conductor, whapping the crop against her quivering flesh with careful, rapid, taps. Ella continued to rub her pussy between her legs. As her desperation crested, she let out a series of high-pitched cries.

At last, she came, arching her back and rocking her hips from side to side as Mr. Harden continued to crop her.

Mr. Harden stopped his steady staccato against her skin as her orgasm receded. Ella leaned her elbows on the mattress and took deep, convulsive breaths.

"It wasn't the lesson I was going for," Mr. Harden said. "But it will do."

Ella stood up from the bed and wiped her

sweaty brow, feeling confused and angry. She had come, but her satisfaction had been hollow, and now it was filling her with impotent rage.

But she plastered a smile on her face before her trainer could see the real state of her emotions behind her eyes.

*"We had a scene this morning. I'm not sure it went well."*

*"Tell me."*

*"She refused orders, and earned herself a punishment. I'd actually been waiting for the chance to test her pain tolerance. I thought this might be the perfect time to take her to her breaking point, make her safeword, but...she somehow turned the tables on me. She came, but...."*

*"But? But?"*

*"But that was it. She had an orgasm—I know she wasn't faking it—but it still felt like all she was doing was putting on a performance. There was no sacrifice of herself, no relinquishment of power. She's not giving up an inch, but I can tell it's beginning to wear on her." He paused. "Mr. Bentmoore, did Lamont say anything to you about getting Ella into subspace?"*

*Mr. Bentmoore's eyes widened, then narrowed. "No, Mr. Harden. Now that you mention it, he did not."*

*"I cannot get her there, either. She has no problem performing humiliating acts for me, as*

long as she doesn't feel like she's giving up any control. But subspace is another matter."

"Yes, it is."

"We haven't managed to push her into subspace, because she won't let herself go. I think, for some reason, she's afraid."

"Afraid? It's possible." Mr. Bentmoore drummed his fingers on his desk. "What do you plan on doing about it?"

Mr. Harden gave it a moment of thought. "Lamont said bondage was a trigger for her?"

"Yes."

His expression turned hard. "Then I think it's time I pulled the trigger."

# CHAPTER NINE: RED

**E**LLA ENTERED HER ACTIVITY ROOM the next day feeling despondent, without any idea why. She had been up the night before until early hours of the morning, writing up her notes, until she had filled up an entire notebook. But she knew her notes were unworkable for any practical use, a pointless waste of her time. They were a jumbled mess of the tangled thoughts inside her head.

Instead of focusing her notes on the machinations of the Hotel Bentmoore, she was beginning to focus them too much on herself. She was using them as a journal, to document her journey of self-discovery.

She was also filling up too many pages with her curiosity about Mr. Cox.

It had to stop. It *had* to. She was not some schoolgirl with a crush on the local neighborhood bad boy. And what did it say about her, that she was intrigued so much by a man like that, one who would whip, grab, grope, and paw a woman at his mercy?

Just thinking about it made her muscles tense with a thrilling pull of arousal.

As she walked into the center of the room to present herself to her trainer, she tamped down her emotions once more, and put on a pleasant smile. Only this time, Mr. Harden wasn't so quickly fooled. He furrowed his brows as he gazed at her pasted grin.

"What is going on inside that head of yours, I wonder?" He asked, his soft voice full of sympathy. His tone touched on Ella's deep sadness, and made it feel even worse.

"Nothing, Sir," she answered. "Why do you ask?"

He continued to study her. "I have not done a fair job with you, Ella. I can make you walk the walk and talk the talk, but I cannot teach you what it means to be a submissive woman until I get inside your head. So that's going to be my number one priority today."

Nervous energy made Ella's skin tingle. "And how do you plan to do that, Sir?"

"With this," he said, holding something up in the crook of his finger.

There, dangling down from his fingertip and swaying slightly with the movement of his hand, was a blindfold.

It was wide and thick, with two sturdy leather buckle straps going across the back, making it easier to adjust, and (Ella assumed) harder to take off. The eyepieces were huge ovals of hard leather, padded with fleece. There was no way Ella would be able to see anything once that blindfold was put on her.

Curiosity leaped into her chest, along with a touch of disappointment. Why did it have to be such a sturdy thick blindfold? Why couldn't it be a simple black sash?

She pushed the thought away.

"How will a blindfold help you, Sir?"

"Not me, Ella. You. It will take away your ability to see what's coming, and help you let yourself just *feel* what's going on. Then you might manage to lose yourself to me a little."

Trepidation surfaced. The last thing Ella wanted to do was to "lose herself." Then she might not be able to get herself back. "Sir, I'm not sure about this...."

"I'm not going to do anything that goes too far, Ella. You'll always have your safeword."

His words did not reassure her. Instead, they filled her with a pining ache. She gave herself a mental shake.

"What would you like me to do?"

"First thing you need to do is get undressed, of course."

"Of course."

Ella sighed and looked down. Despite her trepidation, a small smile played at the corners of her mouth. Some things would never change, she thought.

She began to untie her corset, but Mr. Harden

tsked. "Ah ah ah, Ella. Remember your lessons. Look at me as you get undressed."

"Sorry, Sir." Ella looked up, maintained eye contact with her trainer, and continued to take off her corset. Once it was loose enough in the back, she slowly unhooked the front, one hook at a time, and carefully spread open the delicate satin material. Then she let the lacy corset fall to the floor.

She saw the arousal spring to Mr. Harden's eyes as he shifted his gaze down to her breasts. "Now the skirt. Take it off."

Ella lowered the zipper in the back of the skirt with nimble fingers and lowered the hem of the skirt, shimmying it slowly down her hips and legs. Soon, it was a puddle around her feet, and she stepped out of it gracefully.

The only things left on her were her shoes, but Mr. Harden had not ordered her to take those off yet.

"Come here," he said.

Ella paused. She realized with a start that a part of her did not want to let him blindfold her so easily. She didn't mind the blindfolding—that part actually intrigued her—but walking into her own trap so calmly, acting so blasé about her own possible demise, bothered her a lot. Why did she have to make it easy for him?

Oh, what was wrong with her? She was *supposed* to make it easy for him. It was the role she was playing. It was why she was there.

She walked up to her trainer and turned around, waiting for him to fit the blindfold over her eyes.

The fleece tickled her eyelids before it pressed against her skin, soft and warm. Mr. Harden began to fasten the buckles in the back of her head, and Ella could feel every brush against her hair, every pull and graze of his hands on the straps. It was as if the world had blacked out, and the rest of her senses were now on high alert, especially her sense of touch. It was probably what Mr. Harden had in mind all along.

She could sense him coming around her body.

He grabbed her hands. "Come," he said, leading her forward.

"Where are we going?"

"Right here." He stopped, and his hands lowered. Ella realized he had led her to the edge of the bed, and was now sitting on it.

"What do you want me to do?"

"I'll show you."

He yanked her down, hard. With a single, panicked shriek, Ella was pulled over his lap. She put her hands out in an instinctive gesture to protect herself from falling face first onto the floor, but Mr. Harden held her tight, balancing her across his legs. He spread his knees apart a little more to better support Ella's tense, rigid body.

"Relax, Ella. I'm not going to let you fall, believe me."

He moved up the bed a little, so she could rest her hands on the mattress while still maintaining the lewd pose across his lap. But Ella tried again to get up from his thighs, and Mr. Harden again held her down.

"Stop struggling."

Ella stopped her futile wriggling, but whimpered.

"What's wrong?"

"This feels so—so—"

"What?"

"Humiliating."

Mr. Harden smiled. "Good."

"Good?"

"Yes. Now calm down." He rubbed his hand up and down her creamy haunches, pressing his fingers deep, kneading her firm flesh. Ella began to relax, lowering her legs and turning her head into his lap.

"That's it, Ella," he said as he continued his stroking, spreading his fingers wide, caressing her with lazy sweeps of his hand.

Then his hand disappeared, and Ella heard something slide out from underneath the pillow.

"Get ready," he said.

"For what?"

"This."

With that, he smacked something hard against her ass with a resounding slap.

Ella gasped, and her whole body twisted. She tried to scramble up from his lap, but Mr.

Harden held her down.

"It's just a paddle, Ella," he said. "You've had worse by my own hand. It just feels different now because of the blindfold." He smacked her again with the paddle, and Ella let out another soft, startled gasp.

Then he began to paddle her with quick flicks of his wrist, smacking the hard wood against Ella's cringing bottom, getting a loud *thwack* and a sharp gasp from the startled female after every one.

Ella fought to maintain control over her trainer's lap, keeping her squirms down to a bare minimum. Mr. Harden was paddling her with hard, quick strokes, but allowing her a long pause between each one, so that Ella could collect herself. He was also continuing to rub her butt down between the paddle strikes, working her muscles and soothing her ache.

Ella began to relax her whole body against Mr. Harden's lap, feeling the pain of the paddle diffuse across her ass and thighs. Her angelic face took on a coaxing smile. With each slap, she let out a tiny sigh of contentment.

Mr. Harden noticed the change in her, and commenced with harder, faster, strokes.

Ella was soon crying out after each whack, but it wasn't clear whether she was crying out in pain, or ecstasy.

"Ella, do you want me to go harder?"

Ella didn't answer; she had not even

registered the question. Mr. Harden repeated it louder.

"Ella, do you want me to go harder?"

This time, Ella grimaced. "I...I...can't talk...." Lifting the words in her brain was like pulling on thick taffy; they stuck in her head and wouldn't reach her mouth.

"Just yes or no. Harder?"

"Yes...."

"Good." There was a pause with the paddle, as Ella felt him shift his weight to reach something across the bed.

When she felt him grab her wrists behind her, she felt nothing of it—until she felt cold steel wrapping around them, and heard the click.

"What? What?" Anxiety made her skim to the surface of her hazy state.

"Handcuffs, so you don't try to block the paddle with your hands and hurt yourself."

"No. No, please," Ella whined, twisting and scissoring her hands in the cuffs. Her wriggling almost unbalanced her from Mr. Harden's lap, but he grabbed her just in time, and held her still with his firm hands.

"Shh," he said. "I'm not going to hurt you any more than you can take. Remember, you have your safeword, Ella. Just breathe." He rubbed her ass again, up, down, and around, allaying her fears with soft, quiet words, trying to lull her into complaisance. "You're safe, Ella. You're safe."

Ella relaxed her body, but her face remained a mask of fear and torment. Mr. Harden didn't wait for her expression to change before he started to paddle her once more. He picked up the thick wooden instrument, held her ass still with a tight grip, and let her have it.

*Thwack! Thwack! Thwack! Thwack!*

This time, Mr. Harden's smacks rained down on her ass with choppy, pounding strokes. He spread his reign of torture over huge swaths of her skin, peppering her thighs, ass and hips with blazing wallops of the paddle. Soon, Ella's whole bottom was a fiery red, glowing with throbbing heat.

But Ella was no longer struggling. She was far beyond that: her mind had drifted into a far away corner, where nothing existed but white noise and soothing darkness, punctuated by pulsing light that lit up behind her eyelids every time the stinging paddle lit into her skin.

*Thwack! Thwack! Thwack!*

Mr. Harden's choppy blows continued to rain down on her body, sinking Ella into a space inside her mind she had never been before. White dots painted her view behind her eyelids as cognizant thought disappeared completely. Other sensations rose to the surface, and began to take control over her body—basic, primal responses that felt like nothing but animal instinct.

Exhilaration. Rage. Ravenous sensuality.

Delirious need. And, above all else, the rapturous joy of feeling *alive.*

Ella jutted out her ass further as, from somewhere deep inside her, she bellowed out an echoing peal of laughter.

"Yes, Ella. *Yes.*"

Mr. Harden's voice broke through the wild turbulence of her thoughts. She could not see, but she could still hear, and feel...and remember.

*I reserve the right to punish you myself.*

Where had she heard those words? From Mr. Cox. His voice, hoarse and thick, was nothing like Mr. Harden's; the memory of it filled her with a breathtaking rush of excitement and terror.

But this was not Mr. Cox, whipping her against a concrete slab inside a rundown barn. And she was not tied with rope, or blindfolded with a simple black sash.

She was being paddled over Mr. Harden's lap, naked and handcuffed, like a lewd hussy, a cheap tart, a tramp, a...

Slut.

From the deep recesses of her mind, another memory arose.

*You cheap slut. You think you can just sleep your way to the top? You've only gotten this far because of your looks. You don't deserve to be here.*

In that moment, all her pleasure disappeared, dissolved like melted ice, and in its place jetted boiling hot rage.

"Red!" She yelled. "Red!"

Immediately, Mr. Harden's hand stopped.

"What is it, Ella? What's wrong?"

"Get these things off me!" She struggled against the handcuffs, twisting her wrists inside the hard metal as if trying to break through them. Her voice rose in urgency. "RED!"

"I'll unlock you! Just calm down!" Mr. Harden quickly unlocked the cuffs. As soon as they were open, Ella stood up, shook the cuffs off her wrists, and flung them across the room. Then she pulled the blindfold off her head, tearing out some hair in the process, and wiped her face with trembling hands.

"For God's sake, Ella, what happened?"

"Don't come near me." She took a step back from her trainer. "Don't touch me!"

He put his hands up in surrender. "I won't, I swear."

"I'm not here to become your slut!"

"Of course not, Ella," he said, shocked. "Nobody said you were. You're here to be trained as a Hotel Bentmoore mistress. Isn't that right?"

"I don't know." Her eyes filled with tears. "I don't know why I'm here anymore. I don't know if I *should* be here anymore."

"If you'll just let me—"

"Don't touch me!" Ella yelled again, cringing away as he stepped toward her with his arms outstretched. "Just—just please, leave me alone."

"I can't leave you alone, you obviously need aftercare."

"Red, red, red!"

"Okay, Ella. Okay." He lowered his arms. "If that's how you feel about it, when you're ready, I'll take you back to your room."

Ella nodded, swallowing back a sob. "Yes," she said. "Yes, take me back. I can't do this anymore."

*"We've hit a crisis. I was paddling her over my lap, blindfolded and handcuffed—and she safeworded."*

*"By your expression, I take it you don't have any idea why."*

*"None. She's experienced worse pain from my own hand. She was even enjoying what I was doing to her, at least until she safeworded."*

*"It was the handcuffs, then?"*

*"No, I don't think so. Once she got over her initial fear of being restrained, she relaxed completely. I got her into subspace, Sir. I'm sure of it. But then..." He shrugged, looking resigned.*

*"Are you triggering something else, then? A memory, perhaps?"*

*"Maybe." Mr. Harden scowled. "I don't know what's going on inside her head. She's not letting me in, and I don't think she will. Sir, the truth is, I don't think I'm the right trainer for her. She needs something from me, but I can't figure out what."*

*The confession was short and blunt. It was always a blow to a host's ego when he had to confess he could not give a guest all she needed to grow and move forward on her journey of self-discovery and sexuality. While it was an accepted fact that not every host could be everything for every woman, it was still hard to admit.*

*Mr. Bentmoore tilted back in his chair and looked up at the ceiling. "So who is the right one for Ella?" He murmured.*

*"Shern, maybe?" Mr. Harden suggested. "He has a way of getting inside a girl's head. Or Pierce? His sexual skills might be just what she needs."*

*Mr. Bentmoore paused to think. "No," he said, "not Shern. And not Pierce, either. I think...yes." He sat up straight and pulled himself into his desk. "Please tell Mr. Cox I would like to see him right away."*

*Mr. Harden's eyes grew round. "Cox?" He whispered. "You can't be thinking of giving her to Cox! She's already got one foot out the door—he'll set her running away screaming!"*

*"I don't think so, Harden. I think he's exactly what she needs."*

*Mr. Harden's eyes narrowed. "Sir, do you know something I don't know?"*

*Mr. Bentmoore smiled. "I know many things you don't know, Harden. Now please, send Cox over."*

❦

Ella cried for hours that night. The maelstrom of emotions raging inside her, the commotion going on inside her heart, wouldn't calm. Her wracked sobs finally did die down, not because she felt better, but because she was too physically drained to keep crying the way she was.

But the ache in her chest would not go away. She stared into space, alone in the dark, feeling desolate and exhausted. Her heart felt broken, as if everything she had worked for, all her hopes and accomplishments, had been smashed to bits and swept away, leaving her crushed.

Of course, it wouldn't be the first time.

Why, *why* did things have to be this way? Why did *she* have to be this way? She had come to the Hotel Bentmoore thinking she could slip in and out with no one the wiser, and she would have a great piece of investigative reporting to show for it, one that would help her make her mark on the world. The best thing about it was that it was supposed to be something she had done all on her own, without anyone else's help... without anyone being able to say she somehow cheated the system.

But this place, and these people, had changed her. Or maybe they hadn't changed her...maybe they had just forced her to see parts of herself she hadn't recognized before.

Maybe because she hadn't wanted to know.

She was a masochist. She accepted that now; there was no arguing it, and no going back. But she was supposed to be a submissive, too.

Ella certainly didn't feel like one. Most of the time, she felt nothing but simmering defiance, a deep-rooted need to lash out and fight the men who were there to help her. Wasn't a true submissive woman supposed to feel submissive *all* the time, especially when in the company of dominant males?

She wished she could talk to Mr. Lamont or Mr. Harden about her feelings, but that might lead to them discovering her deception. She had no doubt if Mr. Bentmoore ever found out the real reason why she was there, he would kick her out of the hotel, right on her ass, and she'd be no better off than she had been before. No, she'd be *worse* off, because she'd be left on her own, confused and daunted by her own perverse desires, with no one to offer her any kind of help at all.

She was better off continuing as she was, playing the role, pretending to be the stereotypical submissive female, one who would allow herself to be used through her own sexual needs. In other words, the perfect Hotel Bentmoore Mistress.

Only...how much of it was still an act? She *wanted* to be used, debased, humiliated, spanked and flogged and made to yield completely, with her entire being, down to her shaken soul. But at the same time, she could not give in; she could not offer herself up like a lamb to a sacrifice. Not for Mr. Lamont, and not for Mr. Harden, either. Both were good men, but neither one of them had managed to tame the creature inside her that made her lash out and challenge them at every turn.

Why couldn't she just give in and do what they ordered her to do, instead of meeting them with defiance? Why did her chest swell with rebellion at the simplest command?

Why couldn't she just be a *normal* submissive woman, ready and willing to submit?

She had come so far on her journey, only to reach a dead end. These people had taught her so much about herself, and for that, she would be forever grateful; but they had taken her as far as they could.

With a heavy heart, Ella realized they could not help her, not anymore.

It was time for her to go home.

# PART III: MR. COX

# CHAPTER TEN: THROWING DOWN THE GAUNTLET

THE NEXT MORNING, ELLA ENTERED the activity room like a cloud of depression was hanging over her head. Her back was hunched, and her eyes remained down. She had not bothered putting on any makeup that morning, nor had she done anything with her hair. She didn't care how she looked anymore; it didn't matter anyway.

It was time to tell Mr. Harden she was done; she was packing up and getting out of the hotel. She didn't know why the thought filled her with such overwhelming sadness, but that didn't matter, either. There was nothing he could say or do to change her mind.

With her eyes cast down, she didn't notice the new man in the room. But she heard the change in voice when he spoke to her.

"Well, well, well," the voice said. "We meet again."

Ella's picked up her head in shock. Her eyes went as large as saucers. Goosebumps rose across her arms. "Mister…mister…."

"Cox," he said, raising his brows. "You *do* remember my name, don't you, Ella?"

"Yes, Sir," she stammered, "I just wasn't expecting you here."

"Your time with Mr. Harden is finished. I'm your trainer now. Your *last* one."

"What do you mean?"

"It means, Ella, if you get past me, you're done with your basic training, and you get to stay on as a mistress of the Hotel Bentmoore. But if you don't, you get shown the door. No last chances, no extra credit. I'm the last step in this process of selection, and the hardest trainer to pass. So how about you tell me right now if you have any intention of doing what it'll take to finish this, cause I don't need you wasting my time."

"I—" It was on the tip of Ella's tongue to blurt out she'd had every intention of calling it quits not one minute before. But as she looked at Mr. Cox staring at her so arrogantly, the words died in her throat, and ire rose in their place.

Mr. Cox noticed her moment of hesitation, and pounced on it. "If you can't answer a simple yes or no question now, there's no way you're going to be able to finish this. So why don't you and I just agree right now you're not cut out for the job, and call it a day? Nobody's going to say you weren't good enough." His tone told her clearly there *would* be somebody to say she hadn't been good enough, namely *him*, and Ella's hackles rose.

"What the hell do you know about me?" She shouted. "You have no idea what I've been put through since I got here! I've been flogged, paddled, cropped—"

Mr. Cox waved his hand away. "That's all par for the course. Besides, being a Bentmoore mistress has nothing to do with how much punishment you can take. It's about what's in here." He pointed to his temple. "It's about the attitude. You think you've got it? Show me. At least try to look like a Bentmoore mistress. Since the moment you walked in here, you've done nothing but slouch and flinch away from me." His tone turned mocking. "Poor little girl, what happened? Someone take your teddy bear away?"

Ella's jaws clenched. Fire blazed in her eyes. But without saying a word, she fixed her posture, smoothed her features the way Mr. Harden had taught her to, and served Mr. Cox a derisive stare, one laden with challenge.

She began to walk around her new trainer in a wide circle, sashaying her hips and keeping her shoulders back, using an easy, relaxed gait. As she sauntered around Mr. Cox, she tilted her head to gaze at him, pulling his eyes in to stare at her with potent magnetism.

Mr. Cox turned his head over his shoulder to follow her around, until she had finished her short circuit and was back where she had started. Ella jutted out her chin and put her hand on her hip, looking sure of herself.

Mr. Cox clapped his hands. "Very good Ella," he sneered. "That would have been perfect, if you were trying to model down a runway at a high-school fashion show." He smiled in the face of Ella's scowl. "But really, it was a good try—for a beginner. I have no doubt it was a vast improvement from what Harden had to deal with when he first started working with you."

For a moment, Ella's whole face flushed. Then she smiled.

"Thank you," she said.

Mr. Cox frowned. "That wasn't a compliment, you know."

"I know. You were negging me."

"*Negging* you?"

"You're unfamiliar with the word? It means passing off subtle insults disguised as crass compliments to a woman, just to shake her confidence. Men do it to throw a woman off balance, so she'll be more open to their sexual advances."

Mr. Cox's jaw ticked. "I know what negging means!"

"Then you know men only do it when they think they have to make a woman feel self-conscious and awkward about herself, just so they can have a chance with her—otherwise they wouldn't have a chance at all." She pointed at his chest. "You were negging me, which means you thought you had to throw me off balance just to have a shot with me. It was nice of you to acknowledge that. It was true, of course— you *wouldn't* have a shot in hell with me—but it was still nice of you to acknowledge that. So thank you."

To her surprise, Mr. Cox smiled. "Touché, sweetheart. But you're forgetting one thing: I've got more than just a shot with you—I've *got* you. You're here, and under my care now, which means I can do whatever I want with you. You don't like it? There's the door."

He waited to see what she would do, the smile never wavering from his face.

Ella's expression went from surprise, to anger, to disconcertion, and finally settled on fury...but at the same time, a curious light had leapt into her eyes, one that intrigued him.

"You can't just do whatever you want with me," she said. "I'm not your slave! You have to honor my limits! Mr. Harden said so!"

"Did he now." Mr. Cox's grin was menacing. "Mr. Harden is a much more refined gentleman than I am. He probably did his duty and taught you all about boundaries, and negotiations, and safewords."

"Yes...."

"You're not under Mr. Harden's rule anymore, Ella. You're under mine. I don't put much stock in safewords, and I certainly don't negotiate fair." His eyes grew lecherous as her face paled. "Poor little Alice has fallen down the rabbit hole," he mocked. "Will she run back home, like the scared little girl she is? Or will she follow directions and open her eyes to a whole new world? Which is it to be, Ella?"

"I'm not some scared little girl!"

"Then prove it." Again, he waited, and watched to see what she would do.

Ella wished she could wipe that smug look off his face. She vowed to herself right then and there that somehow, she would find a way.

"What is your first order for me?" She asked in a low hiss, adding as an afterthought, "Sir."

Mr. Cox's grin was huge.

"Oh, this is going to be fun," he said.

"You told her *what?*"

"I told her I don't care about safewords. Well, that's not a hundred percent right....I told her I don't put much stock in them—which we both know is true."

"But *why* did you tell her that? You might have just scared her away completely."

"Oh, I didn't, Mr. Bentmoore, believe me. If anything, I made her rise to the challenge. What I told her is the truth, because I can't expect her to be honest with me if I'm not completely honest with her from the get-go. She needs this from me, I can tell."

"You better be right, Cox."

"I am." His face lit up. "And she finds me exciting, I can see it in her eyes. She's looking for a challenge, and she knows I can give it to her. She's looking forward to some fun, just as much as I am." He chuckled, lost in thought. "She's got courage, challenging me. That girl has spirit."

"Yes, she does." Mr. Bentmoore's eyes narrowed, noticing the look on Mr. Cox's face. "Be careful, Cox."

"She doesn't need me to be careful. She needs me to give her a swift kick in the ass."

"I didn't mean her, I meant *you*. Don't get ahead of yourself with this one."

Mr. Cox looked down at his boss, genuinely confused. "I don't know what you mean, Sir."

Mr. Bentmoore sighed. "Never mind...there's no point trying to warn you, anyway. Have you started in on her yet?"

"Not yet. I'm letting her simmer for a couple hours. Some meat needs to be slow cooked, you know."

# CHAPTER ELEVEN: THE POOL

**E**LLA WAS SURPRISED WHEN **MR.** Cox sent her back to her room; she had thought her "training" with him would start right away. But apparently, he had more important matters to deal with first before he got around to beginning her training.

His treatment of her made Ella seethe. Every time she remembered his haughty, arrogant face, her anger would boil up until it felt like smoke was about to come out of her ears and she wanted to scream. The man got to her like no one else did.

And yet, she was excited to be working with him. Any thoughts she'd had of leaving the hotel were gone now, as Ella wanted nothing more than to prove herself to her new trainer. *Why* this was so important to her, she didn't try to ponder. All she knew for certain was that she had to pass his test. She had to show him he was wrong about her. She was not some scared little girl; she could take whatever he would dish out. She *wanted* it.

She deserved his respect.

He had sent her back to her room with a dismissive wave of his hand.

He'd given her a few parting instructions on her way out the door. "I'm not into controlling what you wear, at least when you're not with me," he'd said. "You feel comfortable in those corsets, wear them. Otherwise, don't. I really don't care. And I'm not into controlling what you eat, either. Just show me I can trust you, and we'll get along fine."

"What is that supposed to mean?"

"It means I'm not into women making themselves sick or putting themselves in danger to get my attention. You abuse the privileges I give you, I'll take them away. It's that simple. Now go back to your room. I'll call for you later."

Ella had retreated back to her room like a banished child, barely stopping herself from stomping her feet in a huff. When she got back to her room, she did stomp her feet, and paced her small, dim room for a good half hour.

She suspected he had brushed her off the way he had just to get her mad. Well, the ploy had worked.

Her anger made her skin flush and her eyes gleam, but there was no one around to see it. There was no one around to watch her punch her pillows, either. Her only comforting grace that she didn't have to wear the damn corsets anymore, and she pulled hers off in fury.

She tried to jot down a few paragraphs in her notebook, outlining the sudden turn of events, but she couldn't. She was too angry. In any case, she was so far behind in her notes, it felt ridiculous trying to catch up on them now, with her head like this.

Thankfully, she didn't have to stew alone in her room for very long. Mr. Cox sent for her about an hour later. By that time, Ella had managed to get her temper under control and her head on straight.

She would not let him see how much influence he had over her. (She would not let herself use the word control; no, it was not control he had over her, it was *influence*.) She had managed to maintain her composure with her last two trainers; she would manage with this one, too.

Even if it was the infamous asshole Mr. Cox.

Mr. Trowlege brought her to yet another activity room. (Ella had tried to ask him more than once how many activity rooms the hotel had, and she'd gotten only vague replies. She was beginning to wonder if even Mr. Trowlege knew.) This activity room was smaller than any of the others she had been in, and with very little furniture: only a St. Andrew's Cross, and the spacious wardrobe. But it had a vast array of bondage equipment bolted into all four walls. There was even a suspension bar hanging from the ceiling.

Ella's eyes fell on the large cotton sheet laid out in the middle of the floor, and the collection of canes, paddles, and floggers spread across it. A pile of terry cloth rags sat in the corner of the sheet, along with a large, nondescript bottle. Ella had no idea what the rags and bottle were for.

Mr. Cox was quick to spell it out for her. "Many of the canes, wood paddles, and flogger handles need polishing," he said. "Usually the staff takes care of things like this, but I thought we could give them a break this once, and put you to work instead. Polishing toys is an easy job; even a pair of pretty hands like yours should be able to handle it."

Ella glowered. "And what does polishing toys have to do with my training?"

He smiled. "Nothing. I just thought you wouldn't mind doing a little work to help earn your keep around here. After all, we're feeding you, housing you, clothing you—"

"Clothing me! Dressing me up like some kind of sex doll, more like—"

"We're taking care of all your basic needs, and in addition to all that, we're teaching you many useful skills. I think you can show a little appreciation, don't you?"

"Appreciation! Appreciation—why you—"

"What's wrong, princess? Didn't think some god-honest work would be part of this arrangement? Thought you'd just skate through your training on your looks alone?"

"No!" Ella's face fell. "I never thought that. *I never thought that.*" She looked down, dejected.

Mr. Cox's eyes narrowed. He had hit a nerve. He hadn't meant to. "Good," he said. "Then get to work. Just take your clothes off first."

Ella's eyes snapped back up. "What?"

"I'm not going to let you claim later I ruined your clothes by making you wear them while you got dirty. Take them off before you start polishing. You can work naked."

"My clothes won't be ruined. I can just wash them."

"Are you arguing with me, Ella?" His tone turned dangerously soft, and Ella pursed her lips shut. "Mr. Lamont told me you had issues with your modesty, but I thought Mr. Harden had that handled by now. If you can't follow a simple request to strip, then that's something we should work on—hard. But for now, my little highbrow princess, please listen to what I'm telling you to do, take off your fucking clothes, and get to work."

"I'm not a highbrow princess!" She shrieked.

"Then prove it." He pointed to the sheet. "Do the job, and do it right."

Ella's eyes shot daggers at him, but she began to take off her clothes.

Mr. Cox watched her take off her clothes with angry jerks and pulls, satisfied with her change in mood. He had triggered something inside her before in a way he hadn't meant to. He would discover what that was all about in time, but for now, he wanted her temper, not her sorrow. His order that she strip, while spontaneous, had done the job.

Once Ella was naked, she sat down cross-legged on the thin cotton sheet, got comfortable, and grabbed a rag. Then she opened the bottle, held the rag over the top, and tipped the bottle over. The rag grew wet with polish.

"Do you care which toys I start with?" She asked, her voice clipped.

"No," Mr. Cox answered. "So long as you get them all done, I don't care what order you go in."

"How kind of you. Sir," she muttered under her breath, grabbing up a thin rattan cane.

"You have no idea how *kind* I'm being to you right now, princess," Mr. Cox replied. Ella didn't answer, nor did she turn her face up to look at him, so she failed to see his eyes filling with fierce heat as he gazed down at her gold-tipped head.

In truth, Mr. Cox thought he was being extremely kind to Ella. He was letting her get on with her task, instead of forcing her on her knees and making her suck his cock.

Ella had no idea when she had gotten undressed, her areolae had crinkled in the cold room air, and her nipples had puckered into pink nubs. She had no idea that with the way she was sitting, her hair was cascading down her back in gentle golden waves, and her ribs were articulating her reedy back. And if she had any clue that by sitting in the position she had chosen, her cunt had spread open just enough to reveal her dusky crease and lovely pink folds, she gave no sign of it.

Ella got down to work, polishing the canes with long pumps of her hand over the rag and an intent look on her face. As Mr. Cox watched her, he wondered if she would pump his cock the same way she was pumping that cane, with her hard, steady grip. He promised himself he would find out eventually.

"Tell me about yourself, Ella."

She still did not look up at him. "What would you like to know, Sir?"

"Do you have any brothers? Sisters?"

"No, I have no siblings."

"So you are your parents' little darling?"

Ella finally glanced at him, but that was all. "My father died when I was little," she said, still working the rag.

"I'm sorry," Mr. Cox replied, contrite.

This time when she turned her head up, Ella's eyes held his a little longer. "It's okay," she said softly. "I barely remember him. For as long as I can remember, it was just me and my mom." She started in on a short paddle that looked like it was made out of a single piece of thick oak.

"What about your mom?" Mr. Cox asked. "What is she like?"

Ella let out a little snort. "Nothing like me."

"What does that mean?"

She frowned. "It means she has different ways of looking at the world than I do. A different set of ideals."

"Is this about politics or religion? Cause if it is, I'd rather move on to something else. Those topics bore me."

Ella glimpsed at him out of the corner of her eye, furrowing her brows. "No, Sir, it's not about politics or religion. She has different ideas about how women are supposed to behave."

"Now this sounds more interesting. What does your mother think? I'm curious."

Ella attacked the flogger she had picked up next, wishing she had never let herself be pulled into this conversation. "She thinks women need to do whatever it takes to get ahead in this world. According to her, the game is stacked against us, so we have to restack the game."

"And how does she think women should do that? Restack the game?"

"I don't know, Sir, it's just something she says." Ella put down the flogger and the rag. "Is there some reason why you want to know about my mother?"

"No," he shrugged. "Just making small talk. But if you don't like the topic, we can move on to something else. What were you doing before you came to the Hotel Bentmoore?"

Ella's eyes darted around before she quickly picked up another cane in the pile.

"I was in Public Relations."

It was true, somewhat. She had been an intern in a Public Relations firm during college, before going on to journalism. So why did it make her feel so uncomfortable to lie?

"Public Relations, huh? I can see that."

Ella glowered. "Why? Because I look a certain way? I fit a certain image?" She sneered. "You know what's funny? I've just realized working in this place is a lot like working in PR."

"How so?" Mr. Cox asked, trying to keep her talking.

"You have to know how to entice people, how to tell them what they want to hear to lure them in. It's all about attraction. Appeal."

"You could say that about a lot of things, princess," Mr. Cox replied. "A doctor who's starting a new practice has to look and sound professional if he—or she—wants to bring in new patients. A teacher has to know how to talk to a school board to get hired at a school. I could go on, but I won't. My point is, to get ahead in this world, people have to sell themselves, and to do that, they have to show their best."

Ella bristled. "You might be able to find a few cases where women are judged on their brains," she said, "but you can't deny no matter what the industry, women are judged on their looks, too. A woman looking for a job as a receptionist or a restaurant greeter is not going to be judged on her talent. She's going to be judged on whether she has the right face."

"I could say the same thing about men. People everywhere are judged on their looks, Ella, women and men both."

"But women are judged more than men."

"Maybe. But why are you so caught up on this issue of judgment? Who's judging you?"

Ella swallowed, thinking fast. "Aren't you, right now?"

Mr. Cox gave her a twisted smile. "Touché again, princess. I guess I am. But not on your looks."

"I think Mr. Harden was. He had me wearing those awful corsets."

"Those weren't about your looks, Ella. Those were about control. Harden gets a kick out of controlling his women even when he's not with them. So do I—so do all of the hosts here—but we control our women in different ways. Harden likes breath play, so he starts with corsets."

"Breath play?"

"If you had stayed with him long enough, he would have been choking you out. Lots of women love to feel the grip of a man's hands around their throats. It takes skill, though."

Ella's eyes narrowed into small slits. "And how do you like controlling your women?"

"You'll find out eventually, if you make it that far," Mr. Cox said. "But back to the subject at hand, I guess it might look like the Bentmoore judges on looks, but we don't. We appreciate talent and skill more than anything else. Now, we do expect our staff to maintain a certain level of fitness, but that's because it's required for the job. I can't do a marathon fuck session if I'm running out of breath after ten minutes, can I?"

Ella's nerves tingled as the words "marathon fuck" came out of his mouth. "I guess not," she agreed. "But my original point still stands. Women are typically judged more harshly than men."

"And what would you do to change that?" Mr. Cox asked, cocking his brow. "The world is what it is, princess. You can't always be banging your fists against a brick wall. Sometimes, you have to accept the obstacles in front of you, and find a way around."

"Now you sound like my mother." Ella turned her attention back to the pile of canes, looking stony. Mr. Cox narrowed his eyes.

"That's enough for today," he said softly, motioning her off the floor. "I'll have the staff do the rest. C'mon, you need some exercise." As he opened the activity room door, Ella gasped.

"Let me put some clothes on!" She yelled, grabbing up her panties.

Mr. Cox looked at her over his shoulder. "No," he said. "We're going to the pool. Go grab a towel from the bathroom and put it around you. That'll be good enough."

"I can't walk around the hotel naked!"

"You won't be naked, you'll be wearing the

towel," Mr. Cox said. "It'll cover you up better than that bathing suit I caught you in the last time. Which reminds me, I owe you a punishment, don't I? So go get the towel and drop the panties, or you'll be facing your punishment right now."

Ella's mouth clenched. Her nails dug into her palms.

But she threw the panties back on the floor and went to the bathroom to grab a towel. When she came out, she had the thick white towel wrapped around her body from armpit to thigh.

"C'mon," Mr. Cox repeated, holding the door open for her. Ella walked through nervously, looking up and down the corridor for any sign of someone coming their way. When she saw there was no one, she ran to the elevator and quickly pressed the button, praying she wouldn't be seen.

Inside the elevator, Mr. Cox admonished her. "You're being ridiculous, Ella," he said, looking at her through the mirrored doors. "Nobody can tell you're not wearing a bathing suit."

"*I* can tell," Ella hissed. The doors opened, and Mr. Cox led her through the back corridors to get outside. Ella tiptoed behind, grabbing the towel around her in tight fists and gripping it tight. Thankfully, she saw only a few people inside the small office rooms lining the hallway, and all of them were busy doing their own things. Nobody looked up as she walked passed.

The pool was empty, as it had been the last

time, but Ella didn't know how long that would last. Anyone could show up at any time.

"Get in," Mr. Cox ordered, pointing to the water. "Do some laps."

Ella eyed the water and gripped the towel around her tighter.

"Do it, Ella," Mr. Cox said, his voice louder. Ella didn't move.

With a sigh and a roll of his eyes, he yanked the towel away from her naked body and pushed her into the pool.

Ella rose to the surface with a scream. "How! You! Oh!"

As he watched her splutter, Mr. Cox sat down in one of the pool chairs, lay back, and put his hands behind his head. A smile curved his mouth.

"You arrogant son of a bitch! You—" Ella reached for the ladder at the side of the pool, ready to pull herself out.

"Don't get out of that water yet, Ella," Mr. Cox sat up to say, a stern look on his face. "Do some laps. I'll tell you when you're done. And unlike Stacey, I'm going to sit right here and make sure you don't go wandering off where you're not supposed to."

"I can't swim naked! Anyone might come and see me!"

"No they won't. This is the private pool. You have to reserve a time to use it. I reserved it this morning, so no one is going to walk over and see you—unless they're wandering around where they shouldn't be, which has been known to happen."

Ella stared at him. "Why didn't you tell me before this is a private pool?"

"You didn't ask. Now start swimming." He leaned his head back against the chair again and closed his eyes.

For a second, Ella debated climbing out of the pool and clawing his eyes out. But the water, now that she was used to it, felt pleasantly cool. The sun shined on her face, and other than some birds' song, Ella couldn't hear a single soul. The area felt entirely secluded. Her anger dissipated.

She began to swim up and down the length of the pool. Mr. Cox continued to sit in his chair with his head tipped back and his eyes closed. Every so often, Ella would glance at him, but he looked to be dozing. After a few minutes, she stopped glancing at him every few seconds, and focused on her swimming.

Mr. Cox was not dozing. He was, in fact, watching Ella go back and forth across the pool with her strong, graceful strokes. She swam like an expert swimmer, like she'd been doing it for years. He would have to find out about that.

For now though, all he cared to focus on was the way her ass swayed and dipped in the water, how her coltish legs rippled under the waves, and how her nipples peeked over the surface with every breath she took. Every time she turned, her hair would wave around her body like a cloud of gold, then pull back behind her in a shimmering train of smooth silk. She reminded him of a water nymph.

Mr. Cox knew the moment Ella relaxed in the water: it was the moment she stopped doing her unvarying laps, gave him one last suspicious glance, and then turned over in the water to start in on a lazy backstroke. The water beaded off her shimmering breasts, and her hips dipped in and out of the water as she smiled up at the sun.

He couldn't take it anymore. "Get out of the water," he said.

Ella stopped swimming and stood up straight in the water. She turned around to glare at him, wiping her hair away from her face with both hands. "Why?"

"Because I said so," Mr. Cox said with a growl.

Surprised by his tone, Ella swam over to the ladder and pulled herself out of the pool. Mr. Cox watched her dry off with the towel, his eyes catching every inch of her creamy skin.

When she moved to wrap the towel around her body, he stopped her. "Not yet," he said. "Before we go back to the hotel, I want you to make yourself come."

Ella froze. "Excuse me?"

"You heard me. Make yourself come. Play

with your cunt, rub your clit, pinch your tits, whatever it takes. I want to watch you do it, and I want you to do it now."

"That's disgusting!"

"Why?"

"We're out here in the open! Anyone might see me!"

"I told you, this is a private pool."

"Still...I can't...."

"Yes, you can. But you know what, I'm feeling magnanimous, so I'll give you a choice. You can come on your own, or you can use my shoe. Which is it to be?"

Ella looked down at his feet in horror. "Your *shoe?*"

He pulled over a short coffee table nearby and rested his foot on it. "Just have a seat and go for a ride," he said. "It's fun once you get the hang of it."

Ella couldn't believe what she was hearing. "You...are...*disgusting*," she whispered. "I am not going for a *ride* on your *shoe!*"

"Fine," Mr. Cox replied. "Then use your own fingers, or whatever else you can find around here to make yourself come. Hell, I'll even let you use the towel if you want. But do it—now!" He waited, and watched as Ella processed what he was ordering her to do.

"Can I at least sit in a chair?"

Mr. Cox smiled at the question. She was negotiating now; she was relenting.

"By all means," he answered. "Have a seat." He pulled another lounge chair over for her, but situated it directly across from his. He would make sure he had a front row seat of her performance, Ella realized.

She sat down slowly, leaning a little to the side, with her legs pressed together. Looking shamefully down at the floor, she moved the towel away just a few inches from the venus of her thighs, and dug her hand inside.

"That won't do," Mr. Cox said. He was sitting up now, and staring at her with rapt attention. "Open your legs. I want to see."

Ella opened her legs another inch.

"Wider, Ella. Wrap your feet around the legs of the chair."

Letting out a small whimper, Ella opened her knees until her feet could bend behind the legs of the chair, and twisted her ankles around.

She curved her fingers into her pussy, but kept her fingers tightly together, so that they covered her mound and soft pink lips from his view.

"Spread your pussy open," Mr. Cox said. "I want to see it."

Closing her eyes in mortification, Ella spread her vaginal lips, revealing her rosy pink folds and spongy clit.

"Now keep it open, and rub it with your other hand," Mr. Cox said. He grew impatient when she didn't move right away. "Go on, rub your clit!"

Ella turned her head away in shame. But she lowered her other hand between her legs and, with two gentle finger pads, began to rub her clit.

She rubbed slowly at first, trying to work up her arousal. But to her alarm, it didn't take more than a few gentle strokes to feel the first stirrings of an orgasm building. She dipped her fingers lower to her cunt opening, and found it dripping wet.

"That's it, get your fingers wet," Mr. Cox said in approval. "Now rub a little faster."

Ella began to rub her clit faster now, but followed a steady rhythm, gliding her fingers along her stiffened clit with soft strokes. She kept her pussy lips open with her other hand, as ordered, and found that in this stretched position, she could get into nerve-rich folds she wouldn't otherwise be able to get into. The strange, sensual stimulation added to her burgeoning distress. Her face scrunched up as if in pain, and her feet lifted onto her tiptoes around the legs of the chair as her mounting desire spread across her body like wildfire.

"Faster," Mr. Cox hissed. "Rub faster!"

Ella rubbed faster, crying out with her rising need. Her fingers moved in a blur of speed between her legs. Her cunt squirted juices.

"You like playing with yourself, don't you Ella? Tell me! Say you like to play with yourself!"

Ella rubbed furiously. "I like to play with myself," she said, her words punctuated by pants and jerks of her hand.

"I thought so. You treat your clit like a private little sex toy that only you get to touch. But it's mine now, Ella. I get to play with it, and I get to decide when you get to touch it. You're my clit-toy. Isn't that right, Ella?"

Ella continued her frantic rubbing.

"*I said, isn't that right, Ella?*"

"Yes...yes Sir." She was very close to coming now, and could only barely respond.

"Tell me you're my clit-toy, Ella."

"I'm your—I'm your—"

"Go on. *Say it.*"

"NO!"

In that moment, something snapped inside her. Ella pushed herself up from the chair so forcefully it fell on its back behind her. Her body shook with strain. "Red!"

"Excuse me?" Mr. Cox had risen from his own chair in alarm, but now stared at her with narrowed eyes that glowed with fury. Ella saw it, but didn't care.

"I cry red! I don't want to do this!"

Mr. Cox's voice was soft and menacing. "I didn't *ask* you if you want to do this. I *ordered* you to. Now get back in that chair and finish what you started."

"But—but I said red! I used the safeword!"

"I told you before I don't put stock in

safewords, Ella. You should've believed me. Now *sit down.*"

"No!" She looked like she was about to cry. Her lip quivered, and her hands clenched at her sides.

She didn't know how he had done it so quickly, but Mr. Cox had sneaked past all her defenses. He wasn't like Mr. Lamont or Mr. Harden; he had a power over her she couldn't overcome.

Maybe because she didn't want to.

She had been so close to losing all control. She had felt herself sinking down, drifting into that strange, dark territory of her mind where everything felt deliciously tranquil and gracefully erotic, even agonizing pain and humiliation.

She wanted him to force her to yield, make her obey, because she knew in the end, she would enjoy it beyond imagination. She just didn't want to go willingly. To acquiesce so easily, without a struggle, without a fight—*that* was what she couldn't do.

"Sit down and make yourself come, or I'll punish you right here and now," Mr. Cox said, his voice hard. "And believe me, Ella, I take my punishments very seriously. By the time I'm done with you, the only thing you'll be crying about being red is your ass!"

"NO!"

Mr. Cox took two long strides toward her. His eyes were dark with fury, and his hands were tight fists at his sides.

Fear overcame her, and she did the only thing left for her to do.

She ran.

She could hear Mr. Cox's voice bellowing behind her: "ELLA!"

# CHAPTER TWELVE:
## TRAPPED

**E**LLA RAN AROUND THE POOL and through the small field of grass, heading straight for the barn. She ran without reasoning or logic; her only thought was to get away.

Mr. Cox was right behind her, and catching up fast. Ella wasn't giving much thought to what would happen if he did catch her. She was focused on getting *away*, and *away* meant getting to the barn before he could tackle her to the ground.

A part of her felt a sense of elation when she made it to the barn and Mr. Cox still had not caught her. She granted herself a single look back, and found him still running through the grass. But he was looking straight at her, savage and bloodthirsty, like a voracious man-eating predator about to take down his prey.

Seeing him looking at her like that gave Ella the rush of a lifetime. She almost crumbled to the ground right then, ready to concede defeat and face whatever punishment he would deliver her. She knew it would mean relinquishing her tenacious self-control, and letting him do whatever he wanted to her…and in that moment, she wanted nothing more.

But a part of her still wouldn't give up.

She had not been caught yet. The chase was still on. She turned around and ran into the barn.

As soon as she was in, she shut the creaky wood door behind her. It had no lock, but the noise of it would at least give her some warning he was inside.

Frantically, she looked around. The last time she had seen the inside of this place, she had been peeking through a window. It hadn't really afforded her a good look around. Now she saw a low, crumbled-down cement wall, divided part of the space ahead.

Ella ducked behind the wall and crouched into the corner in a tight ball, breathing hard. Fear was riding her hard now, along with something else, something even more primal, an emotion she couldn't identify, although the closest word she could think for it was…rapture.

As she heard the barn door shove open with a bang, she hugged her body tighter and quieted her heavy panting.

"Goddamn it, Ella, will you come out!" Mr. Cox bellowed into the barn. "If you come out now, I swear to you, we'll just talk. No punishment, not even a spanking." Ella didn't move. "Ella, get out here now, or I swear to God...." He didn't finish his sentence.

Ella's eyes went wide as she heard him begin to move around the barn, but she took controlled breaths through her mouth, careful not to make any noise. Her skin prickled, and her senses went on high alert.

But she wasn't reacting in fear anymore, she realized. Mr. Cox was almost upon her, there was nowhere else for her to run... her lungs were aching for oxygen, her nerves were fraught, her heart was pounding in her chest... and the only thing Ella could feel from it all was roaring excitement.

She was loving every second of this.

A moment later, a hand gripped her hair from the top of her head. It pulled. Ella screamed.

"Gotcha," Mr. Cox said, pulling her up to stand.

Ella fought to get away, but Mr. Cox's hold on her hair was too tight, and Ella howled, this time with fury. He dragged her around the broken wall and pulled her head back against his body, forcing her to look up at him.

His deep brown eyes, usually so shrouded with veiled secrets, were now bright with wrath.

"Running was a mistake," he murmured into her face. "Hiding was a bigger one, one you will pay for dearly." He dragged her by her hair to the low cement wall, sat down on it, and *yanked* Ella over his lap.

Tears sprang to her eyes from the pain in her scalp. But it had the desired effect, as Ella stopped struggling. She lay tense but still across his thighs.

"You want red?" He hissed. "I'll give you red."

Mr. Cox trapped both Ella's legs under one of his own, making sure she would stay bent over his lap no matter what. But he still didn't let go of her hair.

With his other hand, he ministered a mighty slap across her ass.

*Smack!* Mr. Cox's hand came down right on the meatiest part of Ella's left ass cheek, breaking the smooth surface of her skin like a brick hitting water. Ella's whole butt rippled from the impact; then it tensed and squeezed as Ella screamed.

Mr. Cox lifted his hand away, and saw he had left a bright red handprint pressed into Ella's soft skin.

*Smack!* He delivered her another mighty slap, harder than the first, right on the other ass cheek. Ella howled and jerked, but Mr. Cox pulled her hair up tighter, twisting it around his hand, and Ella stopped struggling quickly.

Mr. Cox began to spank her with his bare hand, using quick, heavy strokes. He never let go of Ella's hair, but used it to keep Ella still and arched over his lap.

As the slaps rained down, Ella began to howl and cry. Tears ran down her cheeks, and while

Mr. Cox couldn't see them, he could feel her body shaking over his legs.

She fought to get away, but it was no use. When she tried to use her hands to shield her bottom, Mr. Cox just pulled her hair tighter until she grabbed his hand on her head with both her own to try and pry his fingers loose. Then he would slap her ass harder, making her cry and shake even worse.

But after a while, Ella gave up fighting. Beaten into submission, she lay passive across his lap, accepting his hard spanks with only instinctive squeezes and shudders of her bottom. Mr. Cox released his grip on her hair, and Ella drooped her head down over his thigh, resting her cheek on his leg. He moved his hand to the small of her back, ready to use it to keep her still should she attempt to get up, but it wasn't necessary.

Ella wasn't fighting him anymore. All her resistance had been pounded away.

That didn't mean Mr. Cox stopped his spanking. Far from it. He kept going with his bare-hand slapping until Ella's entire ass was a shiny, throbbing crimson. He was hitting her so hard, his hand hurt, but he didn't care. Ella's punishment was filling him with heady satisfaction and potent lust, and he wasn't about to stop yet.

Finally, his slaps began to die down, and he rubbed his palm on the outer curve of her butt. Her ass radiated with heat.

Ella moaned in response. To her, his rough fingers on her sensitive flesh felt like sandpaper.

Mr. Cox began to caress her butt with his lazy hand until Ella was shifting her weight across his lap, trying to widen her legs. She was beginning to enjoy her little break from his corporal punishment, Mr. Cox realized.

She was enjoying it a little too much.

He began to spank her again, using flat beefy blows, and Ella screamed in frustration. But a moment later, he grabbed her by the hair again and pulled her up until they were both standing.

Ella was off balance, shaking with apprehension and muscle fatigue. Mr. Cox leaned over her, forcing her to meet his eyes. He looked more in control now, not like the marauding beast that had been chasing her before, but his eyes still gleamed with dark depravity.

"I gave you a choice before, and you didn't take it. Now I'm revoking it. You'll come the way I want you to come."

He grabbed her by both arms, moved her over so that she was standing directly in front of him, put out his foot...and pushed her down by the shoulders until she was sitting on his shoe.

"I can't do this," she cried. "I can't."

"Oh, but I think you can," Mr. Cox replied in that menacing whisper of his. "And I think you know you can, and that's what's scaring you right now. You want control over your own orgasms, but I'm not letting you have it. You don't have control here, princess, I do. Now *rock*."

Ella took a tiny nudge across his shoe, letting the hard leather dig into her pussy lips. She gasped.

Her clit was so sensitive, even the smallest touch felt sharp and intense. She was wet, too; Mr. Cox's shoe was now slippery with her cunt oils.

She slid further back until her cunt was at the tip of his shoe; then, slowly, she shifted her weight forward, all the way to his leg. The thin shoelaces tickled her prickling nerve endings, nipping her, shooting delicious sensations up her spine and down her thighs. Ella moaned and bit her lip in agitation.

Mr. Cox lifted his foot and wiggled his toes in answer. Even through the tough leather, Ella felt his wiggle, and gasped in response.

Soon she was rocking back and forth across his shoe, sliding along the wide strip of polished leather with small surges of her body. She grabbed his calf and hung on for support as she pushed her body back and forth, riding his shoe like a small, short, carousel pony.

Mr. Cox was fine with letting her set her own pace. He was enjoying watching her crisp features contort with growing arousal and humiliation. Through his shoe, he could feel her smooth ride across his foot, and he knew she was pressing down harder to feel every bump and groove along her clit. Her hold around his leg was now desperate, and she leaned her forehead against his calf.

"Ella, look at me."

Ella looked up, her eyes wide and pleading. The sadistic predator inside Mr. Cox wanted to howl in triumph at what he saw there: complete subjection.

"Tell me you're my clit-toy."

"Please Sir, please, please—"

"Say it."

A sob rose in her chest. "I'm your clit-toy. I'm your clit-toy. Oh—oh god!" She rubbed herself madly across his shoe as she came, digging her nails into his calf and howling into the sky.

Mr. Cox put his hands on his hips, wiggled his toes, and smiled.

As Ella's orgasm ebbed away, she slid off his shoe onto the floor.

Mr. Cox gave his foot a good shake to get off all the loose drippings. He debated whether he should have her lick his shoe clean, but after studying her wasted, supine body, he decided against it—this time. He was pleased enough with her progress that he didn't feel the need to subjugate her further, at least not at the moment.

He would take her back to the hotel now, back to their activity room, and they would talk.

But when Ella began to finally recover, she didn't stand up to face him. She pulled herself onto her hands and knees, looking up at him in desperation.

"Fuck me," she said.

The words flummoxed him. *"What?"*

"Fuck me. Here, right now. Fuck me like you did that woman. Take me like an animal. Fuck me raw."

Mr. Cox's eyes narrowed into hard slits. "No."

Ella sat hard on her heels, blown away by the force of his refusal. *"No?"*

"No. I'm not going to fuck you now, not like this."

"But—but I want you to fuck me!"

"I don't want to fuck you."

"But...." She swallowed hard. "I thought you wanted me."

He knelt down to her eye level. "This is the first time a man's ever refused to fuck you, isn't it Ella?" He asked softly. "I'll fuck you when I'm ready, and not before."

As he stood up, Ella looked down at the floor, her eyes flooding like crystal blue pools. Tears dripped down her cheeks. Her emotions were crashing, piling on top of each other like a train wreck: shock, mortification, frustration, bitterness, confusion...all of them flitted through her features.

Her face finally settled on deep, seething rage.

Ella stood up, gave her host a venomous look...and slapped him across the face.

By the time Mr. Cox recovered from the slap, Ella was already on her way out of the barn.

"Where do you think you're going?" He shouted.

"I'm leaving! I'm done!" Ella cried without turning around. Mr. Cox caught up with her and spun her around by her arm.

"I didn't give you permission to leave, princess. We're going to talk."

"No! I don't care about your fucking permission! I quit this place!" She jerked her arm out of his hold and continued to walk away. It was then Mr. Cox realized Ella didn't mean she was done with the scene; she meant she was leaving the Hotel Bentmoore completely.

He spun her around again. "You can't leave yet."

"Yes I can! I can quit if I want to! Let go of me!" She tried to shake off his hold again, but Mr. Cox held her arm tighter this time. "I said let go! You can't just grab me!"

Something dangerous set into Mr. Cox's eyes, something chilling and ominous that made Ella stop struggling and stare at him in blooming panic.

"Can't I?" He said, his voice cold. "We'll see about that."

He dragged her over to the other part of the barn where the mattress still lay in the corner, bare of sheets. Ella saw that next to the mattress was a coil of red rope. She had only a moment to wonder why a coil of rope would just be sitting there in the corner of the barn, as if laying in wait, before Mr. Cox was grabbing it up and flicking it open.

With a strong twist of his arm, he turned Ella around, took hold of both her wrists, and quickly tied them together behind her back.

"What do you think you're doing? Stop it!" Ella fought to pull her wrists apart, but they were already knotted together. Mr. Cox had done such quick work of tying her wrists, there was no way Ella was going to be able to get them free by herself.

At this point, she tried to run away, but Mr. Cox just yanked on the rope, and she stumbled back against his chest.

"Let me go!"

"No."

He coiled the ends of the rope around his hand, giving her a couple feet of lead, and gave her a push.

"Walk," he said.

"Where are we going?"

"Back to the hotel. You're not leaving here until you've calmed down and we've had a chance to talk."

"But—you can't do this to me! This is kidnapping!"

"Sue me." He gave her a stronger push, and Ella stumbled forward.

"I can't walk through the hotel like this!" She shrieked, looking down at her naked body. Her legs were filthy from the floor, her hair was a mess, and her inner thighs still showed the evidence of her recent romp on his shoe.

"Oh yes you can," Mr. Cox replied. "This should get you over your modesty issues, that's for sure."

"Stop it! Stop it!" Ella screamed as he began to force her into a march. "You can't do this! You can't!"

"Watch me."

Mr. Cox pushed, pulled, shoved, and dragged Ella all the way back to the hotel, until they had reached the side door. She continued to squirm and squawk until they were inside; then Mr. Cox grabbed her around her shoulders and held her still against his chest, moving her hair away to whisper in her ear.

"If you're quiet and don't draw attention to yourself, it's likely no one will notice you," he said, tickling the skin on her neck with the warmth of his breath. "But if you scream, people will turn around. They won't help you—I promise you that—but they will see you, and watch me drag you down the hall. They might even laugh. Is that what you want?"

Ella went still.

"That's what I thought." He kept his lips next to her ear a second more than he had to, and Ella shivered.

He walked her down the hallway. Only two office doors were open this time, and the men sitting inside them did not turn around as Ella and Mr. Cox quietly walked past.

But instead of taking her all the way down the hall, Mr. Cox made a sharp turn around a different corner, and walked her down another corridor, this one carpeted and painted in the same tones of the hotel lobby. Ella realized with a start they had entered the corner of the building where Mr. Bentmoore had his private office.

Mr. Cox pulled Ella along until they had reached a pair of thick double doors she recognized all too well. He knocked loudly.

A voice called from the other side: "Yes?"

Ella's eyes went wide. She renewed her frantic efforts to get away as she realized Mr. Cox was about to drag her into Mr. Bentmoore's office—with Mr. Bentmoore sitting inside! But Mr. Cox pulled her in with the rope, dragging her along like a feisty puppy fighting its leash.

"Mr. Bentmoore, we need to use your elevator," he said as he yanked her across the room.

Mr. Bentmoore stood up away from his desk in shock. "What the *hell* is going on here, Cox?"

"Just a minor disagreement, Sir," Mr. Cox replied, working hard to control the struggling woman. "We'll have this worked out in no time, just as soon as Ella calms down."

"He attacked me!" Ella yelled. "He tied me up, and now he won't let me go! This is kidnapping! You can't do this! I want to go home!"

"No," Mr. Cox answered her, pushing her through Mr. Bentmoore's private elevator doors.

"We're not done yet, not by a long shot, princess."

Mr. Bentmoore watched in disbelief as Mr. Cox scuffled with the naked woman to keep her on the elevator. The doors closed, and he could hear her voice descending as she continued to scream: "Let me go! Let me go! *Let me go!*"

Once they were on the dungeon floor, Mr. Cox dragged Ella faster along. "C'mon, princess," he said, his voice thick with effort. "We're almost there."

*"Let go of me!"*

Mr. Cox didn't bother to say anymore, but continued to half push, half carry her down the hall. Once they got to the room he was looking for, he pulled out his card key, opened the door, and pushed Ella inside.

Now that they were inside an activity room, Ella thought he would at least let go of the rope. But Mr. Cox still wasn't done. He pushed Ella hard across the room, trying to get her into the far corner. It was then Ella saw what he was trying to corral her into: a large cage.

"No, no, NO!" Ella twisted and bucked. "You can't stick me in a cage! I'm not an animal!"

Again, Mr. Cox ignored her cries. His sole intent now was to get her into that cage, and it became obvious he was willing to do whatever it took to get her there. When Ella tried to kick him, he picked her up by the waist and hauled her over. She bit his arm, and he pulled her hair until she let go with her teeth and howled in pain.

Finally, he gave her a mighty heave, and Ella went flying into the cage. While she was still trying to catch her balance from the momentum of his push, Mr. Cox was already shutting the door behind her. By the time she could turn around, Ella was locked inside.

"You can't do this! You can't!"

"Come here and put your hands out. I'll take off the rope," Mr. Cox replied, finally speaking to her again.

Ella backed up until her ass hit the bars. She pushed out her wrists out. In short order, Mr. Cox had the rope off, but by the time Ella could turn around and try to make a grab at him, he had stepped back, out of her reach.

"This is against the law," she hissed. "You can't just keep me here against my will."

"Like I said, sue me." And with that, Mr. Cox turned around and left the room.

# CHAPTER THIRTEEN: UNMASKED

"**Y**OU DID WHAT?" MR. BENTMOORE'S booming voice echoed around the office, making Mr. Cox flinch.

"I locked her in a cage, nice and safe. She's not going anywhere, and she can't get herself into trouble. Now please, Sir, give me her file. Not just the notes—the whole thing. I need to read it."

"You can't just keep her locked in the cage, Cox, not against her will!"

"I just need a little more time with her, just until I figure things out. She's hiding something, I don't know what, and I need to find out. It's killing me. We've all missed it, it's why nothing we've done with her has worked so far, and I need to figure out what it is, or we're going to lose her."

"It sounds to me like you've already lost her. She's not going to submit to you now."

"This isn't about submission anymore. This

is psychological warfare, and *I need to win.*"

Mr. Bentmoore frowned and shook his head, but he walked over to his file cabinet, opened the drawer, and handed Mr. Cox a thin manila file. "I don't know what you think you're going to find in there," he said. "You've been told everything."

Mr. Cox opened the file and sat down in one of the plush armchairs to start reading. Pages began to flip as he scanned them with his eyes. Mr. Bentmoore had a seat at his desk, waiting.

Ten minutes later, Mr. Cox's eyes lit up, and his lips spread into a grin. "Not everything," he said, tapping the page. "Not this."

"What? What did you find?"

Mr. Cox turned the paper around and slid it across Mr. Bentmoore's desk. "Right there," he said, pointing. "That's where it started." He rushed to the elevator and got on as soon as the doors opened, tapping the button repeatedly as if he could make it go down faster.

As the elevator doors shut, Mr. Bentmoore squinted his eyes at the page, trying to see what Mr. Cox had discovered. Then his eyes went wide.

"I'll be damned," he said.

Ella heard the bolt unlock before the door opened. She stood up and braced herself, ready to go into attack mode as soon as her oppressor walked inside. But something about Mr. Cox's demeanor stopped her, and her eyes narrowed as he came to stand before her.

He seemed too calm, too sure of himself—not like a man who could face criminal indictment.

"You were an intern at a local news channel," he said. "You spent a whole year working closely with a producer. He was helping you move up the ranks. You even started getting some work in front of the camera after only six months—that's pretty impressive."

Ella took two steps back inside the cage. Her skin paled, and she hugged her arms around her chest. "You know?"

"Yeah, I know."

"How—how did you find out?"

"Ella, we've always known."

"Oh my god." Ella felt frozen with shock.

This whole time, Mr. Bentmoore had known what she was doing there, why she had come... and he had taken her on anyway. He had been letting her pretend.

Mr. Cox, unconcerned about the bombshell he'd just dropped, continued. "Then last year, you quit your job at the station," he said, "and very suddenly. You had no other job to fall back on, no other offers, but you quit anyway. You started working as a freelance journalist."

"You got me," Ella said, her voice full of biting contempt. "I'm a journalist. It's true."

"I don't give a fuck, that's not the point I'm trying to make. You've barely survived the past few months, Ella. An assignment here, a small job there...not enough to make it, not even enough to make ends meet. Why did you quit your job at the station? You were getting juicy assignments, spending time in front of the camera—you were on your way to the top. There was no scandal, no misconduct...or was there?" Mr. Cox eyed her guilty expression. "What happened? What did you do?"

Ella didn't answer. She continued to gaze at Mr. Cox through the bars of the cage, feeling trapped in every way possible.

"Fine," he said. "If you won't tell me, maybe your old producer will. He was working directly over you; he must know what happened." He began to walk away.

"Don't!" Ella yelled, making Mr. Cox turn around. "Don't call him. I don't want him to know where I am!"

"Why not? What's the big deal if the guy knows what you're up to?"

"Because, okay? I don't want him to know. I just...don't." Ella looked away, unsure. Her tongue came out to nervously graze her lower lip. She had no idea how vulnerable or magnificent she looked.

It didn't take long for Mr. Cox to put two and two together. "It was this guy, wasn't it? This producer. Your relationship with him wasn't strictly professional. Something happened between you two." He took in Ella's panicked face. "Did he harass you at work?" His voice lowered. "Did he rape you?"

"No, he didn't rape me," Ella hissed. "It wasn't like that at all. What we had was—special. It was amazing. He taught me so much...and he made me feel...." Her voice trailed away.

She slid down the length of the bars and slumped down to the floor in defeat, hugging her knees to her chest, and pressing her forehead into her legs. Mr. Cox came over and sat down next to her, right on the other side of the bars.

"He gave you your first taste of submission?" He offered gently. "He took control, at least in the bedroom, and you liked it."

"Yes." Tears gathered in her eyes. "But it wasn't just about what went on in the bedroom. It was *all* the time he spent with me. God, he was so amazing. He was dynamic, this force to be reckoned with...everyone at the station admired him, but they feared him, too. But with me, he was more laid back. He was calm, always so calm, he never lost his cool, but he had this power about him, this control—"

"He was a Dominant?"

"Yeah. Yeah, I guess so." Ella wiped her cheek with the back of her hand. "I don't think he would ever label himself like that. He wouldn't even know what that word means. But he was, and he taught me so much."

"Then why did you quit your job?"

Ella cradled her head in her hands. "Because

we fucked up, okay? I sent him an email to his work account, just some stupid note about how I couldn't wait to see him, and he answered me back about all the things he wanted to do to me, and someone in the I.T. department found it, and told everyone how the boss was fucking the young intern, and...." She took a shaky breath. "Everyone started saying the only reason why I was getting the good assignments was because I was sleeping with the producer. They said I was fucking my way to the top." A sob rose in her chest.

"Hey. Look at me." Their eyes met. "Was that true? Were you just sleeping with him to get ahead?"

"No that wasn't true!" Ella yelled, crying hard now. "I didn't give a damn about the assignments he was giving me! I mean, I did, but that didn't have anything to do with why I was sleeping with him! Our relationship...it was...god, it doesn't matter anymore."

"It does matter. It matters a lot. Why did you quit if the rumors weren't true?"

"Cause nobody wanted to believe the truth. They all wanted to think the worst of me. Here I was, some young hot blonde, just started out but already getting herself the good stories, the time in front of the camera. It couldn't be because she actually deserves it, can it? No, she's nothing but a pretty face sitting on a tight ass, sleeping with the producer. She's not getting ahead because of her talent, she's getting ahead cause she's a slut."

Her sobs became anguished, and Mr. Cox gave her a minute to calm down.

"Even my mom didn't believe me," Ella continued in a softer tone. "Of course, *she* thought I was being *smart* to sleep with the producer. She told me I was doing a good job, using what I got to get what I want. She even congratulated me." Another sob rose in her throat, but she put her hand over her mouth to stifle it. "Everyone was looking at me like I was some kind of cheap whore. I couldn't stay there anymore."

"So you left out of misplaced shame. I get that. But Ella, why did you come *here?*"

Her voice rose. "Why do you think? To get inside the infamous Hotel Bentmoore, 'where secrecy and anonymity are guaranteed.' It was supposed to be the report of a lifetime." She shook her head, and her hair stuck to her tear-stained cheeks. "I guess I'm not going to write that report now, am I? Mr. Bentmoore will make me sign some kind of non-disclosure form, and I won't be able to challenge it. Nobody's going to believe you locked me in a cage. It's not like I have the money to get a lawyer, anyway."

Mr. Cox ignored her accusatory tone. "Ella, I understand you wanted a good story to write about, but why did you choose *this* place? Nobody cares about the Hotel Bentmoore out there. It's not on anyone's radar. Nobody would have bought your story—and I think you know it." He stared at her through the bars. "So why did you come here? What made you think the Hotel Bentmoore would turn your life around?"

"I don't know. I don't know." She began to rock back and forth on her butt. With her body folded up, and her hair hanging down her face, Ella looked very pitiful, and to Mr. Cox, very precious.

He sighed. "I'll tell you why you came here," he said. "Deep down, some part of knew you needed what your producer was giving you a taste of, and you figured out where you had to go to get more. You didn't come here for the story, Ella. You came here for the submission, the kink, the desire to be controlled. You did your research, and you learned there's a whole world of kink out there, and we could hand it to you in a platinum package deal. You didn't come here to learn about us. You came here to learn about yourself."

Ella gazed at him. "I guess so," she said softly. "I never thought about it, but...yeah."

Mr. Cox stood up. Then, to Ella's surprise, he unlocked the cage, and opened the door.

"I'm giving you a choice," he said. "If you want to leave, then leave. Nobody will try to stop you. You want to write your story, go ahead." He squatted down to her eye level. "But if you really want to learn about yourself, if you want to learn what your submission is all about, how far it can take you, *how powerful a force it can be*, then stay here, with me. I'll stay on as your host, and I'll teach you as much as I can." He stood back up. "But there'll be no more lies between us, Ella, no more games. You'll have to be completely honest with me, and trust me to do what's right by you. That means you'll have to submit to me completely. I will see you through this—if you stay." He moved aside, giving her space to walk out of the cage. "Which is it to be?"

Ella remained in the cage, hugging her legs, thinking. She took a long time.

But when she began to crawl out of the cage on her hands and knees, looking up at Mr. Cox with both veneration and adulation in her clear blue eyes, he knew he had her.

"I want to stay," she said quietly, coming to a stop by his leg and pressing her forehead into his calf. "Please. Please teach me, Sir."

Mr. Cox wanted to shout in triumph. Instead, he walked over to the wardrobe, got out a thin leather strap, and brought it back to where Ella sat on her heels, waiting for him with her head bowed.

"You will have to obey me, Ella, at all times. Do you understand?"

"Yes, Sir," she said without raising her head. "I understand."

Mr. Cox walked behind her prostrating form and moved her hair away from the nape of her neck. Then he circled the soft leather strap around her slender throat, cinched it tight, and buckled it closed.

Ella took a sharp breath as she felt the leather fasten around her throat, but said nothing.

Mr. Cox smoothed down the leather, making sure it was flat against her skin. Then he ran his fingers down her silky shoulders, grazing her flesh. Ella didn't move, not even when his fingers came around to trace lazy circles over her breasts, but held still, letting him touch her however he wanted, only shivering now and then in response.

Behind her, Mr. Cox smiled.

Now Ella's real training would begin.

# PART IV: ELLA

# CHAPTER FOURTEEN: MR. COX'S CLIT-TOY

**E**LLA EYED THE TWO PIECES of braided rope snaking across the bed. They were thin, but long, and strong enough to restrain her if that's what Mr. Cox had in mind.

They filled her with foreboding.

"Sir, what's the rope for?" Ella asked him. He was standing by her side, watching her reaction to the rope.

He was wearing a thin white shirt today, open to the chest, and tucked into a pair of dark blue pants that in Ella's opinion, made his ass look marvelous.

Not that she would admit to him such a thing. The two of them had come to a new understanding yesterday, but she was not ready to start handing out compliments yet, especially when she was still getting used to the brand new collar around her neck.

"The rope is for you," he said. "You have a problem with restraints. I happen to be a rope master. I'm going to make you get over your aversion to being restrained very quickly." His smile was twisted but alluring, and despite her apprehension, Ella had to smile back.

He continued, "What you have to understand, Ella, is that your problem is not with the restraints themselves, it's the idea of relinquishing control, not just of your body, but of what's happening up here." He tapped the side of his head. "So before I start using the rope to tie you up, I'm going to show you that being restrained has nothing to do with submission."

"How can you say that? If you're tying me up, you're making me submit."

Mr. Cox shook his head. "No, Ella. Your submission has to come *first*. You are consenting to being tied up—that is your first act of submission right there. The restraints are a result of your relinquishment of power, not the other way around." He picked up a length of rope. "Come here. You won't really understand what I'm trying to say until I show you."

Ella stepped forward, cautious and scared. "What do I do?"

"Just raise your arms up and stand still," Mr. Cox said. "This will take some time. You'll have to be patient."

As Ella stood tall and graceful before him, a vision of feminine beauty, Mr. Cox began to wind the rope around Ella's body. His warm hands felt like they were touching her everywhere, with light sweeps around her thighs and tingling grazes under her arms. His eyes were bright, and furrowed with concentration. Ella wondered if it was her enticing body making him look at her like that, or just his joy working the rope.

After a while, she stopped thinking about much of anything. Her mind drifted, and she closed her eyes. Mr. Cox kept up his work with the rope, repositioning her now and then like she was nothing more than a pliable doll. Ella relaxed into the process, letting his hands roam where they would, feeling surprisingly calm.

She had sunk into a sort of daze by the time Mr. Cox announced he was done. "Test it out, see how it feels. Then go to the mirror and see how you look. Tell me if you like it."

Ella looked down at herself. She could still move her body however she wanted; he had not used the rope to restrict her movements in any way. But the thick weave and web of rope felt alien on her skin.

She went to the full-length mirror and stared at herself. The rope followed a diamond pattern around her breasts, down her torso, and across her hips. Intricate knots hemmed the rope right under her thighs, partially shielding her sex. Ella turned in front of the mirror, admiring her reflection.

"It's beautiful," she murmured.

"You're beautiful," Mr. Cox replied, coming to stand by her side. "I take it you like it?"

"Yes." Ella continued to turn in front of the

mirror, studying Mr. Cox's intricate skill. Then she ran her fingers up and down her body. She shivered.

Mr. Cox smiled. "I'm glad you like it, cause I'll probably be tying you up every chance I get from now on. Be honest now: do your movements feel restricted in any way?"

"No," Ella shook her head. "It's like I'm wearing a dress."

And yet, she did feel different somehow. She still felt free in her movements, her body and joints could move however she wanted...but she felt bound in a way that was more mental than physical. She felt *claimed*. Everywhere the rope touched her skin sent a little shock through her, a small reminder than Mr. Cox was in control of her now. She was not confined by the rope; she was confined by his will.

"I want you to remember that," he said, as if he could read her thoughts. "No matter how much rope is around your body, it's not the rope making you give up control. It's what's up here." He tapped the side of her head this time.

Then, to Ella's surprise, he began to unbutton his shirt. "Submission comes with trust," he said as he worked the buttons free. "Your mind needs to tell your body it's okay to accede control. But it's hard, especially for someone like you."

As Ella stared at him in growing excitement, Mr. Cox peeled off his shirt and began to unzip his pants. Then, as if thinking better of it, he stopped.

"Come here," he said. Once Ella stood in front of his naked wide chest, he pointed her down. "Kneel."

Ella wanted so badly to run her hands across his chest, feel the muscles and soft skin under her fingers. But she knelt down on her knees and looked up at him, waiting.

"Open my pants, pull them down," he ordered. "Free my cock."

Ella smiled now. This was much better than running her hands across his chest. She lowered the zipper the rest of the way and pulled down his pants. Mr. Cox's prick, already semi-erect, sprang free and proud.

"I know Harden had enough time with you to work on your oral techniques," he said, his voice hoarse. "Show me what you got. Go on, take me in your mouth."

Grinning, Ella grabbed the base of his cock, brought her mouth down to the tip, and pressed her lips against the smooth head before opening her soft lips and letting his prick slide past. Mr. Cox didn't make a sound, but stared down at her with an intent look on his face.

Ella slid about half way down, paused, and swirled her tongue around his shaft. Then, she began to pull her face back up, careful not to scape her teeth along his cock. Mr. Cox moaned and lifted his head, but quickly recovered and met her eyes once more.

Ella squeezed her hand around his base and began to pump up and down the shaft in time with her mouth, treating Mr. Cox's warm prick to slow turns of her palm. As she sucked his cock into her mouth, she widened her tongue around the base, pressing and undulating it across the pulsing veins. Mr. Cox gasped in tingling delight and shifted his legs open wider.

Now Ella began licking his stiff cock in quick rhythm, twisting her head up and down, letting her tongue slide around the upper shaft, and stabbing at the tiny hole in the center. While her mouth tormented the top half, her hands worked soft magic on the bottom, circling and rubbing the base with the tight grip of her fingers.

Mr. Cox's brows furrowed, and his eyes went dark with passion; but after a few minutes of this blissful torture, he tapped her arm.

"Take yours hands away," he said. "Put them behind you. Use only your mouth."

Ella paused what she was doing, suddenly scared. But she followed orders, taking her hands away from his cock. She folded them behind her back.

Pleasuring his cock with her mouth alone was a completely different kind of task. She continued her face pumping and sucking, but it was harder for her to maintain control over his hard prick. It seemed to want to slide between her teeth and further down her throat without reservation. Ella had to use her tongue to block him from going too far back, but when she did that, she couldn't use it to lick and suck.

Mr. Cox made a sound of impatience and raised a gentle palm to her cheek, holding it there to keep her head still. Then, he began to pump his hips—not a lot, just enough to gain some momentum in her mouth. Ella closed her eyes and scrunched up her face; she couldn't handle the large cock gaining ground down her throat. She pulled back.

Mr. Cox pulled her head up with his palm. "Why did you pull back?" He asked, his voice kind. "What scared you?"

"It's too big. I can't take all of it."

"You can, if you relax your throat. I'll go slow. Just let your muscles open for me."

He pushed his cock in her mouth...deeper, deeper, until Ella felt it slide down the back of her tongue. She tried to calm herself and be still, but her panicked reflexes got the better of her, and she pulled away, coughing.

Mr. Cox gave her a minute to recover. "You're not letting your throat open, Ella," he said. "Tell me what you're afraid of."

"I'm afraid I'll gag and throw up on you," she admitted.

"You won't gag if you relax and don't fight it. Let your throat stretch for me. Accept it's going to be blocked, and that you'll be okay. Give me control of your mouth, your throat, even your most basic reflexes. Understand?"

"I...yes, Sir."

"Good. Let's try this again." He began to push through her lips into her mouth once more, and this time, he grabbed Ella by the back of the head to hold her still.

Ella's brows furrowed with concentration as she took deep, even breaths, trying to calm her nerves, trying not to tense up and gag. But just as she felt his cock hit the back of her tonsils, her anxiety got the better of her; her throat clenched, her esophagus closed, and she brought up her hands to physically push him away.

Mr. Cox didn't move, but the force of Ella's push managed to throw her head back. Her chest heaved as she fought to get some air. She wiped her mouth with the back of her hand, and it came away wet with saliva.

"You're still not relinquishing control," Mr. Cox said, sighing. "Somewhere in the back of your head, you still think that by servicing me in this way, it's all about you. It's not. You have to let me take control over what happens."

"I'm trying to, but I can't stop my reflexes," Ella said, her voice thick with remorse. "I'm sorry."

Mr. Cox tipped her head up. "Don't be sorry for who you are," he said. "Never be sorry for that."

With his thick erection bobbing in front of him, he went back to the bed and retrieved the second piece of rope. "Let's try something. Move your hair away from your neck."

Wary now, Ella held her hair up on the top of her head with both hands. Mr. Cox removed the thin leather collar from around her neck and began to wind the rope around Ella's throat, looping it in the back and making a series of vertical knots.

Ella could feel the coils of rope going higher and higher up her neck. "Sir?"

"Try moving your head around. Is the rope too tight?"

Ella moved her head in a wide circle, testing the pressure of the rope around her neck. She found it was loose, much looser than what she'd been afraid of; she owned necklaces tighter than this.

"It's not tight at all," she said, "but it feels strange." She cocked her head to the side, and felt the fibers of the rope rub against her sensitive pale skin. The rope felt scratchy, and a little bulky, like an unfamiliar weight.

"It's okay if it feels strange," Mr. Cox said. "I just don't want it to feel like it's choking you. That's not the point."

"What *is* the point?"

"I'm getting to it." He tied the last knot at the back of her head, and draped the two long ends of the rope over her shoulders, so that they dangled over her breasts. Then he moved around to face her once more. "Touch the rope," he said. "Feel it on your neck."

Ella ran her hands up and down her throat,

and felt the loops going all the way up to her chin.

"I assert the right to use your throat, Ella," Mr. Cox said softly, looking deep into her eyes. "You don't control it anymore. I own it. Everywhere the rope touches is mine. Understand?"

Ella nodded, her crystal blue eyes wide.

"Good. Let's try this again." Mr. Cox grabbed onto the two loose ends of the rope to pull Ella toward him. He pulled her in slowly, but firmly; Ella had no choice but to bring her face right up to his swollen cock. She opened her mouth and let Mr. Cox pull her down.

When her lips were about half way down the shaft, he stopped. "Take a breath," he ordered. Ella grimaced, feeling her throat contract. "No— relax. It's not your throat anymore, remember? It's mine. Open my throat for me. Open it. That's it...relax."

Ella's features smoothed out as her muscles finally relaxed. She opened her mouth wider and let her neck go slack, easing the way for Mr. Cox's approaching assault.

"Now breathe in, and hold it."

Ella sucked in some air through her nose. As soon as she did, Mr. Cox pulled on the ends of the rope, forcing Ella's head and mouth all the way down his cock. In one smooth pull, his prick hit the back of her tonsils. Ella opened her mouth wider, letting her lips rest around his thick shaft, and relaxed.

Mr. Cox held his prick down her throat for a

good long moment, letting her feel it, enjoying his success. Then he pulled back, giving some slack to the rope. His cock popped out of her mouth, and Ella took a deep breath.

"Breathe easy," he said. "Easy now."

Ella slowed her heaving chest, trying to regain a measured tempo for her lungs to work.

"Again now: take a deep breath and hold it."

Once more, Ella took a deep breath and held it; and once again, Mr. Cox pulled her mouth all the way down his prick, until the entire length had disappeared inside her mouth and her neck distended with his large presence. He didn't ask her to suck it, or lick it; merely accept it.

Ella accepted it now without qualm.

This time, when he pulled away, he could feel Ella's tongue pressing against his cock as it slid past. He smiled.

"We're going to go faster now," he warned her. "Control your breathing. Remember, the throat is mine. Keep it open for me."

He began to pump in and out of her mouth with long, slow strokes, dipping his cock all the way down her throat each time. Ella held still and let him block her air passage as much as he wanted, breathing when she could, and holding it when she could not. Her face contorted now and then with her efforts, but her muscles remained malleable, and easy to penetrate.

"Good, Ella," Mr. Cox murmured, moving faster now. "Very good." He gripped the pieces of rope in both hands tightly, pulling her to him now with greater urgency. Ella let herself be moved, giving in to his demands on her body.

No, not her body. His body. His throat. He could use it as he pleased. The thought calmed her, and filled her with contentment.

"Use your tongue now," he ordered. Ella began swirling her tongue against his cock again, this time adding some sucking motions all the way up his prick each time he thrust it down her throat. Mr. Cox moaned, and a look of deep concentration took over his face.

"God, Ella," he groaned, tipping his head back. He let go of the rope and grabbed her hair instead, digging his fingers into her scalp. Ella smiled serenely around his cock and bore down with her face, pressing her eyes and nose into his groin each time he buried his prick down her gullet.

Unable to control his movements any longer, Mr. Cox rammed down her neck with quick pumps of his hips, rubbing her soft tissues raw and pummeling her throat. Ella held still and took it, feeling an incredible sense of power she wasn't expecting.

A minute later, Mr. Cox was holding himself still inside her as his balls erupted down her gorge. His sperm shot thick spurts down her throat, and Ella relaxed, swallowing it all.

Mr. Cox was soon staggering away from her, leaning against the bed for support. "That was amazing, Ella."

"Thank you, Sir," Ella said, licking her lips. The power she had felt before was still pumping her heart. It bloomed now into a new realization: she could give into Mr. Cox's demands, relinquish control of her body and mind, and by doing so, grant him even greater pleasure. She had that power.

The knowledge opened her eyes to a whole new array of possibilities.

Mr. Cox studied her as she sat on her heels and smiled.

"You're beginning to understand now, aren't you?" He whispered.

"I believe so, Sir," she said, nodding. "It feels...good."

"Let's see if you can apply what you've learned," he said. "Here, get on the bed."

Ella climbed in on her hands and knees, feeling adventurous. "What do I do now?"

"Get on your back. Lie down," he said. "Spread your legs and bend them in at your knees."

Ella eagerly spread her legs, but Mr. Cox spread them wider as he settled himself between them. He looked down at her soft, wet pussy. Then he lowered himself even further down, getting comfortable with his elbows on the bed as he spread her cunt lips wide, studying her pink folds.

Ella squirmed a bit, feeling uncomfortable. It always embarrassed her to have a man look at her pussy this close up. "Sir?"

"Shh. I'm admiring the view." He began to rub two fingers up and down her folds, making Ella gasp and squirm. But when he squeezed her clit lightly between two fingers, he felt her stiffen in response.

"We're going to need more lube," he said. He moved away from her sprawled legs long enough to reach over to the bedside table and pull out a bottle of lubricant. He poured a large glob over his palm.

"Sir, what are you doing?"

"I'm going to have some fun," Mr. Cox said, a wicked gleam in his eyes. "Now relax."

He brought his hand, now covered in lube, back to her pussy. His fingers rubbed along her slit, spreading it wide, getting it nice and wet, and Ella propped herself up.

"It's cold!"

"It'll warm up. Now lie back down and be still."

"Sir, please, I—"

Mr. Cox plucked on the rope crisscrossing her body. With it being all one piece, the fibers pulled and brushed across her skin everywhere. "Mine, Ella," he reminded her. "All mine."

Their eyes met, and Ella lay back down, looking up at the ceiling.

Mr. Cox continued his slow exploration of her velvety soft pussy folds and secret valleys. Ella gasped and sighed now and then, but did not try to pull away.

Then she felt him push two fingers deep inside her cunt.

"I'll know if you're tensing up, Ella," he warned her. "Keep your body relaxed." Ella let her breath out and forced her body to go limp.

"Very good," she heard Mr. Cox say. Then she felt him slip another finger inside her.

With slow, gentle thrusts, Mr. Cox eased his fingers in and out of her, letting her muscles stretch around them. With the lube easing his way, and Ella's natural arousal taking over, he soon had all four fingers tightly packed up her cunt.

Mr. Cox didn't pump in and out anymore, but calmly, steadily, began to push his fingers deeper and deeper inside Ella's cunt, until they were in all the way to his knuckled thumb.

When the third knuckles of all four fingers pressed inside, Ella flinched, feeling her skin stretch and burn. In that moment, all her sinews contracted, and she tried to pull herself up the bed, away from his hand.

"Red," she said, scrunching up her face. "Red, please...." She took a deep breath, trying to get on top of the sensation of his hand invading and burning her clenching cunt. Mr. Cox stopped, but did not pull his hand out.

"No safewords with me, Ella," he reminded her. "I'll give you a minute to relax, but we're not stopping."

Ella breathed, willing her body to calm down.

Soon, she was able to ease her body back down the bed.

"Good girl," Mr. Cox said. "You can take it." He pressed his fingers deeper into her. Ella whimpered, but said nothing.

But when the knuckle of his thumb tried to slip past her cunt opening, searing her open with its wide stretch, Ella cried out.

"Sir, please! It hurts!"

"It's going to burn a little. Just relax. You can take it."

He pushed in more, and Ella could feel her whole cunt ache. Even her inner tissues were beginning to burn.

A second later, something hard pressed against her pelvic bone from the inside.

"Wait! Wait! Oh god."

He stopped again. "What's wrong?"

"You're going to tear me open!"

"No, I won't. Relax, Ella."

"Please, Sir. Please."

"Do you trust me?"

Ella paused, making a pained face. "Yes, Sir."

"Then relax. I'm not going to tear you, I'm going to give you an orgasm like you've never felt before. But you have to trust me."

Ella lay back, and this time, she closed her eyes in surrender.

"That's it, Ella. I can feel your body yielding to my hand. Just relax." Ella gave up the last of her fight, and relaxed.

She took deep breaths at Mr. Cox's hand eased into her cunt, pushing her soft innermost tissue aside and making room for itself within her tight grip. Her cunt throbbed and burned as it stretched open further and further. She could feel his hand pressing, pressing...and slip through.

His whole hand was now inside her cunt, balled into a tight fist.

"Oh God," was all Ella could get out. "Oh God."

Mr. Cox placed his other hand softly on her belly. "You're good, Ella," he said. "You're doing fine. How does it feel?"

"Oh God."

Mr. Cox smiled. "It's not my name, but I'll take it."

He began to pull his fist in and out, only a little, only enough to give Ella that push/pull sensation of his hand stroking the deep cavern of her body. But Ella, impaled on his hand and feeling completely stuffed, felt every twitch and rub at her insides. His hand was huge inside her, a ball of pressure, heat, and need.

"Your clit is all swollen," he said. "It looks delicious. It needs some attention, don't you think so, my little clit-toy?"

"Yes...yes, Sir."

Ella stretched her legs open wider, trying to accommodate him. His hand didn't hurt so much anymore; pain was orbiting into pleasure, and an overwhelming feeling of possession. She was his toy now, his personal little clit-toy, just like he'd said. He could do whatever he wanted, and make her do whatever he wanted.

She was his puppet, and with his hand lodged well up inside her, it felt like he was literally pulling her strings.

He brushed against her lower lip with his other hand. "This is my mouth, right Ella?"

"Yes, Sir."

"I want to hear it saying 'I'm Mr. Cox's clit-toy.'"

"I'm Mr. Cox's clit-toy," Ella repeated. "I'm Mr. Cox's clit-toy. I'm—Oh God!" Mr. Cox had begun to rub Ella's stretched, stiffened, throbbing clit. He didn't have to rub very hard. Ella was so close to coming, her thighs were quivering.

As Mr. Cox pumped his hand back and forth inside her, he rubbed her spongy little clit, and Ella came with a howl, jerking her body against his hand and twisting her head back and forth.

Mr. Cox grinned as she came. He could feel her orgasm from the inside—it made all her muscles spasm around his hand.

As Ella's breathing began to calm down, Mr. Cox slowly eased his hand out, letting her body expel it. Ella made a series of tiny grimaces, feeling the burn of his retreat more acutely now. But soon, his hand was free, and she gave him a languid smile.

"Well?" He asked her. "Was it like nothing you've ever felt before?"

"Yes. How did you know it would be like that?"

"I'm not exactly new at this, you know," he said wryly. Then he went to the bathroom, got a towel, and wiped Ella down.

When he was done, he ordered her to rest. "Close your eyes. You've earned a nap."

"I'm okay."

"Sleep, Ella, or I'll be claiming your ass next."

Ella promptly fell asleep.

# CHAPTER FIFTEEN: PREDATOR AND PREY

"**I** HAVE A QUESTION."

"Okay," Mr. Cox replied. His voice came out smooth, but Ella could detect a hint of wariness.

"Yesterday you said it's hard for someone 'like me' to give up control. What did you mean by that?"

Mr. Cox looked at her in that probing way of his, as if he were already predicting Ella's next three moves, and deciding the best way to counter-attack....

Which, Ella guessed, he probably was. The thought pleased her. Here was a man who thought he could beat her at her own game. Time would tell, but the prospect of a challenge made her smile with wicked revelry.

He had just told her to "get naked and come here," but Ella had not obeyed, had instead ignored his order and asked him her question. If her recalcitrance had bothered him, he gave no sign of it, other than that probing look of his.

He answered, "I meant a woman like you, who will only submit to the right man, and only under the right circumstances."

"I thought all women are supposed to be naturally submissive." Ella's smile turned smug. She thought she had scored one against him. She frowned when Mr. Cox began to laugh.

"Oh, princess, I don't know where these ideas in your head come from, but that is so not true, it's ridiculous," he said, chuckling. "Why would you ever think that?"

"Isn't that the basic philosophy of this place?" Ella answered, scowling. "That women everywhere are naturally submissive, they just need someone to show it to them, namely a dominant man?"

"Oh hell no," Mr. Cox said, crossing his arms and pealing with laughter. "You've just managed to insult every dominant woman everywhere." He calmed himself down, but continued to grin at her. "People are people, princess, they all have their own weird habits and idiosyncrasies—and their own kinks. They can't be categorized and labeled just to fit inside someone else's idea of how they *should* behave."

Ella's scowl deepened. "Mr. Harden and Mr. Lamont were certainly trying to get me to behave in a certain way."

"Because they were trying to show you what your body is capable of, strip away all your inhibitions and your fear of judgment that was holding you back. *That* is the real philosophy of this place: we give people a chance to indulge in their desires, without them having to worry about what anyone else thinks. There's no condemnation here, no looks of disapproval. Now I grant you, it's more common for us to host submissive women. But we have submissive male guests, too."

"You do?"

"Oh yeah. Life out there is even harder for them. Society doesn't look too kindly on submissive males. Men are taught from an early age they have to be strong, aggressive, non-emotional...a guy who likes to be cuffed, whipped, ordered around? He's not looked upon well in the outside world."

Ella thought for a minute. "Are you comparing me to a submissive guy, then? Is that how I'm different?"

"Fuck no, Ella. No no no." He laughed again, and Ella's eyes became stormy blue. "I'm saying, there are many different kinds of kinksters out there, and many different kinds of subs. You can't point to a submissive woman and think you know all there is to know about her, just because she's a submissive; what her submission *means* is completely up to her. Now you—" he uncrossed his arms and pointed to her—"you are still discovering yourself, so I wouldn't make too many assumptions about you just yet. But...I think it's safe to say, you're a special kind of sub. One who identifies as Prey."

"Prey?" Ella's voice was sharp. "What the hell does that mean?"

"It means, princess, that you don't submit to just any man, not even if he's a Dominant. You need to be hunted; you need to be taken down. You respond to the chase. Your play, if that's what you want to call it, is about you making sure your Top is stronger, faster, and smarter than you. Once you're in the paws of the beast, that's when you feel comfortable enough to let yourself go."

"You make me sound like a weakling. Like a lab mouse, happy in its cage."

"Then you misunderstand. Tell me, have you ever heard of a lion hunting a mouse?"

Ella paused, thrown off. "No, lions don't hunt mice. Do they?"

"No, and that's my point. Lions hunt the big game: the zebras, the buffalo, the wildebeest. They take down animals no other predator can, because they are the apex predators, the very top of the food chain. You're prey, Ella, but not just any predator can take you down. Only the apex predator, the guy at the top of the chain."

"And you think that's you." She pursed her lips.

Mr. Cox didn't smile. "You better believe it, princess. When I play the game, I don't just play to win. I go for the kill. I *never* just walk away. I think you know it; I think you could tell that about me the first time you saw me in action, in the barn. I think that's what drew you to me in the first place."

Ella rolled her eyes. "Really, I'm drawn to you, huh? It all makes sense now. I'm drawn to the guy who compares me to a wildebeest."

"I never said it's logical, princess. I think it's totally primal. It's the oldest game on the planet: predator and prey. Kill or be killed." He pointed to her again. "You want to submit, you love the rush, the way your body feels when you've been caught. But you'll never go meekly—that's not the kind of woman you are. And you know what? I wouldn't want it any other way." His smile made Ella's blood hum.

"I submitted pretty easily yesterday," she reminded him.

"Yes, you did. And now look at you: you're contentious, belligerent, combative—you want a fight on your hands." He opened his arms wide. "So let's fight."

Ella's veins pulsed. Her eyes lit up a sky blue. Excitement unfurled deep in her belly.

"I thought I'm supposed to submit freely," she said, her voice hoarse. "That was the deal."

"For you to submit freely? Ha. No woman's submission is every free, Ella. I have a feeling yours is going to cost me some skin—but it'll be worth it, when I take you down. You want to try taking me on? C'mon. Go for it."

Ella let out her breath slowly. His words had

stirred her own inner animal, one that was all too willing to rise to his challenge.

"Don't think you know me so well," she spat, feeling the adrenaline rushing her blood. She was already scanning the room, weighing her options.

"Really? You know you want to." When she didn't move, his tone went dangerously soft. "Come here, Ella, now, or else."

"Or else what?"

"This." In one swift movement, he had grabbed her arm, pulled her to his chest, and pinned her hand behind her back. Ella had no time to anticipate his attack, or try to defend herself.

"This is how easy I can take you," he said, gazing down into her face full of outrage. "But since it's a fight you want...." He let go of her arm and pushed her away. "This time try harder, Ella, because it's *on* now. Once I get you, I'm not letting you go again." He furrowed his brows, as if deciding something. "You know what? Let's raise the stakes. I owe you a punishment. I catch you, you'll get your first caning."

"I've already had one. Mr. Lamont caned me."

"Not the way I'm going to cane you, sweetheart, believe me. This is going to be your first *real* caning, and you're going to know exactly what that means. The question is, how badly do you want to find out?"

Ella's eyes flared. Then she ran.

Of course, there wasn't much space for her

to run. The room was large, but contained, and the door leading to any real escape was locked. Ella could evade his capture for a while, but deep down, she knew it was only a matter of time before he caught her.

But she would not make it easy for him, not by a long shot. The beast inside her, the one which now carried the name of Prey, controlled her actions, and Mr. Cox was right, giving into it was a thrilling rush.

He began to stalk her, trying to maneuver her into a corner. Ella avoided that at all costs, scooting around, faking turns, and running over the bed, barely missing Mr. Cox's hand slipping out and making a grab for her. A padded sawhorse sat in the middle of the room, and she tried to lift it, thinking maybe she could throw it at him; but it was bolted down tight, and her attempt only seemed to amuse her pursuer, who chuckled from the other side of the room.

She could see in his eyes, the chase was turning him on.

It was turning her on, too.

But he let her duck and weave around him, letting her escape his grasp for as long as she could, letting the chase play out. It took some time, but he finally corralled her into the corner.

She had nowhere left to run.

Baring her teeth, she turned to fight.

Mr. Cox was ready for her: he spread his arms wide and bent his body in, preparing for anything she might try to pull on him as he inched his way closer.

When he got close enough, Ella dodged, trying to slip under his arm as she had once before. But he caught her by the hair, making her shriek, and yanked her back.

He thought she would try to grab his hands off her hair and duck. She surprised him by stepping back into his chest and elbowing him in the ribs.

He folded in with an "umph." But he managed to keep his grip on her hair, and this time, when Ella tried to jerk away, he grabbed her around the waist and folded her in with him.

Ella struggled and fought, outraged by the turn of events. Mr. Cox dragged her along with him across the room until she was facing the wall.

He pressed her into it, hard, using the length of his body to restrain her. As Ella continued to yell out her rage, he pulled her hands high over her head and locked them in one of his, pressing her fists into the cool, smooth wall.

Ella was locked in place now between hard drywall and Mr. Cox's hot body. Her breathing came hard and fast, and she still jerked now and then in a futile attempt to gain her freedom.

She screamed when she felt Mr. Cox's wide fingers slip under her skirt and begin a leisurely rise up her leg. She kept screaming as his hand slipped under her panties to rub her ass. Then, he reached around, dipped his hand down the front of her panties, and lightly cupped her cunt.

Ella let out a primal yell that sounded like a battle cry.

Mr. Cox flipped her around and pinned her back against the wall facing him, so he had better access to her front. Ella was momentarily struck speechless, the breath knocked out of her. But then she was screaming again, kicking, thrashing, and fighting him for all she was worth.

Mr. Cox smiled in the face of her tantrum. He let her struggle for a while, watching in amusement. Then he pressed his free hand on top of her mouth to quiet her, looking directly into her fury-filled face.

"Ella, will you please shut the fuck up," he said. "I want to hear it when I rip your clothes off."

Ella's deep blue eyes went wide. When Mr. Cox pulled his hand from her mouth, she remained still, her mouth agape, dumbfounded by what he had just said.

Placing his hand squarely in the V-neck opening of her button-down shirt, Mr. Cox pulled the material down. They both heard the loud tear as it ripped away from her body. He pulled at her skirt the same way, ripping the zipper open, and letting the frayed material fall to the floor.

"Maybe Harden had the right idea all along—I should start telling you not to wear underwear," he growled as he pulled at her bra without any success.

"Don't! Please!" Ella begged as he continued to grapple with the stubborn fabric and lace. Mr. Cox stopped his ineffective attempts to tear off her bra so he could put his hand over her mouth again.

"Shh," he quieted her. "You don't get to talk anymore. When I'm ready, I'll let you beg. I'll *enjoy* hearing you beg. But right now, you get to stay fucking quiet. Understand?"

Ella nodded and closed her eyes, turning her head away so she wouldn't have to watch him tear her bra. But Mr. Cox pulled the wire and delicately laced cups over her breasts instead, leaving the bra intact.

He slapped her right nipple. "I said, *do you understand?*"

Ella turned her head back quickly, eyes wide with pain. "Yes! Yes Sir! I understand!"

He slapped her left nipple. "I told you to stay fucking quiet."

"But—"

He slapped both her nipples, making her writhe and yell. "I take it back. You don't have to stay completely quiet," he said. "Feel free to cry." Then, holding her hands tight above her head by the wrists, he reached down his face, and bit into her right breast.

Ella screamed, feeling his teeth sink into her. The shock and pain of it was acute, a breathtaking jolt of agony, and Ella's cry was harrowing even to her own ears.

But as Mr. Cox pulled his face away, smiling at her with his devil eyes, a tiny bit of blood staining his lip, Ella could feel the animal inside her surrender the fight. She was caught now, taken down like prized game. She was his to do with as he wanted.

A part of her sighed in delighted relief.

Mr. Cox's monstrous smile grew wider as he sensed the change in her, saw the capitulation in her eyes. With her surrender came a surge of arousal for them both, but Mr. Cox was far from done with her.

The prey had been caught. It was time to play.

He dragged her over to the high and wide padded sawhorse, yanked off her bra and panties, and pushed her over it. He had her quickly cuffed down. Ella was now bent over the sawhorse, legs and arms spread, soft, subdued, and defenseless.

Mr. Cox took a moment to circle the sawhorse, admiring the picture she presented, her lush body and wanton pose. The sawhorse was low enough that her feet stood flat on the floor, but in her bent and stretched pose, her calves strained, and her thigh muscles quivered with strain. With her legs spread so far apart, her ass cheeks opened just enough to reveal a shadowy crease between them, and where her thighs diverged, Mr. Cox could see the sealed glistening pouch of her pink-lipped cunt.

Ella didn't move, save for the tense rise and fall of her back with each breath.

Mr. Cox went to the wardrobe and got out a long, knotted, wooden cane. He stepped over to Ella's head and bent down to her face.

"Ella, can you hear me?"

"Yes," Ella said softly, with great difficulty. Her eyes were already cloudy and dazed, void of all cohesive thought. With her capture and surrender, her mind had fled. She was somewhere else now, somewhere light and free. Her prey instincts were in control, and they were telling her to relax, and revel in her fate.

"I'm going to make you hurt now. Do you understand?"

"Yes." Her voice cracked.

"Good. Just making sure." He went back around to her spread buttocks, and without preamble, swung at her with the cane.

Mr. Cox had spoken the truth: this felt *nothing* like the caning Mr. Lamont had treated her to. Mr. Cox's strikes with the cane were brutal and merciless. They struck her everywhere, on her hips, her thighs, her legs, her rump...they left wide crimson impression lines wherever they landed.

Still, it took a while for Ella to react to the pain. Her mind was so far gone, every lick felt like sizzling glory to her spirit. But slowly, the pelting began to have its desired affect.

By the tenth blow of the cane, Ella was crying.

By the twentieth, she was screaming. And by the time Mr. Cox had gotten to somewhere in the thirties, she was sobbing uncontrollably.

Mr. Cox kept going, marking up her blotchy skin with more strokes of jolting agony.

Ella struggled in her cuffs now, twisting and flailing after every impact of the vicious cane. Mr. Cox knew her thrashing was not any lucid attempt to get away; it was just her body's natural reaction to the agony. But the cuffs insured she did not move in any way that would interfere with his aim, and possibly cause her harm.

Ella was a mess now, overwrought by all the sensations flooding her body. Her back and legs glistened with sweat, and she let out a ragged wheeze with each breath, her voice hoarse and raw.

Her ass and legs were a maze of lines in varying shades of crimson, many of them already turning purple. Mr. Cox struck her again with the cane, right across both buttocks, and listened as Ella screamed once more, her voice fading into a wracked sob.

He came around and knelt beside her, picking up her head by the chin. Ella's face was a mask of red eyes, swollen nose and lips, and running mascara. Mr. Cox watched, fascinated, as her tears fell down her cheeks and made new track lines across her smeared makeup.

Then he kissed her lips hard, holding her head still and pressing it against his own. He was surprised by how hard Ella kissed him back.

"I really must fuck you now," he whispered, once he had broken his lips away from hers.

"Oh god, yes please," Ella whispered back.

Mr. Cox threw the cane on the bed, moved back around her splayed body, unzipped his pants, yanked them down, and thrust his rigid cock right into Ella's cunt.

Her cunt lips curled into his thrust as if trying to push him in deeper. Mr. Cox slapped his body against hers, burying himself to the hilt. Ella's cry now was low and breathless.

Mr. Cox grabbed her by the hips and began fucking her just as brutally as he had caned her, with quick, powerful thrusts of his hips, marveling at Ella's tight hold and incredible heat. She was very wet, and very tight, and after the exhilaration of the caning he had just given her, he didn't know how much longer he could hold on.

It turned out, he didn't have to hold on very long at all: Ella was already coming with his next thrust. Her orgasm rolled on as Mr. Cox continued to pump into her, awed by the vise-like grip of her pussy around his cock. Her delicate ripples of pleasure as she came thrilled him to the core.

He kept pumping as her orgasm ebbed, trying to hold out for as long as he could, trying to prolong the pleasure for them both. He was rewarded for his trouble when he felt her come again just as he did, letting out a deep-rooted cry.

He pushed against her body with powerful blows of his hips, rubbing his rough thighs against her tender and bruised ass. As his own orgasm faded, Mr. Cox could hear her quietly keening.

He uncuffed her as soon as he felt stable on his feet, and helped her off the sawhorse. Then he picked her up in his arms, carried her over to the bed, and lay down next to her.

He gazed into her dirty, tear-stained, swollen face.

"God, you're so beautiful."

He kissed her eyes, her cheeks, her nose, and finally her lips, pressing against her mouth tenderly.

Ella kissed him back, albeit weakly, and gave him an angelic smile. "Thank you Sir," she said. Her features began to smooth out as she fell into a doze.

"No, Ella. Thank you," Mr. Cox said, still gazing at her in awe.

# CHAPTER SIXTEEN: SUBDROP

**M**R. COX GAVE ELLA A few days to recover from the severe caning he had administered. During that time, he did nothing to hurt her ass or legs; in fact, he barely even touched her there. But he would often ask her to turn around and stick out her butt, so he could admire her welts and bruises.

And he certainly wasn't leaving the rest of her alone. He would call for her whenever he could, and expected her to come whenever he called—in more ways that one.

With time, Ella learned that Mr. Cox's view of play involved a lot of rope, a lot of fucking, and often, hefty doses of humiliation. Now that Ella's spirit had been conquered, Mr. Cox enjoyed taking full advantage of the power he had over her.

Sometimes he would attach a leash to her collar and order her on all fours, so he could parade her around the room like a prized pet. Other times he would order her inside a cage, and have her pleasure herself until she was near coming; then he would order her out and fuck her from behind, pushing her face down on the floor, making her knees scrape and burn.

When he was feeling particularly devious, he would put nipple clamps on her nipples, watch the way her nipples paled and distended under the bite of the little teeth, and smile as Ella's face contorted with pain. Then he would attach the leash to the nipple clamps instead of her collar, and pull her around the room by her breasts. When that was done, he would sit in a chair and put his feet on her back, treating her as if she were nothing more than his footstool.

Ella didn't know why, but she found being his play toy incredibly satisfying, and wildly erotic. When he was ordering her around, her mind didn't have to think; it could go away on a little vacation for a while, and when it came back, she felt renewed.

Her debasement turned her on.

She would often beg Mr. Cox to fuck her.

Sometimes he agreed; sometimes he made her wait. Her orgasms were his now, he said, and it was his sole discretion if and when she had one. When Ella was deep in her degradation, bowing before his feet, flushing with shame and desire, he would order her to refer to herself as his clit-toy, and Ella would beg him to fuck his clit-toy hard, to make his clit-toy come...and Mr. Cox would grin with pride.

But when he treated her gently, with great tenderness and care, Ella would relish those times, too. They helped her see that while Mr. Cox enjoyed hurting her, disgracing her, and basically treating her like the personal play toy she was, he cared about her, too.

Ella was walking around in a constant state of simmering arousal now. Mr. Cox only had to look at her with his piercing stare, give her that twisted grin of his, and Ella's cunt would flood with wetness.

But once she was sent back to her room to spend some time alone, doubts would creep in. Her thoughts would grow muddled with confusion and shame.

She didn't understand why she enjoyed being degraded the way she did; she didn't understand why she found giving up power and control so cathartic. And when she grazed her hands against her ass and thighs, pressing into the bruises here and there to feel the last remnants of the caning, she couldn't understand why the prickling pain and the haunting flashbacks made her smile instead of cringe.

Being under the care of Mr. Cox was a whirlwind ride of agony and ecstasy. Being left alone was torture.

Thankfully, she wasn't left alone very often. Mr. Cox instructed Ella to spend a good portion of her free time sitting in open areas around the hotel, like the bar and the lounge, so she could watch the way other guests interacted. Ella learned a lot about different kinks and fetishes that way, just by observing people from afar.

But Ella began to feel as if she was on information overload. Her mind had been opened up to a whole new world of possibilities and pleasures, and she was having a hard time processing it all. Worse, she was still harboring a deep suspicion that her desires were perverted and wrong. She began to fear what her life would be like once she left the hotel and she was stuck back in the real world, alone.

Her visit to Mr. Cox that night was cut short when he received word his immediate help was needed with another guest. Ella was quickly sent back to her room. She knew it was something bad when he didn't even escort her down, but trusted her to go on her own.

Ella hoped that whatever the emergency was, Mr. Cox could help handle it...but she still felt bereft by the sudden dismissal. She knew it wasn't rational, or even fair—clearly, he had not sent her away out of choice—but she had been looking forward to her time with him. She needed to feel his anchoring presence and calm control.

She was depending on it.

That night, she had a horrible time falling asleep. Her chest felt filled with sadness, and anxiety made her restless, like she couldn't stand being in her own skin. She hated this feeling, like she was drifting in a cloud of doubt and despair. But most of all, she hated feeling so weak.

Finally, after berating herself long enough, she managed to fall into a light sleep. But she awoke in the middle of the night, crying and trembling.

She tried washing her face with cold water. It didn't help; she still felt shaky and miserable, like she was going mad, alone in her dark room... like the room was closing in on her, stifling her very breath.

There was no way she could go back to sleep now. She needed to get out of there. Without even bothering to put on a pair of shoes, she slipped outside, and into the corridor.

There was no one in the hallway. It was far from quiet—Ella could hear moaning, screaming, and maniacal laughter from behind many of the doors. But just being outside her own small, empty room helped her to breathe again. Her nerves were still shaking, though. She needed to get upstairs, among people, and out of this dark narrow hallway.

Ella strode to the elevator and pressed the button, fidgeting on her feet as she waited for the doors to open. She didn't know exactly where she was going; all she knew was that she had to go somewhere where she could escape all the chaos going on inside her head.

"Ella, what the fuck are you doing out here?" Mr. Cox's voice came from her left, a few steps down the hall. He sounded angry at first, but that changed when he took in Ella's tear-stained face and shivering lip. "What the hell happened?"

"I don't know...nothing happened."

"Obviously something happened."

Her face crumbled. "Nothing happened! I'm just...I'm just...." She burst into tears, and covered her face with her hands.

"Oh, Christ," Mr. Cox said, sighing deeply. He came forward to wrap his arms around her shoulders. "C'mon, Ella. I'll take you back to your room."

He led her back down the corridor as Ella cried in her hands, unable to see where she was going. As soon as they got to her room, Mr. Cox opened the door and led her inside. To Ella's surprise, he shut the door behind them both, and helped her back into bed.

To Ella's further surprise, he climbed in the bed beside her, and cradled her in his arms as she continued to weep.

"I don't know why I'm like this," Ella said between sobs. "I'm sorry."

"Don't be sorry," Mr. Cox said gently, holding her tighter. "Your body is going through subdrop. This is normal. It will pass."

Ella peaked at him between her fingers. "Subdrop?"

He smoothed some hair away from her face. "It's like a crash after a high. When we play together, and you're floating through subspace, enjoying that rush you get from the pain and surrender, all the endorphins are flooding your body, and you feel that high. Your energy feeds off of my energy, but it fuels it, too. We both end up pushing each other higher."

"You mean, when you're Topping me, you get high, too?"

She could hear the smile in his voice. "Of course. It's one of the reasons why I do what I do. But I've been doing this for a long time, Ella. You're a newbie, you're still processing everything. What you're feeling is the drop some subs go through, especially after a difficult scene or a new type of play. Everything we've put you through is new to you. I'm actually surprised you didn't go through subdrop before now. I guess it's because of that iron will of yours."

Ella cried harder. "I don't have any iron will," she said between hiccups. "I'm pathetic, and I'm weak, and I'm a horrible person."

Mr. Cox's brows rose in surprise. "Why do you think so?"

"Because I like to be treated like—like some kind of animal. You said it yourself, I like being your prey. I want you to hunt me down and catch me, do all these perverse, disgusting things to me—"

"Why do you call them disgusting?"

"Because they are!"

"No, Ella," he said softly. "That may be what

you've been brought up to believe, but it's not true. You're happy when I'm doing all these perverse, disgusting things to you, aren't you?"

"Yes, but that's wrong, too!" She cried louder.

"Oh, Ella." He held back his chuckle. "You're still judging your submission like it's some sign of weakness. Being submissive doesn't make you weak—far from it. Only a strong woman, a woman who knows her own mind, who has a strong enough will like yours, can give up control the way you do. You don't submit because you're weak. You submit because you know it gives you power."

Ella wiped her face a little. Mr. Cox could tell she was listening very hard.

"Let me tell you what I see when I look at you," he continued. "I see a woman who was working her ass off to get what she wants in life. I see a woman who was making it on her own, without any favors or payoffs from anyone else, despite what others might've thought. I see a woman who couldn't stand her reputation being dragged through the mud, and who decided she'd rather quit and make it on her own than have people think she cheated her way to the top. And I see a woman who never gave up on what she wanted, who was willing to risk everything, just to get what she was looking for, even when she didn't know exactly what that was." He paused to smile. "So if you need to judge yourself based on how others see you, try doing it based on how *I* see you. Cause I see a beautiful woman before me, inside and out."

Ella could only stare at him. No one had ever complimented like Mr. Cox just had. His poignant words touched her soul, and melted away all her misery.

"Thank you, Sir," she whispered.

"You're welcome, Ella," he whispered back.

She closed her eyes and snuggled into his warm body, feeling comforted in ways that finally brought her peace.

"Christ, I'm tired." Mr. Cox shifted her into the crook of his arm and closed his eyes. "Go to sleep, Ella. We'll talk more in the morning."

"But Sir, are you sure it's okay for you to be in my room? I don't want to get you into trouble—"

"Ella?"

"Yes?"

"Please shut the fuck up and go to sleep."

Ella's mouth pressed shut. She wanted to think up a good retort, but before she could say anything, she heard the unmistakable sounds of Mr. Cox snoring. She smiled.

The notorious sadist was still human after all. Imagine that.

"Oh, man."

Ella woke up, turned over, and opened her eyes to see Mr. Cox sitting at the edge of her bed, rubbing his face.

"Hey," she said.

He twisted around to look at her over his shoulder. "How are you feeling?"

"Better," she said. "Much better than last night."

"Good."

Mr. Cox didn't look better. His eyes were red, his hair was a mess, his clothes—the same ones he had worn the day before—were wrinkled, and his face was all puffy on his left side.

Ella had to smile at the picture he presented. *I guess no one looks their best in the morning, not even the great Masters of the Hotel Bentmoore*, she thought.

Without turning around he asked, "Will you get squicked if I use your toothbrush?"

"Squicked?"

"Grossed out."

"Oh. No, go ahead."

"Thanks."

He got up, and a second later Ella heard the unmistakable sounds of him taking a piss in her bathroom. Then he was using her toothbrush, and Ella smiled again.

When he came back out, he looked marginally better. "I better go find out what happened last night after I left," he said. "Christ, what a mess." He shook his head, looking vaguely away. "One of our regulars came in last night, a long-time slave, freaking out, with burns all over her body."

"Whoa."

"Yeah. Apparently her Master had negotiated a scene for her to be used by another Dom, some big hotshot who was in town visiting. The two men flogged her and beat her senseless—which was fine, that part had been negotiated—but then the other Dom brought out some candles and lighters, stuff they *hadn't* negotiated beforehand, and he started using them on her when she was already high in subspace."

The glare of his eyes and the tick in his jaw told Ella Mr. Cox wasn't just angry, he was furious.

"He wasn't supposed to do that?" She asked in a small voice.

"Fuck no, he wasn't supposed to do that," he growled. "And it was her Master's fault. He should have stopped the other guy immediately. His first concern, his *only* concern, should have been the safety of his slave, not impressing some other celebrity Sadist." His eyes continued to smolder. "You know what's sad? This couple has been together for seven years. *Seven years.* And now, this Master might've just flushed the relationship of his life down the toilet, because he decided impressing another Dom was more important than protecting his slave."

"But, Mr. Cox...if the burns were so bad, why didn't she put a stop to the scene? Didn't she have a safeword?"

"Yeah, she had a safeword."

"But then...." Ella's brows creased. "Why

didn't she use it?"

Mr. Cox exhaled slowly. "Ella, you don't get why I don't trust safewords, do you?" He sat on the edge of her bed again. "For many subs, safewords are a lifesaver. They can put a quick stop to any scene, for whatever reason. A sub who holds that safeword secure in the back of her head can usually go farther in a scene than she could without it, because she thinks of it like her safety net." He paused. "But for some subs, for some women—" his voice lowered "—like you, safewords become a hazard."

*"What?"*

"Think about it. The day I caned you, when you were high in subspace. Were you able to think clearly at all? Would you have been able to put two thoughts together to form a word? Even your safeword?" He paused as Ella's eyes grew wide and she shook her head no. "You were flying so high, you wouldn't have safeworded no matter what I'd done to you. I could have pulled out a dozen needles and used your clit as a pincushion, and you wouldn't have said a peep in protest."

Ella recoiled in horror. "That's...."

"That's the truth. It's not what I did, because I knew it's not what you wanted. But a Top who uses a woman's safeword as a crutch, to feel free to do whatever the fuck he wants to her as long as she doesn't safeword, that's a dangerous Top. I've seen women who've ended up burned, scarred, marked in ways they never wanted and never would have consented to, because their Top decided non-use of the safeword implied consent." His jaw ticked again.

Ella's face paled, and she looked away in shock.

All this time, she had thought Mr. Cox didn't allow her the use of a safeword because he didn't want to give her any control, or any way to stop the scene. But now she understood: he just didn't want to depend on something so precarious as a safeword to keep her safe. Somehow he had known, from the beginning, a safeword would be useless to her. He wasn't taking her control away...she never had it to begin with.

"You make it sound like safewords are dangerous," she said.

"Safewords are incredibly useful, and necessary, for most subs," he said, grabbing her hand and entwining her fingers in his own. "But they're dangerous if they're the only thing a Dom is using to judge how far his sub is flying, especially for women—"

"Like me," Ella finished. "You're scaring me now."

"Maybe that's a good thing. You should be scared a little; it'll keep you safe. You should never enter any scene with any Top until every part of what he's going to do to you has been negotiated, with limits set in place. You should be very clear with the Top you're playing with what you want, because once you enter into subspace, Ella, he's going to have control over you."

"You never negotiated with me," Ella said softly. "I never had to tell you what I want. You just knew."

"Well." He smiled. "Some people just click, don't they? We connect somehow. We have since that day at the barn. You felt it, didn't you? I know I did."

They were quiet for a few moments after that. Ella couldn't stifle her smile, feeling happiness unfurling inside her chest and warming her heart like a soothing balm.

She had not been the only one who felt the connection between them. Mr. Cox felt it, too.

He rubbed his forehead and sighed deeply. "The woman who showed up here yesterday evening...the slave...she was burned, hysterical... we finally got her calmed down enough to get the story out of her...and then her Master shows up, out of his mind, demanding to see her so he could apologize. We had to tie him up just so he wouldn't go tearing through the hotel looking for her. He was starting to hurt himself, too. He was going crazy with guilt."

"That sounds really sad."

"It was. It is."

"What do you think will happen to them?"

"I don't know. According to the doc, her burns are bad, but they'll heal without scarring.

Whether the relationship can be salvaged, I don't know. Dean is working with them. He's their host now. He's good at this relationship mediation stuff."

"Dean?"

"Mr. Dean." Mr. Cox passed her a look. "You didn't meet Mr. Dean? No, I guess not. Mr. Dean is another Master here. He's a quiet, no-nonsense kind of guy." Mr. Cox smiled. "He's also an ass-man. Stick him in a room with a willing female ass, and he'll get it stretched wide enough to fit a man's arm." He chuckled, then turned serious. "Speaking of...mmm."

The look he gave Ella made her suddenly nervous.

"What?"

"Take off your pajama bottoms and spread your legs. I feel like fucking you."

"In the ass?"

"No...unless you want me to?"

"No!" Ella yanked off her pajama bottoms, lay down on her back, and spread her legs. "But this isn't exactly romantic, you know."

"Princess, when have I ever given you the impression I'm a romantic man?" He removed his pants, but didn't bother taking off his shirt or socks before planting himself between her legs.

Ella pouted her lips. "But, you know, usually there's some kind of foreplay, or buildup, even if it is—oh!" She gasped as Mr. Cox nudged her thighs open wider, pulled her to him by the hips, and thrust his already hard cock deep into her cunt.

He fell on top of her, smiled, and finished her sentence for her. "Even if it is something disgusting? Perverted? Kinky and erotic and totally hot?"

"Yes!" Her eyes widened as Mr. Cox rammed once more into her quickly flooding pussy, fast and deep.

"It's all about ownership, princess," he said as he pounded into her. "I can choose to take you however I want." He sat up and raised her legs around his torso. Ella could feel his thick cock hitting her all the way down, and closed her eyes.

As he continued to thrust in, she heard Mr. Cox growl above her, "don't come yet."

"Okay," she said breathlessly, enjoying the pleasure pulling at her insides with each one of his thrusts.

"I mean it, Ella. Don't come."

"I...I won't, Sir."

"Good." He let her legs go and fell on top of her with all his weight. Ella relaxed and lay still, forcing her body to hold back the rising tide of pleasure growing in her core, threatening to crash down with every delicious grind of his hips.

Her face contorted with concentration as Mr. Cox continued to fuck her. Ella could feel her orgasm building, but she held it back, ready to let it go as soon as Mr. Cox gave her permission.

But a moment later, he shuddered and held himself still inside her.

Ella's eyes widened in surprise. Her mouth froze in a wide O as Mr. Cox rolled off her and stood up. She fairly shrieked as he began to put his pants back on.

"What the...you finished? I don't get to come?"

"Nope," he said. "Not yet. Later, when the timing is right. For now, I just want you very horny. Did it work?" He smiled when Ella's face turned into a mask of fury, and she threw a pillow at him.

"You—you're mean!" She cried as he opened the door to leave.

"I'm a sadist, princess," he reminded her as he walked out the door. "It comes with the title."

Ella threw another pillow at him, but it hit the back of the door.

# CHAPTER SEVENTEEN: ASS TRAINING

"**W**ELL NOW, DID YOU HAVE a good morning?" Mr. Cox asked her, smiling wickedly.

"Yes, Sir, as a matter of fact I did," Ella replied. "I took a short hike around the hotel with one of the tour guides, and took a long hot bath before lunch." She met his eyes head on.

His brows creased.

They were back in the activity room they had used the night before, facing each other for the first time since Mr. Cox had left her wanting in her room.

He looked fresh and clean again, his features sharp, his eyes clear. He wore a different suit now, crisp, starched, with his fresh white shirt tucked into his pants above a thin black leather belt.

His arms were slack at his sides, and Ella noticed the cuffs of his shirt were fastened tightly around his wrists, accentuating his wide knuckled hands.

He studied her expression, pursing his lips. "So you're nice and relaxed now, are you?"

"Yes, Sir."

"Because of the hike, and the bath."

"Yes, Sir."

He crossed his arms. "Did you masturbate after I left your room this morning, Ella?"

Ella blushed at his use of the word, and turned her head away.

"Answer me," he said. "Did you masturbate?"

"I...yes, Sir. I did." She crossed her own arms now, facing him with obstinacy.

After he had left her room, Ella had been so angry, she'd pounded a crater into her pillow. The hike had taken her mind off her goading problem somewhat, but when she'd slipped her naked body into the hot bath, all she could think about was her unsatisfied arousal, and how unfair Mr. Cox had been to her.

She deliberated only a moment before slipping her hand between her legs under the hot soapy water and rubbing her pussy until she came. After that, she had let her body float, languid and limp.

She'd felt a certain measure of guilt, but not much. It hadn't been fair, the trick Mr. Cox had pulled on her; and anyway, there wasn't much he could do to punish her for it. He was still refusing to do anything to her ass and thighs until her bruises healed. The bruises were almost gone now, but Mr. Cox insisted her skin had to be completely flawless before he could mark her again.

Ella could feel the force of rebellion growing inside her once more. Her impulse to defy, to push her boundaries, test the confines of her limits, was rising in full force. Words of mutiny were whispering in the back of her head.

He wouldn't know if she pleasured herself, would he? There was no way he could, not for sure. And if he figured it out, what would he do?

It was that bold voice which now made Ella give him an insolent, daring smile. But to her surprise, Mr. Cox didn't meet her look of challenge with a firm stance of determination, the way he had before. His face fell, and his eyes looked sad.

"Ella," he said, "I am *so* disappointed in you."

His words hit her so hard, Ella felt like she'd been delivered a physical blow. Her mouth opened in shock as she took a step back to steady herself.

All her bravado evaporated by his six simple words. A second ago she had been feeling so smug and sure of herself; now she was sinking into shame like a stone in a puddle of quicksand.

"Sir, I...." Her voice died away. She didn't know what to say; there was nothing she could say. "I'm sorry," she managed.

Mr. Cox sighed and turned his head away, as if, Ella thought, he couldn't even stand the sight of her. "Go stand in the corner," he said.

Ella flinched at his tone. "Sir, please, I'm sorry," she said again, trying to get him to turn his eyes back.

*Look at me. Look at me, damn it.*

"In the corner," he repeated. "Now. Just—go."

Her eyes brimmed with tears as she walked into the corner, dragging her feet along the way. As she stood facing the corner like an unruly child, shame and remorse made her tears fall thick and fast, until she had to breathe hard through her mouth to try and calm the choking sobs rising up her throat.

She didn't know how, but Mr. Cox's simple declaration of disappointment had managed to make her feel worse than any act of discipline ever could. No punishment could make her feel worse than this.

After a few minutes, Mr. Cox came to stand beside her. "Look at me," he said.

Ella turned, trying to convey with her eyes all the guilt she felt, hoping she would see a spark of forgiveness in his.

"Ella, when we're together, if you want to fight me, defy me, even provoke me enough to do a whole take-down scene with you, that's fine. We'll play however hard you want. Hell, I'm more than willing to rise to the challenge."

He paused.

"But when you're on your own, and I can't see what you're up to, you need to obey my rules. I need to know you're not doing what you *know* you're not supposed to. It's how I can keep you safe when you're not with me, but more importantly, it's how we build trust. If you don't respect me enough to follow my orders unless you know I'm right there watching you, how can I trust you? Do you understand what I'm trying to say?"

"Yes. Yes, Sir," Ella said, her voice cracking on a sob.

He opened his arms, and she flew into them.

"I'm sorry. I'm sorry. I'm sorry," she repeated over and over.

"It's okay," he said. "I guess it was inevitable for you to try to get away with something when my back was turned. But now you know better, so you're not going to do it again. Right?"

"Right," Ella answered, offering him a weak smile. "From now on, when we're not together, I follow your orders to the letter."

"And when we are together?"

Ella gazed at him, confused.

"You should still follow my orders," he finished.

Ella pouted her lips, feeling some of her previous impudence returning. "I wouldn't expect *too* much, Sir," she said.

Mr. Cox laughed and kissed her on the forehead. "Never change, princess." He pulled away. "You still need to be punished for masturbating without permission, but—we'll see. What I have planned for you today might be punishment enough."

Trepidation crept up Ella's spine, raising the hairs on the back of her neck. "Sir...?"

"Go ahead and get undressed, then lean over the spanking bench."

"Yes, Sir." With all her previous defiance quelled, Ella removed her clothes and bent over the spanking bench. She could hear Mr. Cox moving around and getting things out of the wardrobe, but she waited for him to return, unmoving, looking nervously down at the floor.

"I think your ass is healed enough for some light whipping," he said from behind her. "Don't you agree?"

"Yes, oh yes, Sir," Ella concurred in a breathy voice.

"I had a feeling. You've never felt a cat o'nine tails whip, have you? Would you like to?"

"Yes, Sir. Please."

"Then ask me, princess."

"Sir, use your cat o'nine tails whip on me."

"That's not a question," Mr. Cox said, amusement clear in his voice. "Ask me, don't tell me."

Ella took a breath. "Sir, will you please whip me with your cat o'nine tails?"

"Yes, princess. Don't mind if I do." He flung the whip against her tender ass, and Ella moaned.

The cat o'nine tails was thinner, stiffer, and less supple than most of the floggers Ella had felt up until now. She imagined it felt closer to what a real whip would feel like: stingy and sharp. This cat o'nine tails had at least half a dozen cords snaking out of the handle, and they all whapped against her skin with piercing, biting heat.

Mr. Cox started on her ass, but quickly moved up her back, hitting her sides and shoulder blades. Ella relaxed against the bench and enjoyed the whipping, moaning and gasping now and then with pleasure. She could feel herself sinking into subspace, and while before she would have tried to stop the scene before it went too far, now she let herself go, enjoying the ride.

After a few minutes of blissful torture, she heard Mr. Cox's voice next to her ear.

"You like?"

"Oh, yes, Sir," Ella whispered without opening her eyes. "It's wonderful."

"Good. Now get up." He yanked her up by the hair, and Ella let out a tiny cry. The sudden assault on her hair had not been expected.

Mr. Cox, holding her by the back of the head, pulled her to the bed and threw her on. Ella turned over to gaze at him in flustered surprise, and watched him undress and climb onto the bed.

He lay down on his back. "Fuck me," was all he said.

Smiling now, Ella climbed on, happy to comply. She straddled his hips and reached around to grab his cock, aiming it right into her pussy. As she slid down, she could feel his prick rub against her sensitive inner folds, filling up her hot wet cunt. She bit her lip and furrowed her brows, trying to accustom herself to the positioning.

Mr. Cox reached up his wide hands and pinched her nipples, making her eyes widen and refocus on him. "Fuck me," he said again.

Ella braced her hands on his chest and began to slide up and down his cock, slowly, letting her natural oils ease his way. She let her body stretch and relax around his hard length; then, after a few careful thrusts, she began to add a slight rocking motion to her hips with each one.

Mr. Cox let her set her own speed and rhythm. He rested his hands on the mattress and didn't touch her in any way, but after a few moments, when it was clear Ella had found a rhythm she enjoyed and was starting to work herself up nicely, he stopped her.

With one hand outstretched, he reached over and opened the bedside table drawer. He pulled out a bottle of lube, and....

"Do you know what this is?" He said, as he held up the hard shiny black thing in front of Ella's eyes.

"No, Sir," Ella replied, fear clouding her face.

"I think you do." His lips curved up in a devious smile. "It's a butt plug." He turned it over in his hand, admiring the shape. "It's one of the smallest we have. Despite your transgression this morning, I decided I should still go easy on you, and start you out small." He stopped gazing at the butt plug and looked at her shrewdly. "Lean forward."

Ella sat up straight across his thighs, feeling his hard erection pushing against her cunt wall. "Please, Sir, I've never—it looks so big—please, can we—"

In one fluid movement, Mr. Cox sat up, grabbed her by the back of the head, and pulled her down to his chest. "There," he growled by her ear. "Now don't fucking move, not until I tell you to."

"Sir, please, please...." Ella's pleading voice died away as Mr. Cox lubed up the thick black butt plug. As soon as he deemed it wet enough, he flung the bottle of lube back on the side table, and got down to work.

Holding the butt plug by the handle, he reached around Ella's body, felt up and down her narrow ass crease, and stopped when he found what he was looking for: the puckering, cringing grommet of Ella's asshole. As soon as he found it, he nestled the tip of the butt plug against it, and pressed in.

"Sir, please, Sir please!" Ella began to chorus as Mr. Cox pushed the tip of the butt plug further and further into Ella's resisting ass. Her cringing muscles tried to close up and block him entrance, but the smooth wet butt plug slid through her clenching gate with ease.

Mr. Cox pressed his free arm across her back to keep her locked against his chest as his other hand continued to press the handle of the butt plug against her puckering, stinging asshole.

He pumped it gently in and out now, getting her delicate portal nice and lubricated before pushing the hard silicone further up her passageway. Ella squeezed her eyes shut and let out little cries of agony in his ear.

"While I enjoy listening to this, it would help if you relaxed," Mr. Cox said. He slid the butt plug in, then out...then *in,* further up her butt.

"I can't, it hurts," Ella cried, grabbing pieces of the sheet in her fists as she felt him press the butt plug further still. Her asshole felt like it was on fire.

"It won't hurt so much if you relax." He pushed the butt plug another half inch into her ass, pressing his palm against the flat handle, sundering her opening wide. Ella let out a loud cry.

He held the butt plug still, but pushed Ella back up into a sitting position. She was double penetrated now, feeling stuffed and sore.

"Fuck me," Mr. Cox ordered, his voice a low growl. "C'mon, move."

"I can't," Ella breathed. "I can't!"

"Do it," Mr. Cox snapped. "Or I'll push this thing in the rest of the way right now."

Ella let out a terrified squeak and rocked her

hips the tiniest bit. When she rocked forward, Mr. Cox's prick tickled and grazed her cunt in the most delicious way; but when she rocked back, she could feel the butt plug stretching her ass, widening the breach.

"Please Sir, I can't," she repeated, bracing her hands on his chest.

"Yes, you can," Mr. Cox replied. "You'll fuck yourself on the butt plug until it's buried all the way up there, and then you'll come. Now rock."

"Please!"

"*Rock.*" He pushed and pulled her hip with his hand, forcing the butt plug further up her ass.

Ella forced herself to rock. At least when she rocked, the feel of his prick grinding her cunt distracted her somewhat from the butt plug assaulting her ass. But every time she moved back, her own body pushed her down on the hard silicone, and it slid in a little bit more.

Wincing and straining, she rocked.

Her tissues stretched, and her asshole burned. It was like she could feel nothing except the flaming, piercing agony of her afflicted ass. At one point, Ella pulled her body up onto her knees, trying to get away from the pressure and pain, but Mr. Cox slammed her back down, driving up the butt plug. She howled.

"It's almost all the way in, Ella," he said. "Keep going."

"Oh, please...."

"Keep going."

Ella succumbed. She rocked against both Mr. Cox's hard cock and the smooth butt plug, letting go of the last shreds of her resistance, and feeling the monstrous plug plunge into her body without hindrance.

She continued to rock, knowing she had no choice, that she would rock until Mr. Cox told her otherwise, because he could make her do whatever he wanted, he had that power over her....and as she continued to rock, the burning, aching feeling bloomed into rising pleasure. Her clit throbbed, and her cunt drenched with juices as it squeezed around Mr. Cox's prick. Ella moaned as she began to rock harder, faster, unable to stop the growing need to come.

"That's it, Ella. Let it in." He pushed the butt plug, and Ella pushed back, letting the thick presence of stiff silicone fill her up with pain and ecstasy.

Her clit tingled, her skin flushed, and her anal sphincter clenched in a fiery ring of white-hot agony. Ella rocked hard and fast now, with violent movements of her hips and thighs, trying to bring herself off on cock and plug.

The pain was stirring her on. Ella reached around, put her hand over Mr. Cox's fingers holding still the plug, and pushed them hard, reaming herself on the rigid stopper. She could hear Mr. Cox's chuckle.

His hand was pressing into her ass now, the handle of the plug buried between her buttcheeks, the plug sunk all the way up inside her. Ella bounded on top of him like a happy rabbit, bouncing and jiggling, enjoying the thrilling pleasure and searing pain, trying to make herself come. After a few moments, her churning orgasm broke free, and she bucked her ass and hips against him with loud slaps of her body.

Each spasm milked his prick, but Mr. Cox held on until his balls felt like they were about to explode. In the last minute, he reached around and pressed the butt plug hard against Ella's writhing body, making her stiffen and cry out. He could feel the tight sinews of her thighs across his legs, the shivering throes of her pleasure, and above all else, the incredible squeeze of her cunt around his prick.

He came himself, erupting right up her tight pussy. His body strained up as he came, pushing himself deeper inside her, as deep as he could go. Ella shoved herself back down, grinding her clit against his groin, and came again.

Tiny aftershocks shook them both as Ella fell forward onto his chest. They stayed like that for a few moments, breathing hard, shivering now and then in the cool room air.

Then Mr. Cox pulled her off by the hips, and Ella slid over.

She lay on her back, regaining her senses. But as she recovered, the butt plug lodged inside her ass began to make its presence felt with greater urgency.

"Uh, Sir," she said. "The, um...the, you-know?"

Mr. Cox turned his head. "The butt plug?"

"Yes."

"Say it right, then."

"The butt plug. It's still inside me."

"I know." He pulled himself out of bed, went to the wardrobe, rummaged around, and got out what looked like a mess of black rubber strips and buckles. "Get on your hands and knees."

"Sir, what—"

He grabbed her ankle and twisted. Ella turned over with a short cry, realizing her ordeal with the butt plug was not yet over.

"Head down, ass up."

"What are you doing?"

"You'll see."

Mr. Cox began to encircle the strips of black rubber around her waist and thighs, cinching them, fastening them with the tiny black buckles...and then he slipped a rubbery strip right between her ass cheeks.

He pulled.

The stretchy rubber plunged between her creamy cheeks, nestling itself right against the handle of the butt plug, nice and tight.

"Ow! God, it's pushing in!"

"I know." He buckled the naughty strip of rubber into place. "It's a training belt," he finally explained. The straps felt tight everywhere, but especially inside her ass crease, where the resilient rubber held still the fiendish butt plug.

At least that strap split into two and diverged on either side of her cunt lips, instead of digging between them and pressing against her clit. Ella was thankful for that, since she had a feeling she would be wearing this diabolical contraption for a long while. She didn't have to wonder what kind of "training" Mr. Cox had in mind.

The rubber belt would keep the butt plug from slipping out for as long as her sadistic trainer wanted to keep it in there. It would stretch her ass, and make it ready to take something even bigger.

This was the smallest plug they had, he'd said. How big did they go?

"How long do I have to wear this thing?" She asked, looking over her shoulder.

"Until you see me again," he said, looking at her bent form and smiling.

With the black straps hemming her supple thighs, accentuating her smooth rear cheeks, and forming a perfect dividing line disappearing straight up the middle, Ella's ass looked like it was just begging for a spanking...or something far worse.

His vague answer made her uneasy. "When will that be?"

"In a few hours."

"What if I have to, you know...."

"Answer nature's call? I suggest you hold it in until you see me again, princess. If you can't, you can remove the plug, but then you'll have to put it back in yourself. Think you can do that?"

"I'll hold it in, Sir," Ella said, scowling.

Mr. Cox laughed. "Get dressed. I'll see you in a few hours."

Ella stood up, very, very carefully. Her eyes grew wide in shock every time the plug shifted inside her.

Mr. Cox laughed harder. "You'll get used to it," he said.

"I don't know about that, Sir."

"You'd better. You'll be taking something much bigger up there by the time we're done."

# CHAPTER EIGHTEEN: ELLA FLIES

**"P**LEASE EXPLAIN TO ME WHY** you spent the night in Miss Peterson's room."

Mr. Cox rubbed his cheek and sighed, feeling the stubble there. He had managed to shower that morning, but not shave, and he could feel the lapse now on his face. He wondered if he should skip shaving another day, and see if Ella liked his prickly cheeks rubbing against her nipples.

"Answer me, Cox."

Mr. Cox creased his brows as he gazed at Mr. Bentmoore, sitting tall and somber behind his desk. The old man looked concerned, but not as angry as Mr. Cox had feared he would be.

"I found her wandering the hallway, crying and shaking. She was going through subdrop," he said, choosing his words carefully. "She needed someone with her."

"I shouldn't have to tell you going into her private bedroom was a serious transgression. You should have found an empty activity room."

"I was tired," Mr. Cox replied. "I wasn't thinking straight. It was a difficult night."

"That's true; but you still knew better." Mr. Bentmoore paused. "This thing between you and Miss Peterson, I don't know if I like where it's going."

"I don't know where it's going, but I like where it's been," Mr. Cox said, looking vaguely away and smiling his twisted smile.

"Cox."

"Yes Sir."

"This is exactly what I'm talking about. You're losing focus."

Mr. Cox gave Mr. Bentmoore an impassive stare. "No, Sir. I know exactly what I'm doing."

"Do you now." The two men studied each other, but Mr. Bentmoore blinked first. "I'll let your mistake slide—this time. Like you said, it was a difficult night."

"Thank you, Sir. If I may ask, what's the status on the Martins?"

"Sandy's agreed to stay here and try to work things out with Shawn. But she's refusing to wear Shawn's collar until she believes the relationship can be saved. The two of them had an uncollaring ceremony this morning. Mr. Dean was there—he told me both of them were inconsolable. The whole situation is heartbreaking."

"I hope they can work things out."

"As do I."

"If that will be all, Sir...?"

"Yes, that will be all."

Mr. Cox took a few steps toward the door, but was halted once more. "One more thing, Cox. You didn't discuss the Martins' situation with Miss Peterson, did you?" As Mr. Cox turned around, Mr. Bentmoore continued, "You know discussing our other guests and their issues with Miss Peterson, even without mentioning names, would be a severe breach in conduct. Such an offense would force me to take drastic action."

The moment stretched, and this time, neither man blinked.

"I realize that, Sir," Mr. Cox finally replied. "Like I said, I know exactly what I'm doing."

"I'm glad," Mr. Bentmoore murmured. "Thank you, Mr. Cox. Please continue to keep me posted on Miss Peterson's progress."

Mr. Cox kept Ella in the training belt for three days. She didn't have to wear it all the time, thank goodness; he gave her long breaks. But when she was wearing it, he made sure to check on her often, both to make sure the plug was sufficiently lubricated, and sometimes, to change the size of the plug itself.

When they were playing, he would sometimes yank it in and out of her asshole like a fucking dildo, just to listen to her yelp and moan. But most of the time he would just ignore it, and fuck her pussy while she still had it on. Ella would feel his cock rubbing against the hard plug through her thin membranes, and she would wonder if he could feel it, too. (She didn't ask.)

Their play sessions involved more rope now: Mr. Cox was spending an inordinate amount of time tying her up in different poses. He seemed to favor the hemp rope, although he also used braided nylon and, on occasion, cotton.

Ella was slowly beginning to love her bondage sessions. Perhaps, under other circumstances, her prey instincts would have risen up, and she would have fought him harder. But with the butt plug lodged firmly up her ass, she was hardly in any position to fight. It was both a physical, and psychological, restraint.

By the afternoon of the third day, Ella could tell something was coming. Mr. Cox had been working her up to something big, and now, by the light she saw in his eyes, she could tell he thought she was ready.

He told her to be ready for his summons late that night, and she was: when she walked into their activity room, she wore nothing but a cupless PVC bra, the rubber training belt, and a pair of outrageously wicked high-heeled shoes. She had parted her glorious gold hair into two pleats, and brushed them over her breasts. Her thick blonde locks covered her pink puckered nipples, but her crotch and ass were well on display.

Mr. Cox stared at her in wonder. "Ella," he

said. "My god."

She swept her hair away from her breasts and turned around in a slow circle to show him. "You like?"

"Like is not the word. Where did you get the bra?"

"I asked the seamstress to make it for me."

"That woman needs a raise," Mr. Cox breathed. Ella grinned and looked down. Mr. Cox had never served her with false praise; he had never offered her kind words just to appease her. For him to compliment her like this felt extra nice.

Then she looked around. She had never been in this room before. But there was nothing in the room she had never seen before, nothing but a pair of stainless steel hoops hanging down from the ceiling by thick pieces of chain, about two feet apart. They reminded Ella of the men's gymnastics rings she had seen at tournaments on T.V. A heavy square pad lay under the rings.

"They're hard points," Mr. Cox explained, following her eyes up and down the thick dangling pieces of chain. "Either one of the rings can hold a man's weight."

"Do you do exercises on them?"

Mr. Cox began to laugh, hard. "No, Ella."

Ella scowled as Mr. Cox fought down his laughter. "Then what are they for?"

Mr. Cox grinned and crossed his arms. "They're for you. I'm going to tie you up and make you fly." He stepped up in front of her and looked down at her bewildered face. "I have a scene in mind for you, all planned out in my head. I've been picturing it for a while now. I want everything to be perfect...but it's going to be brutal. Are you willing?"

Ella eyed the rings. "How brutal?"

Mr. Cox went to the bed and yanked the top blanket away, uncovering a vast array of rope, rings, hooks, and other BDSM equipment. Scanning the bed, he picked up a large metal hook: it had an O-ring on one end, and a monstrous metal ball on the other.

"This is an anal hook," he said, holding it up for her to see. "I'm going to put it up your ass. The end will curve up your back," he pointed up the length of the hook, "and I'll tie your hair to the ring."

Ella's eyes went wide. "You're going to put that thing up my ass? That's what all this training has been for. I thought...."

"I'm going to tie you up, rig you up, fuck you up, and play with you for as long as I want. I'll beat you raw. Some parts you'll enjoy, and some parts you won't, but I can guarantee you this will be one of the most erotic memories you will ever have. You have to agree to it first, though. What do you say?"

He waited patiently for Ella to give it some thought.

"I want to," she said quietly. "But I have my

own way I want to start the scene, and you'll need to take this plug out of my ass. Can you do that?"

Mr. Cox's mouth curved into his notorious twisted smile, and his eyes darkened with anticipation. "Of course," he said, motioning toward the bed. "Bend over."

"First...." Ella peeled off her bra and slipped her feet out of her shoes. After putting them under the narrow bedside table, out of the way, she bent over the bed.

Mr. Cox barely touched her skin as he unbuckled the belt from around her waist and thighs, but Ella felt every whisper-soft skim of his fingers. When the rubber straps were away, he tapped her feet wider apart with his toe, and pushed her back further down on the bed.

"Take a breath," he said, digging his fingers into the large handle pressing into her buttocks. Ella took a deep breath, and as she let it out, Mr. Cox dragged the butt plug out of her ass in one single pull. Ella tensed, but in a second, it was out.

"I think I'll just leave this right here for now," Mr. Cox said, putting the butt plug on the bedside table, standing straight up, shiny and obscene. "Now what do you have in mind?"

"This." Before Mr. Cox knew what she was about, Ella ran around the bed and grabbed a short wooden paddle from among the collection of toys. She waved it in front of herself, wiggling her hips and grinning at Mr. Cox, who stared at her from the other side of the bed in surprise.

"I'm armed this time," she said. "You might take me down, but I'll get a few licks of my own in first."

Mr. Cox's whole demeanor changed. His jaw clenched, and his eyes danced with glee. He radiated devious determination and cunning savagery.

"Oh, princess, you have no idea what fire you're playing with. You're going to get burned—badly." He was smiling as he said it, but the storm in his eyes blew turbulent.

As Ella watched, he began to unbutton the cuffs of his sleeves. Her mouth went dry as he rolled them all the way up his arms, uncovering tanned skin and thick muscle. All the while, he never took his eyes off her.

"You want to come after me? Go ahead. Just know you'll pay for it later."

Ella swallowed, trying to get some spit back in her mouth. "It sounds to me like I'm going to pay later no matter what."

"That's true."

He gave her no warning: one second he was staring at her, the next he was sprinting around the bed, trying to make a grab for her. Ella ducked away just in time, and thwacked his bottom with the paddle as she pivoted, laughing in triumph.

"Gotcha," she grinned.

"My turn," Mr. Cox growled, putting his hands out like claws.

The chase was on.

Ella felt like she was fleeing for dear life. She ducked and ran, eluding him time and again, keeping herself clear from the corners. They both laughed as if it was a game, but each of them knew differently: Ella was goading him on, teasing him to pursue her harder, and Mr. Cox was giving in gladly.

She knew she would be caught; it was only a matter of time. The truth was, she wanted to be caught. She was the ultimate prize. But Mr. Cox would have to earn his prize. He had to conquer before he could pillage.

She got in a few good thwacks with the paddle, and yelled in victory with each one. But her last one was her undoing, as Mr. Cox baited her first, waited for her to venture an attack with an outstretched arm, and grabbed her by the wrist before she could pull away. Ella howled as he pried the paddle out of her palm.

"Now," he whispered, "you pay."

He dragged her over to the bed, yanked her across his lap, and began to spank her upturned bottom with the same paddle she had just been using on him.

"I was only trying to be funny!" She cried over the cracks of the paddle.

"So am I," Mr. Cox replied. "Why aren't you laughing? I won't stop until you're laughing."

"I can't laugh, it hurts!" Even through the wallops of the stingy wood, she let out a short giggle. Now that Mr. Cox had won, they could both celebrate in her defeat.

"This is barely a warm up, and you know it," Mr. Cox said, paddling her harder. "Now be still."

"No!" Ella writhed across his lap. Mr. Cox grabbed her arm and twisted it painfully behind her, spanking her faster with the paddle.

"Goddamn it, Ella, be still!"

"No!"

He dropped the paddle on the bed, grabbed the anal hook beside it, and pressed the hard ball against the crack of her bottom, digging it between her cheeks. Instantly, Ella went still.

"This can go in with lube, or without," he said. "Which is it to be?"

Ella's whole body tensed. "With," she cried. "Please."

"Then fucking lie still."

He reached his hand to the bedside table, pulled out the bottle of lube, and began to coat the shiny metal ball until it slipped and slid inside his hand. Ella lay inert across his lap, listening to him coat the slick ball, feeling nervous.

She jumped when she felt Mr. Cox's hand inside the crack of her ass.

"Relax, Ella, or this'll hurt more."

Using all her training, Ella took deep breaths, and willed her body to relax.

"That's it. That's it, my little clit-toy."

He began to rub her down, soothing her like a skittish horse, using words he knew would help her sink into subspace. Ella sank quickly, lulled by his soft murmurs and gentle caresses.

Mr. Cox rubbed her legs, ass, and crack, gliding his fingers across her soft skin, feeling her let go. When he thought she was ready, he slipped a lubed finger up her ass, and met no resistance at all.

But she moaned as he pumped his finger in and out of her asshole. "Good girl, Ella. Good girl. Relax." Ella moaned again, but kept calm.

She felt something cold and hard press against her sphincter, and knew he was inserting the ball.

It didn't scare her until it got to the widest part. Then Ella began to fight it.

"Please Sir, it's too big, please, just give me a minute to—uh!" Her tight sphincter muscles cringed around the ball, and all of Ella's sinews went taut.

Mr. Cox didn't push the ball forward, but he didn't pull it back, either. He grabbed Ella's fingers, and fit them around the stiff metal curve of the hook behind her.

"You push it in," he said.

Ella held onto the hook with weak control. "Please, no," she begged.

"Do it. Do it yourself, or I'll do it my way."

"Oh god."

"Here, I'll help." Using both hands, he

spread Ella's ass cheeks open wide, forcing her already straining asshole to stretch even more. The ball slipped in another millimeter, and Ella whimpered.

He held her cheeks apart for her and watched in rapt attention as Ella pushed the ball into her back channel. Her sphincter distended and throbbed; the ball stuck out of her asshole obscenely. Ella heaved for breath, letting out a series of plaintive cries and desperate moans, and all the while, Mr. Cox duteously kept her ass cheeks spread wide, a perverse smile lighting up his face.

The ball began to disappear up her ass. Once it was through the widest diameter, her contracting muscles sucked it in the rest of the way. Finally, her asshole squeezed shut around the thick metal ball, and Ella went limp.

"Good girl," Mr. Cox said in approval, rubbing the side of her ass. "My good little clit-toy." He pushed the hook into her a bit further, getting a breathy moan from the hooked female, and smiled wider.

Then he yanked her head up by her hair, just enough to pull her out of her haze. "Get up," he said. "Get under the rings."

Awkwardly, taking wobbly, drunken steps with the metal hook curving up her back like a lewd silver tail, Ella walked under the hanging metal rings. Mr. Cox pushed her onto her knees, and Ella tumbled down, grabbing onto Mr. Cox's hand on her shoulder for support. He let go as soon as she was stable, and went to the bed to get some rope.

The rope was twisted red hemp, thick and supple. "Hold your arms behind your back," he ordered her now. Ella closed her eyes and grabbed her forearms behind her back, bending both arms at the elbow.

Mr. Cox began to tie her arms together behind her. First he tied her wrists; then he created a crisscross of diamond shapes across her svelte upper arms and lithe shoulder blades.

He winded the rope around her front, above and below her springy breasts. He would cup and squeeze her breasts as he worked, as if unable to stop himself from the distraction they presented; but most of his attention was on the rope. Ella let out tiny sounds of strain now and then, but other than that, she did not move.

When her arms were well anchored behind her, he helped her lie down on the mat, and went to get more rope.

Now he worked on her bent legs, braiding, looping, and knotting the rope so that her ankles were tucked to her thighs. He left her a little slack, so Ella would have blood circulation to her feet; but her legs were now well tied.

She felt like a trussed up pig.

When he was done, he helped her back up on her knees in a kneeling position.

"Now the hair," he murmured, grabbing a

fistful of her golden mane and giving it a tug before going to the bed to get the final piece of rope. He tied her hair behind her, high up on her head, and coiled the rope around her thick mop. Then he reached down, looped the rope into the ring of the anal hook, and cinched it tight. Ella's head came up and stayed up, tied securely in place by the rope around her hair, anchored to the hook in her ass.

Mr. Cox caressed her shoulders and neck now, running his fingers along her soft arms, around her articulated collarbone, and down to her breasts that trembled with each breath. He cupped the soft tissue and hefted her weighty tits in his hands, fondling them softly, but was careful to leave her nipples alone. He would get to them soon enough, but it wasn't time quite yet.

He came around to her front, and admired the view.

With her arms tied behind her and her back arched, Ella's luscious breasts thrust out, lined with the rope, naked and ready for him. She sat on her heels as if in prayer, her knees pressing into the padded mat, facing him in benediction. Her legs were spread wide as she balanced on her knees, and her pussy lips stretched open, revealing red, wet, swollen cunt lips inside.

Her head was up, but her eyes were closed, her face smooth in soft repose. Her mouth was a tiny bit open, revealing two perfectly white teeth.

Now it was time to get busy.

Mr. Cox went to the bed and came back with a pile of clothespins in his hands. Sitting down next to her, he lined up the clothespins on the mat next to him—all except one.

He began to work her right nipple; pinching it, pulling it, and getting the skin nice and plump.

"Ella," he said. "Ella, open your eyes. I want you to see this."

Ella struggled out of the deep subspace she was in to open her eyes. Mr. Cox was holding open the clothespin for her to see. She didn't have to ask what he was about to do; he was already pulling hard on her nipple, holding it ready.

Ella closed her eyes again and whimpered as she felt the wicked pin close on her nipple.

Mr. Cox did the left nipple next, working it the same way he had its sister: getting the puffy pink tissue good and hard, and then squeezing it into the pin. Ella cried out with this one; the pin felt twice as tight.

Now Mr. Cox began to line her breasts with clothespins, grabbing tiny pieces of skin to pinch and snare next. Ella's whimpering grew louder with each one. Thick tears pooled in her eyes.

But she did not plead or struggle, a fact Mr. Cox noted with pride.

By the time he was done, four straight lines of clothespins went straight across each of Ella's reddened, swollen breasts. Again, he took a moment to step back and admire the view.

Ella was sweating now. Tiny beads were shining on her face like pearls. She was flushed, breathing hard, and trembling with strain.

He got the whippy braided flogger...the one Ella hated the most.

"Time for the pins to come off," he said. It was the only warning Ella got before he began to flog the pins off her breasts.

Ella began to wail now, her face contorting with agony as each strike of the flogger felt like a thousand tiny bee stings piercing her soft tit-flesh. But the prickling slashes of the flogger were nothing compared to the pins being ripped off her areolae and nipples; those made her feel like she was being shredded to pieces.

Ella howled and cried, unable to move, unable to control the rush of sensations coursing through her, pulling her down into the deep void of subspace.

When all the pins were off and Ella's breasts were free, mottled with pale impressions of the pins, Mr. Cox took a moment to breathe. Then he came around and began to flog her shoulders and back, whipping her hard, making Ella cry out once more in shock and pain. The rope going across her shoulder blades protected her a little, but not much, and Mr. Cox was putting all his force in each strike. By the time he was done, he was breathing hard himself.

He threw the flogger on the bed and peeled

off his wet, sweaty shirt. "Time to fly, Ella," he said. She couldn't make out his words; she was already too far gone.

He tied more rope to her ankles, her arms, and, to Ella's dismay, the ring of the anal hook. Ella wasn't paying much attention to what he was doing anymore; she was in a sort of vacant haze where rational thought couldn't exist. But she could feel it when the ball buried deep in her ass shifted and pulled.

And then, her whole body was being pulled up, and up, until Ella was off the ground and floating in the air. Her arms and legs were still tied behind her, and her head was still held back by the anal hook...but Ella was free of the world.

Her mind took that last plunge, and she went flying, soaring, rocketing into a soft cloud of oblivion.

She could see Mr. Cox's face beneath her. She could feel his hands on her dangling breasts, his hard nails digging into her tender skin. He spun her in the air, and Ella went dizzy, weightless as a feather drifting on the wind. He bit her inner thigh, and the pain broke through her trance, just enough to make her cry out. He bit her other leg, and she cried out again.

Then he was an inch away from her face, looking into her eyes, and giving her a second to really *see* him before he was kissing her hard across the mouth.

Ella felt his soft lips on hers, the brutal attack

of his mouth...and she kissed him back, feeling the current running between them, the energy looping their two bodies in one endless circle of synergy. When he pulled his lips away, Ella felt a sudden sense of loss, like he had ripped a piece of her soul away. Fresh tears dripped from her eyes.

With a push of his hand on her shoulder, he spun her again, and Ella felt nothing but wild euphoria, a weightless exhilaration that intoxicated her senses.

There were a few moments of confusion when she felt her body touch the mat again. Mr. Cox had lowered her down slowly, careful to let each one of her limbs make contact with the floor before she came to a complete rest.

She felt disconcerted, helpless, and shaken by the weight of her own body.

Mr. Cox began to untie her quickly, freeing her of the rope with deft fingers. He made her stretch her limbs as he freed them, manipulating her body across the mat like a rag doll.

Ella let him move her as he wanted, her mind barren of any cognition. She was lost, bewildered by the strange body that was her still own, yet now felt foreign and strange. She was an alien in her own skin.

Mr. Cox pushed her chest down on the mat and knelt between her spread knees behind her. Ella lay with her arms stretched in front of her in a position of supplication, her head turned to the side. Her body was free of the rope; only the anal hook remained.

Mr. Cox began to pull the ball out of her ass.

Ella shrieked, and tried to pull away; Mr. Cox pressed her down with a firm hand on her back, and continued to steadily pull the ball out of her ass. Ella yelled and panted, clenching her hands into tight fists. She screamed as the ball stretched her thin tissues to the breaking point; then she let out her breath in one long blow as the ball popped free, releasing her muscles to clamp shut.

Mr. Cox rubbed her back now, giving her a few seconds to recover. But as soon as her breathing had evened out, he stood up, grabbed her hands, and began to tie them together over her head.

Ella could only get one word out: "What...?"

"We're not done yet, princess. Not by a long shot. You flew...now you'll burn."

Ella's face cringed. Mr. Cox stretched her arms up and used one of the lengths of rope to tie them to the ring above her. She was still on her knees, but her wrists were tied tight, her arms locked straight above her head. Ella rested her head on her arm, swaying a little in the rope, wondering with a vague sense of fear what lay in store for her next.

She heard a scrape, a spark being lit...and then a tiny point of white-hot fire pressed into her back.

Ella screamed so loud, the sound ricocheted off the walls.

It felt like lava was being dripped onto her skin. Ella tried to jerk away, screaming every time another drop of agony seared a small circle onto her quivering flesh. But the pain kept coming, yanking Ella out of her subspace and into a realm of terrifying anguish.

Mr. Cox crawled on his knees to her front. As he faced her, he sat back on his heels, looking vibrant. In his hand he held a long white candle, the font of Ella's torture.

He waited for Ella's eyes to focus on the candle and fill with horror.

"Please, Sir, *please, Sir*, PLEASE, SIR—"

Mr. Cox held the flame of the candle right above the sloping summit of Ella's left breast. As he tipped the candle, tiny beads of wax fell right onto the fat crinkly nipple.

Ella screamed until she had no voice left. The heat scorched into her nipple, melting blazing agony into her flesh.

As soon as Ella was done screaming over her left nipple, Mr. Cox did her right, and Ella began to scream all over again. Her vision went blurry as her eyes flooded with tears, but she could still make out Mr. Cox mere inches away from her shaking body. Even if she could not have seen him, she still would have known he was there.

Despite the pain—or maybe because of it—

the current of energy running between them was still pumping fast and hard.

Mr. Cox fell into a pattern now: he would tip the candle over one of her breasts, listen to her scream, watch her struggle with the pain, and let her regain her breathing. Meanwhile, the candle would burn down some, and another small pool of wax would form around the wick. As soon as he felt like she had calmed down enough and he had enough liquid wax at his disposal, Mr. Cox would tip the candle again, this time on her other breast.

He watched in rapt attention as Ella screamed and flailed.

He took his time, working methodically, coating the upper parts of her breasts in soft wax, letting the scalding drops of liquid fire dribble down her heaving tits. Within moments, the wax would cool, dry, and harden. It created white creamy tears down her flaring, throbbing flesh.

Now Mr. Cox gripped her by the shoulder and held the candle still, letting the flame dance and lick below her quaking breast. Ella screamed and writhed, her face a mask of pain and terror, but Mr. Cox dug his fingers into her shoulder, seizing her tight, and moved the candle under her other breast.

Ella was sobbing now, existing only in her pain.

Her sobs turned into those of relief when Mr. Cox stood up and blew the candle out. But she continued to cry, overwhelmed by everything he had just put her through.

He still wasn't done yet.

"I told you you would burn, my little clit-toy," he whispered. "And you will...inside and out."

As he walked to the heavy wardrobe and disappeared behind the wide door, Ella leaned her face against her arm and let her tears fall, feeling utterly spent.

Mr. Cox came back holding a bottle filled with thick reddish liquid. Ella had no idea what it could be, but dread filled her heart.

Mr. Cox sat the bottle on the edge of the mat and began to untie the rope fastening her arms to the rings above. As soon as they were free, he loosened the rope tying her wrists together in front of her, so that Ella could put her arms to her sides. But her freedom did not last long, as Mr. Cox grabbed her wrists and tied them once more, this time behind her back.

With her arms now locked behind her, Ella was off balance. Mr. Cox pushed her face down into the mat.

"Face down, ass up," he said. Ella could hear him grabbing the bottle.

"Please, Sir, please," Ella begged, her voice barely above a whisper. Begging was instinctive now; she knew it would do no good, but she couldn't seem to stop.

She could tell Mr. Cox had squeezed some of the liquid onto his hand. With a steadying hand pressed firmly in the middle of her back, he rubbed his slick fingers between her pussy lips, digging into her flesh, coating her cunt lips and clit with the gummy lube.

Then he crawled on his knees to her front, to wait...and watch.

It only took a moment for the fiery lube to work. The slimy thick sap coating her cunt began to sear and burn into her most fragile, tender skin. Ella yanked her head up and fought the rope tying her hands behind her, trying to free herself, but her efforts were futile.

Mr. Cox watched her flop around the mat, crying, shaking, scissoring her legs and yanking her arms inside the rope. Finally, when all the strength had left her body, Ella was reduced to a ball of wretchedness, pressing her head into the mat and keening pathetically.

Only then did Mr. Cox remove the rest of his clothes.

He stepped up behind her, situated himself between thighs, spread open her ass, aimed his cock against her asshole, and pressed.

Ella was still sufficiently lubricated from the anal ball that his whole helmeted head slid into her with one push. With her arms tied behind her back, Ella couldn't brace herself, or control the force of his thrust; all she could do was feel his thick cock inexorably push into her hot rear channel.

She howled and shook with fury as Mr. Cox

pressed his whole length deep into her ass. Her cunt burned, her clit throbbed, and her asshole strained against this new assault.

Mr. Cox began a slow, steady fucking of her asshole.

Ella couldn't help tightening her muscles around him. The burn from her pussy was still wreaking havoc with her senses, and making her whole body tense up in response. But his slow pumping became a welcome relief from the roasting heat still raging inside her cunt; it spurred her on, helping turn her fiery pain into surging pleasure.

Ella lifted her ass a little more, pushing back against him, trying to bury him deeper with each thrust.

"My little clit-toy is enjoying her ass reaming," Mr. Cox said from behind her. "Would my clit-toy like to come?"

Ella didn't answer right away. She was too lost in the heady sensations. His rigid prick felt like it was splitting her open with each slap of his thighs against her already sore ass. He grinded his cock against her tender tissues, bearing down into her straining sphincter, stretching her open like he was trying to tear her apart. Her cunt throbbed in rhythm with the blood pounding in her head.

Mr. Cox's hand come around and rubbed her swollen clit, and Ella almost shrieked from the staggering surge of pleasure and pain.

"I said," he growled as he rubbed, "would my clit-toy like to come?"

"Oh god!" Ella spread her legs and lifted her ass as much as she could. Her shoulders and cheek pressed hard into the mat. "Yes, Sir, your clit-toy would like to come!"

"Then come, clit-toy," he said, pumping harder. "Come for me."

"THANK YOU SIR!"

Ella screamed as she came, engulfed by blinding white light. She heard more screaming, and realized it was still coming from her, but she had no way to stop it. She had lost all control of her body.

Mr. Cox continued to pound his solid cock into her hot rear channel, relishing the way her raw tissues squeezed and milked his entire length. He held back his own release for as long as he could, feeling every spasm of Ella's multiple orgasms roil her wracked body and pulse around his cock. Every time she would come down from another orgasm, he would spread her cheeks wider and thrust harder, and feel the exquisite thrills of her coming again.

Only when Ella was fully depleted, a sobbing, limp heap before him, did he let go of his own release and plow in his cock up to the balls, shooting his come right up her back passage.

She fell prone on her stomach as soon as he slid out of her. Splayed over the mat, breathing hard, with welts, bruises, and wax covering her body under a thin layer of sweat, Ella was a beautiful wreck.

Mr. Cox freed her hands and gathered her up in his arms. He smoothed the hair away from her face and rocked her in his lap, holding her tight.

He was expecting some sort of outburst or torrent of tears. She had just been through a grueling suspension scene; her crash from subspace back to earth was bound to be traumatic.

He was shocked when she smiled at him instead.

"That was pretty kinky, wasn't it?" She whispered, her blue eyes gazing at him in soft repose.

Mr. Cox's own eyes lit with wonder. "Yes," replied. "Yes, it was."

# CHAPTER NINETEEN:
# PARTING WAYS

**E**LLA WAS SUMMONED INTO **MR.** Bentmoore's office the next day.

"Well, Miss Peterson, your training period has officially come to an end. I trust you have learned a lot with us."

"Yes, Sir. I have." She tilted her head and gave him a wry grin as they shared a laden look, one filled with deep understanding.

She was wearing the same clothes she had worn the day she had arrived to the Hotel Bentmoore, but the woman inside them had gone through a drastic change. Her eyes were free of all the self-loathing and shame they had been filled with before. Now her whole demeanor held strength, gentle confidence, and a vast wealth of knowledge.

"Mr. Bentmoore, I can't thank you enough for everything you've done for me."

"It was nothing, Miss Peterson. It's what we do here."

"But you knew I was lying to you all along,

and you still took me in."

"You needed our help, didn't you?"

"Yes," she sighed. "I did indeed."

"If you don't mind me asking, what are your plans now?"

Ella's expression turned inward. "I think I'll go back to the station, and ask for my old job back. I left it for the wrong reasons. I'm not going to let other people interfere with my plans and goals like that again."

"And the producer you were involved with?"

She made a face. "Maybe I'll try to work thinks out with him. Maybe I won't. I haven't decided yet...but whatever I decide, it will be my choice."

"That's good to hear. You've spoken to Mr. Cox already?"

"Yes, Sir." Ella turned wistful as she remembered. Her last conversation with Mr. Cox, just an hour before, had been short and sweet.

"You've learned enough to have a strong foundation," he'd said. "Now you need to build on it. Go back out in the real world, be the woman I know you can be. Make your mark— and remember that your submission can never be a sign of weakness. Give it to the right man, and it will only make you a stronger woman."

Ella swallowed back threatening tears. "When can I come back?"

Mr. Cox had kissed her then, gently, holding her head still with both his hands so she couldn't get away. When he had finally pulled away, he looked at her with an intensity in his eyes Ella had never seen before.

"Don't come back," he'd whispered.

He had walked out the door then, leaving Ella behind, stunned.

She thought maybe she understood why he had left her with those last parting words: he didn't want her using the Hotel Bentmoore as a place to run away from her problems. He wanted her to be strong, and make it on her own.

At least, that's what she hoped he had meant. The alternative was that he never wanted to see her again, and that idea was too painful to contemplate.

Mr. Bentmoore cleared his throat. "I'm sorry I have to bring this up, but—any thought of publishing that story about the Hotel Bentmoore...?"

"Won't happen, Sir. Your secrets are safe with me."

"I'm happy to hear that, Miss Peterson. Very, very happy." He gave her a warm parting smile. "I'll have someone show you to your car. Have a safe drive home."

# CHAPTER TWENTY:
# SEVEN WEEKS LATER

**H**E SCANNED THE HORIZON, SHIELDING his eyes from the glaring sun with both hands. He was standing in a square field of short green grass right below a knobby hill. To his right was the private pool, from where he had just come; to his left was the abandoned barn.

Mr. Cox continued his scan of the area.

He was hunting, but to his consternation, his prey was nowhere to be seen. He had caught sight of her at the private pool, bending over next to one of the sturdy lounge chairs, dripping water, glistening in the sunlight. She was drying off her lithe legs with a thick white towel, but somehow, she had detected his covert approach, spotted him in the distance, and had made a run for it before he was in range of capture.

Now, much to his confusion, she had disappeared.

Mr. Cox knew these parts better than almost anyone—or at least, he thought he did. So where had she gone?

There was only one place for her *to* go, he decided. He headed off toward the barn.

From his direction, it was easier for him to follow the path to the front entrance. He stopped when he saw the wide red barn door, wavering and swinging back and forth in the breeze.

She was there.

Mr. Cox took heavy footsteps toward the door, making as much noise as possible with his feet. Then he grabbed the shaky door and slammed it shut. But he hadn't walked through it first; he waited on the outside.

He didn't have to wait long. As soon as the bang of the door rent the air, his prey bolted out of her hiding place behind the corner of the barn, trying to make a run for it. She thought he was inside the barn, looking for her.

She was silly for thinking she could outsmart him.

Mr. Cox was well within range this time, and caught her on the edge of the field.

He brought her down hard, tackling her to the ground, bellowing like an animal. Stunned by the crash, she screamed and tried to brace herself before she hit the ground; but as soon as she was down, she began to fight, struggling to escape his arms and make another run for it.

Mr. Cox was not about to let that happen. Gripping her tight, he stood up with her in his arms. When she continued to tussle, he moved one hand up to dig into her hair and pull brutally. Instantly, she stopped struggling.

"Back to the barn," he ordered her, his breath blowing over her face like soft silk dragged over ragged stone. "*Move.*"

She moved, taking tiny steps in his arms. He opened the creaky barn door wide, making sure to keep a tight hold on her hair, and as soon as they were through, he pulled the door shut behind them with another bang.

Before she could think of struggling again, he was pulling off her damp bathing suit, peeling it off her moist skin with hard yanks, forcing her to twist this way and that so it wouldn't tear.

"I ought to flay you bloody for running from me," he growled once the bathing suit was off. "Get against the pillar. Go!" He pushed her forward without letting go of her hair, and she stumbled into the cement column.

She thought he would have to leave her for a moment to get some rope to tie her up. She debated whether she should try to make another run for it; but the question became moot when he stepped around the column, grabbed both her hands, and cuffed them together using a pair of metal handcuffs he had pulled out of his pocket.

Now she would get it.

As she rested her cheek against the coarse cement, her lips curved up in a shaky smile. She had been caught faster than she planned... but she had been caught, which was exactly what she wanted.

The first flick of the flogger was a painful surprise. The second made her gasp. But she was soon relaxing against the pillar, only jerking now and then when she felt a particularly vicious strike, feeling very much subdued.

He flogged her with an easy rhythm for a while, warming her back and ass, lulling her into calm repose. Then he began to put more force into every strike, snapping the tails of the flogger into her flesh with quick flicks of his wrist, and listening to her cry out. Soon, she was trying to twist her body away from him, screeching in pain.

He stopped when her back and ass were a grid of angry red lines, and she was trembling with strain.

"Shall I beat you bloody?" He asked, his lips right next to her ear. His warm breath tickled her prickling skin, and she shivered.

"No, Sir, please," she begged him. "Don't do that."

"Then how will you make it up to me, that little chase you put on to make me find you? Mmm, let me think...will you get down on your knees and suck my cock?"

"Yes," she nodded her head. "Yes, Sir. Please, let me suck your cock."

"Very well then."

He came around, unlocked the cuffs, and forced her down on her knees before him. Then he unbuckled his pants and yanked them down.

"Suck me off," he hissed, "and thank me for being so kind."

"Yes, Sir. Thank you for being so kind to me. Thank you for allowing me to suck your cock."

She took his cock in her hand and pointed it out toward her mouth, lowering her face on it like it was the most delicious looking thing in the world. Mr. Cox inhaled sharply as he looked down and watched his prick disappear into her soft pink lips and her hot, tight mouth.

She slid him down her tongue, gliding him towards her throat, removing her hand from his cock so she could get her lips all the way down the base. When his cock was down the back of her tongue, she stopped, and took a breath; then she sank down on him, pushing him into her throat.

Mr. Cox moaned in delight. He wiggled his hips, rubbing his cock against the velvety tissues of her throat, relishing in her struggle to hold still. When her brows furrowed and she moved to pull away, he dug his hands into her hair and held her still for just a moment, just long enough to sense her desperation to breathe. Then he let her go, and she pulled off him completely, taking deep, ragged breaths.

He gave her a moment to recover before he grabbed her head and pulled her on him again, hard, pushing his thick cock right down her gullet and making her eyes widen in fear. He pulled back halfway, letting her airway open up, but not giving her full liberty of his prick. He slammed her head back down his shaft, holding her head against his groin as she pushed against his legs in a weak attempt to get away.

Within moments, he was fucking her face, holding it tight in his hands and jerking it up and down his ramming hips, using her mouth like a tight, wet, luscious cunt. She held her mouth open to him, letting him pound his hard tool into her face and cram it down her throat without hindrance. Drool dripped down her lips, and her eyes squeezed shut; but she offered him no resistance as he used her mouth for his own pleasure.

She was afraid he would come in her mouth, and make her wait for her own orgasm. But he pulled away, popping free of her mouth, and ordered her to bend down. As soon as she did, he stepped up behind her, aimed his rigid cock, and rammed it right into her needy cunt. She moaned in delight.

He pounded into her pussy just as hard as he did her face, with brutal, quick, gorging thrusts. She spread her knees and raised her ass, offering him better access. He grabbed her around the hips and held her still, plowing deep, getting rich groans of pleasure from the pummeled woman.

Soon, she was coming with wild abandon, letting out a series of high-pitched cries with each crashing wave of ecstasy. Her wet pussy contracted around his long prick, and with each spasm, she drew him in, gripping his cock like a vise and rippling down his hard shaft.

Her squeezing orgasm was his undoing, and he came as well, pounding into her contracting pussy and letting go of his raging lust with the cry of a savage beast.

He held himself still inside her until he was done shooting his load. Once he was done, he pulled out of her slowly, letting his shrinking cock fall away from her dripping cunt.

She turned to look at him over her shoulder, grinning like a happy puppy.

"Hello, Ella," he said, grinning back at her. "It's nice to see you again. How've you been?"

They relaxed on the mattress for a while, catching up, talking about mundane things. Then Ella grew pensive.

"Are you mad at me?"

"Oh, yes. Furious. Livid—can't you tell?"

"I'm serious."

"You mind telling me what I'm supposed to be angry at you for?"

"You told me to never come back." Her lip quivered.

"Oh. That." He sighed as he squeezed her into the crook of his arm. "Well, that was wrong of me, and I'm sorry about that."

"I thought, at the time, I understood why you said it. Now I'm not so sure."

"Does it matter?"

"Yes, it does!" She sat up and gazed at him. "Did Mr. Bentmoore tell you why I'm here?"

"We had a conversation, yes." His jaw clenched as his mind flashed back to that morning...the first time he had ever shouted at his boss.

*I can't believe you'd ask her to work here,* his voice had boomed. *You know what kind of woman she is. You know what will happen to her if she works here!*

*I had no choice when I learned you'd told her about the Martins,* Mr. Bentmoore had replied, his own voice threatening. *You forced my hand.*

*Bullshit,* Mr. Cox had thrown back. *I never gave her names or details—and you know she'd never say a word in any case!*

*And* you *knew what you were doing when you told her—you told me that yourself.*

*Things were different then,* Mr. Cox had whispered. *Now....*

Mr. Bentmoore had scoffed at him. *Now, what? This hotel still has a reputation to uphold, Cox. I did what I had to do. Once Miss Peterson accepts her position, I can have her sign a non-disclosure agreement, and that'll be it.*

Cox had paused at this point, trying to think up a way out. *How do you know she'll take the job?* He'd finally asked, knowing he was grasping at straws and hating every second of it. *She might be happy wherever she is. She might turn your offer down.*

*I don't think so.* Mr. Bentmoore's reply had been confident. *Believe me, I've made it worth her while.*

Mr. Cox had stormed out of his boss's office at that point, feeling like an animal caught in a bear trap.

Now, seeing Ella again after so long, and holding her secure in his arms, he couldn't find the strength to be angry. But he knew, beyond a doubt, that all the rationale he'd used to ask her to stay away still held true.

"Since you're here, I'm assuming you told Mr. Bentmoore you'd take the job," he said.

"Yes, I did."

"I'm asking you to reconsider."

Her lip began to quiver again. "Why? Why don't you want me here? Am I that much of a bother to you? You can't bear the thought of seeing my face in the hallways now and then?"

"Goddamn it, Ella, no." He leaned his head on a balled fist. "I've always asked you to be honest with me, so I'm going to be honest with you. We both know what kind of woman you are— strong, confident,"—he brought her eyes back to his with a finger under her chin when she tried to look away—"and a woman with an incredible spirit to submit. But you need to be taken down before you submit, and...goddamnit, Ella, when you submit, it's...it's beautiful. It's like breaking a butterfly out of its cocoon, and watching it fly free."

He paused then, looking away himself. "If you work here, this place will change you. Maybe not right away—you'll be able to fake it for a while. But eventually, you'll find a guest who'll be able to tell you're holding back. He'll want your full submission, and he'll break you to get it. I don't want to see that happen."

Ella pulled back from him, upset. "You always told me my submission isn't a weakness. That I'll always get to decide who I give it to."

"That's true."

"Then do you think me so weak that I'd let someone force me to give them my submission?"

"No. I think once you surrender to a man, when you yield to him and become his prey, you'll do it freely."

"Then what's the problem?"

Mr. Cox scowled. "The *problem* is, I can't just stand back and watch you offer your submission to someone else besides me!" He stood up and looked down at her with fire in his eyes. "When you left the hotel, I knew you'd end up with some Dom who would have to earn the right to call you his. And that was okay, that was fine, because I knew it was what was best for you. But it was happening out *there*, where I didn't have to watch it happening. You can't ask me to stand back and watch you pleasure man after man, fulfill their fantasies, and make me constantly wonder if *that's* the guy who manages to take what's in *here*." He pointed to her heart. "I don't care about you fucking other guys...but to know one of them might manage to see the real you, the animal inside you, the part of you that I... no. I can't do it, Ella. I'm begging you, please don't ask me."

He turned away from her. Ella stared at his back in surprise.

"Cox," she said gently, "did Mr. Bentmoore tell you *which* job he offered me?"

Mr. Cox's turned back, his brows creased in confusion. "I assumed it was to become a new mistress of the hotel...."

"No, Cox." Ella shook her head. "Mr. Bentmoore asked me to head up the international PR department."

*"What?"*

"I'll be travelling all over the world, meeting with executives, VIPs—in very discreet circles, of course. Mr. Bentmoore says he wants to 'spread the Hotel Bentmoore influence.' He says I have the right background and expertise for the job."

"So you wouldn't be...?"

"No. I wouldn't be."

"Oh."

"Yeah, oh."

Mr. Cox smiled and looked away. "Why that crafty old son of a bitch...you never even told him I told you about the Martins, did you?"

This time, it was Ella's turn to look surprised.

"What the hell are you talking about?"

"Nothing," he said, shaking his head, chagrined. He grew quiet for a moment, thinking. "Look, Ella, you should still take some time to think about this," he finally blurted. "You've been away from this place for barely two months. That's not enough time for you to see what else is out there—"

"I think you mean *who* else is out there," Ella said as realization crept in. "You didn't want me attaching myself to you, the first guy who got me to surrender myself. You wanted me to go out there, and have new experiences with other men."

"Yeah. I was trying to do what was best for you."

"How noble," she sneered. "Telling me to go outside and play, like I'm a little girl bored with her dolls. What a high opinion you must have of me."

"God damn it, Ella."

"You'll be happy to know, I tried to work things out with the producer. We had another go of it."

"You did?" His eyes narrowed. "What happened?"

She shrugged. "It didn't work out. We had a fun time in bed—he was *very* happy to find out about all the things I'd learned while I was here. But he wasn't interested in the kind of relationship I want. I wanted him to take more control all the time, not just in the bedroom. It turned out, he wasn't much of a fulltime Dom. He wasn't much of a Sadist, either."

"Oh. That's, um, that's too bad."

She sighed. "It happens. I know what I want now, the kind of commitment I need from a guy. Thanks to you, I'm not willing to settle for anything less." She gave him a piercing stare. "Look, Cox, I'm taking Mr. Bentmoore's offer. This job is an opportunity of a lifetime, and I'm not going to pass it up. So the question is, what are you going to do about it?"

He stepped in front of her and delved his fingers into her glorious hair. "I'm not a kind man, Ella. I'm not going to shower you with pretty words of love."

"I know."

"Life with me won't be easy. People around here call me an asshole. I've earned the title."

She smiled. "I know that, too."

His face grew tight. "We'll hardly have a traditional relationship. I'm going to be working here, doing what I've always done. You know what that means. Will you be okay with it?"

"As long as I know that I'm special. That I hold a part of you in *here*." She pressed her hand over his chest, right above his heart.

"Oh, fuck yes, Ella."

Ella's smile was radiant; then her expression turned somber. "I'm going to be travelling a lot. I'll be meeting with some very important clients, all over the world. You'll be in charge, but you're not going to be able to micromanage my life. Are you okay with that?"

He held her cheek and smiled, his eyes bright. "Princess, I'll be your number one fan, cheering you on. I'll be the proudest Dom in the world—just as long as no matter where you go, you remember who is master."

"Master, huh?" She leaned her face into his palm. "Then can I be slave?"

"Sounds good to me."

"Sounds good to me, too." She closed her eyes, pressing her face into his hand, and sighed with pleasure. "You're right, we'll hardly have a traditional relationship. We won't even have a conventional Master/slave relationship."

"Like I always say, the dynamics of a relationship are up to the people in it."

"True," she grinned. "But I would still like a collar. Something tasteful, something that I can wear all the time, no matter the company I'm in."

"That, princess, can be arranged."

"And everything else...rules, protocols...."

"We have time. We'll figure all that out. But I'd appreciate it if you'd shut up now."

"Why?"

He stopped her mouth with a kiss. By the time he broke his lips away, Ella was in a daze.

"Oh," she said.

"Yeah, oh."

He smiled and tried to kiss her again, but this time, Ella broke away.

"Count to ten," she said.

"What? Why...?" As understanding set in, he lifted his brows in surprise. "You're completely naked," he reminded her.

"I don't care. Nobody's out there to see me, and if there is, well, we'll put on a show. Come on, Cox. Count to ten."

"I think you mean 'Master, please count to ten.'"

Ella's smile was huge. "Master, please count to ten."

Cox seemed to take a moment to think about it; then he began to count, articulating his words loudly. "One...two..."

Ella, naked and glorious, ran out of the barn.

Mr. Cox made it all the way to seven. Then he ran after her.

And the chase was on.

# OTHER BOOKS BY SHELBY CROSS

### Novels
*The Edge of Jasmine: A Hotel Bentmoore World Novel (BDSM Romance)*
*The Taming of Red Riding (A BDSM Fairy Tale)*

### Short Stories
*Tales from the Hotel Bentmoore: Alice*
*Tales from the Hotel Bentmoore: Deborah*
*Tales from the Hotel Bentmoore: Mark and Audra*
*Tales from the Hotel Bentmoore: Elizabeth*
*Masters of the Hotel Bentmoore: Khloe*
*Masters of the Hotel Bentmoore: Evie*
*Masters of the Hotel Bentmoore: Michelle*
*Masters of the Hotel Bentmoore: Samantha*

### Compilations
*Masters of the Hotel Bentmoore: The Complete Collection*
*Tales from the Hotel Bentmoore: The Complete Collection*

**Coming Soon**

*Untold Stories from the Hotel Bentmoore*
*King Thrushbeard: A BDSM Erotic Fairy Tale*

# SPECIAL THANKS

*Special thanks to Dr.Yo, who taught me the wonders of Shakespeare by means of a cross.*

5301658R00200

Printed in Germany
by Amazon Distribution
GmbH, Leipzig